HOOPER

Books by Geoff Herbach
Hooper
Cracking the Bell

HOOPER

GEOFF HERBACH

KATHERINE TEGEN BOOKS
An Imprint of HarperCollins Publishers

Katherine Tegen Books is an imprint of HarperCollins Publishers.

Hooper

Library of Congress Control Number: 2017943389

ISBN 978-0-06-245312-9

Typography by David Curtis

19 20 21 22 23 PC/LSCH 10 9 8 7 6 5 4 3 2 1

❖

First paperback edition, 2019

To this whole great nation of ballers.

ONE

I AM A HOOPER

This is where I first found happiness in America. I am a hooper.

I leap high, grab the rebound over all the Wauzeka boys. I drop the rock to the point guard, Caleb Olson, then jog down the court.

Shoes squeak. The pep band drummer drums. Cheerleaders cheer. The air smells like popcorn and nachos and the heat of all these people, a packed gym full of Northrup Polar Bear fans.

This is February. Sophomore year.

I jog underneath the hoop. The defender tries to push me out. I am already too big. He is six foot one, maybe. I am six foot six and all bony arms and legs. I back him down just for fun. Caleb Olson, a senior, takes his time coming down the court. He is so good with the ball in his hand. He is such a fine shooter, too.

We are far ahead. No need to rush things.

I swing outside the paint to the left wing.

The drum drums. The crowd cheers.

Our offense runs through me and Caleb and no one else.

Caleb moves into the frontcourt. The Wauzeka defense sets. I cut again underneath the basket, then explode from the post to the top of the key, where I set a pick on Caleb's defender.

Caleb drives.

I roll.

Caleb lobs the ball high at the rim.

I leap. I catch. I throw it down.

It's like water breaking through a dam.

The crowd goes crazy, even a kid at the end of our opponent's bench. He looks like me when I was a little boy, or like my little brother would look if I had one. Blond hair spiked up. Long arms. Long legs. So skinny. He wears a red T-shirt with a big yellow corncob on it. "Fear the Cob" is written in big letters.

That boy is so happy to see me dunk the basketball, and I do not fear the Cob.

Wauzeka, known as "the Cobbers," won the Minnesota Valley Conference three years in a row, but this victory claims the crown for us.

Northrup Polar Bears reign supreme. We are the champions.

Me and Caleb high-five.

But I don't like him.

You would think this victory makes me a popular guy. You would be wrong. After the game, no girls come to kiss my cheek. No teammates want to meet me for pizza at Patrick's. And I don't want to be with any of them. Instead, I leave the gym fast. I don't shower. I grab my bag of clothes from my locker and fire out the door into the night air.

In the parking lot, Barry Roland waits for me. Nobody in school likes him, but he is a good person. Barry Roland takes me to McDonald's down on the highway. I eat two quarter pounders and a large order of french fries.

While I eat, Barry talks about tae kwon do. Although he is small, he is good at this martial art, the star pupil at Bob's Champion Tae Kwon Do Studio. He is so good, in fact, he helps teach the little kid classes and old people classes. Sometimes when we're at McDonald's a little kid or old person will come to say hi. He may not be popular in high school, but little kids and old people love him.

This February night he is excited because he has just begun to kick trees with his shins. He thinks he can have the most powerful shins in all of Minnesota by the time he attempts his second-degree black belt test in April.

"I saw it on YouTube? If you micro-splinter the bone on

your shins it grows back harder? You can turn your shins into steel?"

I stop eating the quarter pounder. "Your shin grows metal?" I ask.

"No, it grows more bone. Strong bone! It just gets as hard as metal, okay?"

"Okay," I say. "Sounds good." I take another bite of my quarter pounder.

Barry Roland ends many sentences with the sound of a question, even if there is not a question. I once thought he was asking many questions, but I learned that this is just his conversation style.

He has much style. He often wears his karate-style headband on his head, and he has thick glasses that make his eyes look big and surprised. He has puffy blond hair and a fluffy blond mustache.

Food also fires from his mouth while he talks. It's only because he is so excited about life.

"Maybe, if my shins get hard enough, I can get on TV for breaking logs?"

"Yes. Dope," I say. I make my voice deep to sound like a TV announcer. "Mr. Strong Man can kick down your house."

"That's right, dude!" he says. "I thought of my TV name, too. Do you want to hear it?"

"Yes."

He lowers his head and whispers like a snake. "The Shinja."

"The Shinja? Like a ninja with great shins?"

He nods.

I nod. "That is very, very dope, bro."

When we finish with the burgers, Barry Roland drives. He talks all the way to my dark home on the edge of a small college campus, on the outskirts of a tiny Minnesota town. In the house, Renata, my adopted mom, is fast asleep. Barry gives me a high five when he parks. "See you for breakfast," he says, because he will come to eat breakfast with me and Renata in the morning.

I point and say, "Catch you in the morning light."

He smiles in his piece-of-shit Pontiac. This car has rust holes in its bottom. When there is rain or snow, there is rain or snow in the car. Barry doesn't mind. He is happy for what he has.

He drives away, and I go into the dark house across from the darkened college buildings, on the edge of all those dark farms.

TWO

TALK MORE

A girl named Carli Anderson says I should talk more. So here.

I come from Poland. My name was Adam Sobieski, but I changed it to Adam Reed, because my adopted mom, Renata, has the last name Reed. I have been in America for four and a half years. I just moved to Minnesota last summer. I like basketball. I sound funny when I talk in English, but that's not my fault. I work on it a lot. But I'm bad at school, even when I was in Poland and could do school in Polish.

That's me.

Is that enough, Carli Anderson?

THREE
EN VEE PEE

A week after we defeat the Wauzeka Cobbers, the playoffs come. Because Northrup is the conference champion, the first round is in Northrup High School's gymnasium (small and old, but okay).

Like it has been the last couple of games, the gym is filled. The old farmers and businessmen and hairdressers and dental assistants and the guys who hang out in bars, they all pack the stands to cheer us on. Cheerleaders shout and kick higher than ever. So many fans cannot find seats, they have to stand at the doorways. Almost everyone in Northrup attends, except Renata. She did not come to any game all season, which is okay. She did not attend games in Philadelphia when we lived there, either. Big crowds and noise give her migraines in her eyes and temples. I don't mind who is in the stands, because all I do is play basketball.

Caleb Olson lobs a pass. I dunk so hard and shout and raise my arms above my head like a warrior.

That morning, a newspaper wrote how I make more dunks than anyone in all of Minnesota. The chemistry teacher, Mr. Burton, taped the article to the door of his room.

"Did you know you were so good, Adam?" he asked.

"No," I said. I ducked and looked around because I didn't want people to make shit of me.

No one I could see made shit.

The coach from New Ulm screams, "Watch for thirty-four! Watch out!" We are on defense and that coach is right: they should watch out for me. As he shouts, I peel off the center and steal the ball from the shooting guard and explode across midcourt. Nobody from New Ulm's team can catch up. I sky into the air and throw the ball down and pound on my chest.

We are up by fifteen points.

The wild drummer, Derrick Oppegaard, pounds his drum, and the crowd begins shouts of "En Vee Pee!"

Coach high-fives me, brings me off the court so subs can get some minutes. The crowd stands and continues to chant. I try not to look over my shoulder at them, but I don't like them making a chant.

In the "good game" line, the center from New Ulm, who

is as tall as me, but not an athlete, says, "You're too good, dog. *En Vee Pee* for sure."

"Okay," I say.

Then I leave school fast. Barry Roland waits for me in the parking lot. It is icy and below zero. The wind cuts through my warm-up, but Barry's shit Pontiac, even with the holes in the floor, is warm and toasty.

"Hey, dude!" he says. "Ready for some grub?"

At McDonald's, I ask Barry Roland what *En Vee Pee* means.

He scrunches up his nose so his fluffy mustache gets small underneath. This is what his face does when he thinks. "Maybe it's like when people envy your skills so much they have to pee their pants?"

I do not trust Barry in matters of fact, but this seems like a possible explanation. "Okay. Maybe," I say.

"Yeah. Uh-huh," Barry says, nodding. "I'd be willing to bet on it."

Then I am sure he is wrong.

The next morning, during breakfast, I forget to ask Renata what she knows about *envy pee*. We always listen to jazz (because Renata's dad, Papa, loves jazz). But Renata is not humming along as she usually does. Barry is there. She is staring at him. He explains to her why he is limping, why he has blood on the shins of his blue jeans.

"I don't know if that's a good idea, Barry," she says to

9

him about his tree kicking. "You could permanently injure yourself."

"It's worth it, Mrs. Renata," he says. "I can feel the steel growing in my shins already." He always calls her Mrs. Renata, even though Renata is her first name.

I forget about *envy pee*.

But at school, before class begins, a tall girl with thick, shiny brown hair, who walks on crutches, says, "Look who's here. It's the *envy pee*." She smiles as we pass in the hall. I recognize her from being around, but I don't know yet that her name is Carli Anderson. And I don't say nothing in reply. I mean *anything*.

First hour, I motion to the gym teacher, Ms. Hader, to come speak. She is a very nice woman who doesn't make shit of dumb people. "Excuse me," I say. Other students stand by the volleyball net. They stare at me while I ask my question. I don't want them to hear. "What does *envy pee* mean?" I whisper.

She smiles very big across her whole face. "*M*, Adam. Not *N*."

"Oh yeah?"

"The *M* stands for *Most*. The *V* stands for *Valuable*. The *P* stands for *Player*. The crowd was chanting Most Valuable Player at you last night. That's pretty cool, huh?"

"Oh," I say. "It's okay."

"Just okay?" she asks.

I shrug. The other students are smiling now.

I don't smile back, because I don't like people and I don't like to be stupid, but inside I am getting warm. I know in my heart it is more than okay to be MVP, because now I know what MVP means, only I never imagined American kids would shout about me like that.

LeBron James is MVP. Steph Curry is MVP. Kevin Durant is MVP. Michael Jordan was MVP before I was even born.

I walk through the halls of the school. There is a bounce in my step. How did I become MVP?

I was not the very best basketball player back in Philadelphia. In fact, I didn't want to play any basketball. Renata made me go. She was worried I didn't make friends at my school.

She was right to worry. I didn't want friends. I wanted to be home, where there was always food and always the TV and the couch and a blanket.

But my gym teacher told her I was a natural athlete and that I was a good player in my class. So Renata said, "Adam, you need to do this. I'd be a bad mother if I didn't encourage you to get involved. Do you want me to feel like a bad mother?"

"No," I mumbled.

"That doesn't mean I don't like having you around, okay? I really do."

"Oh," I said.

I didn't believe that she liked having me around, even though she had to work for almost two years to adopt me. I went to basketball because for most of the time I've known her, I do whatever Renata tells me to do. I need a mom.

And I knew right away that Renata had made a good parent decision. Although I sucked at first, I loved playing this game.

My teammates were mostly new from Nigeria, and we ran and ran and ran and I got better at layups and passing and defense and then I worked on basketball all the time and went to three camps at Temple University and did drills in the hallway of our apartment building and on the sidewalk even when there was snow falling and on the park courts in the sun and in lightning and in sleet, and I got much, much better, and me and my team were far superior by the next year, and my growth has taken me from average-size to quite tall over a couple years. By the time the Minnesota kids shouted MVP at me, I was dribbling so well, crossing over, breaking ankles, and dunking like a crazy man. I played killer defense. Even though I didn't shoot great all the time, I knew I was good at this game. And the competition in Northrup was not as good as in Philadelphia. So I seemed very good.

But MVP? Me? Adam Reed, who was born Sobieski on a small Polish dairy farm a million miles from anyplace? Why would my classmates cheer and call me MVP? Also, don't all these kids hate me?

Some kids do.

I walk past Kase Kinshaw, who leans against his locker. Other students are smiling now, saying "good game" to me. But he glares and shakes his head like I am shit on the ground. My heart accelerates. I feel adrenaline rise. Kase Kinshaw has hated my guts from the moment he noticed me. His hate is getting worse.

I go fast to get past him.

I don't understand some things. Kase Kinshaw is a large football player, but he never messes with people big like him, only those smaller or dumber or weaker. This behavior does not make everybody hate him. Most kids act like he is a dope dude. They get quiet and listen when he talks. They smile at him. They laugh at his jokes, which are not jokes but shocking things that no one else would say out loud. He calls Barry Roland the r-word and he calls me "Duh" because I have pauses in my speech. When he learned I was from Poland, he started to call me "the Refugee," too. Poland is troubled, maybe, but not at war. His meanness got worse. "Don't breathe," Kase Kinshaw said at his lunch table as I walked by one time. "You could catch AIDS."

He was talking to Caleb Olson. Caleb laughed. Why would I like Caleb even if he is good at basketball?

In Philadelphia, there were a million people. I played

basketball against boys with tattoos on the playground who liked to shove me.

Okay. Basketball is rough.

I played against a team who were in a juvenile home because they committed violent crimes.

No problems with those guys.

The worst were some guys from a public school who called me Forrest Gump and who flipped hand signals at me that my teammate Mobo Bell said were gang signs (I don't know why they would flash gang signs at me). I was thrown from that game because I elbowed a boy in his nose and then we brawled so bad he got a dislocated shoulder. The cops talked to me after and the other boy's coach begged there to be no charges, because that kid had already had bad troubles and he didn't need any new ones. My coach called Renata about the fight, and she was so shocked and scared and troubled. She grabbed my shoulders and yelled at me, and I thought she might throw me out onto the streets. Luckily it was the last game of the season, or I maybe would have a suspension. My Philly coach met with me later and said I have to learn to control my emotions or I will have future suspensions.

Worse, I thought, Renata could abandon me. She doesn't know I had violence problems in Poland, too, and so I try hard to be a good kid, to stay clear of any trouble.

But Kase is worse than everyone. He insults me not because I am his opponent on the court, but because he hates who I am as a person. I have seen some bad people in my life. My dad was one of them, too. But of all the people I have encountered, Kase Kinshaw is the worst.

Kase makes me want to hurt him.

But after Ms. Hader explained MVP to me, I don't care about Kase. All day long I jog between my classrooms because I am MVP. Other students want to high-five me because I am MVP. In English class, Zachary Hilderbrand says I need a good nickname.

"How about the Polish Hammer?" he asks. "Because of your dunks?"

I know this nickname has been used before, but I also like it. "Okay," I say. "That is dope."

"Yeah, it is!" he says.

Yeah, it is. Very dope.

Who cares about Kase Kinshaw?

FOUR

HATE VICTORY

It is the second round of the playoffs. I jog out onto the floor. Caleb Olson is right behind me. "Let's get after them, Adam. Let's do this," he says. Before now he has called me Duh, because, like everyone, he thought that was no problem.

"Okay," I say.

There is one opposing player who is taller than me on the Blue Earth Spartans. His name is Percy Reynolds. He is well known in Minnesota. He is actually huge, six foot ten. He averages over twenty points a game and six blocks.

I watch him warm up. Nice stroke, but very slow. He dunks the ball and looks at me like he is a warrior. He clenches his fist and glares. But he has barely jumped. Everything about him is slow. In fact, Coach Jenson has said to the team at practice during the week, "Attack Reynolds! Attack that guy! Make him work on defense. His feet are lead balloons!"

The game is at Minnesota State University in Mankato, at the Taylor Center, which is named after the owner of the NBA Timberwolves. It is a big arena that looks like the ones on TV. I breathe deep, and I get goose bumps. Maybe this move to the "middle of the middle of nowhere," as Renata calls Northrup, Minnesota, will work out? Maybe this was the best move? Maybe things are getting better all the time?

Not really.

The gym is only a twenty-minute trip from Northrup, so the old farmers have driven in their pickups, and so have the dentists and hairdressers and all the city workers. Many, many students from school have made the drive, too, which is okay, except Kase Kinshaw. He sits with two girls behind our bench. One girl is Carli Anderson, the tall one, who has crutches and wears a brace on her leg. She has been very nice to me all week. She has told me she wants to play one-on-one against me when her leg is better. But how can she be sitting with Kase Kinshaw? How can she be laughing at his jokes? As I pass him, I make eye contact. He shakes his head, then looks away like I make him so sick to his stomach.

I hate Kase Kinshaw. Adrenaline grows.

The whistle blows.

I use this energy to destroy Percy Reynolds. I crush Percy Reynolds, bash away his weak shots, slam the ball through the hoop and onto his stupid face. I play so mad, I am almost scared, almost dangerous. I get whistled. I get warned. I don't hear the crowd. I feel shaky in my insides. I don't hear the coach. I have no fun playing my game, because I hate Kase Kinshaw. His voice comes to me during time-outs. He makes Carli Anderson laugh more behind us. I want to turn and whip the ball into his face and make him bleed, but I can't hurt people. Instead I destroy Percy Reynolds and his lead feet. I leap over him. I run past him. I punch the ball out of his hands whenever he catches it.

Averages twenty a game? No. This game Percy Reynolds scores four points, and all on foul shots (I fouled him).

We win huge.

Caleb Olson scores twenty-two. He makes six three-pointers.

I score twenty-eight. The gym once again echoes with chants of M-V-P near the end of the game. But I don't care.

Carli Anderson stands, propped up on crutches. "You're going to get recruited big-time, dude!" she says. "Huge!"

I don't care.

Coach Jenson huddles us up. "On to the next round! We're going deep!" he says.

I don't care.

I pull on warm-ups, run off the court and out the gym door, and find the school bus so I can sit in the last row and everyone will leave me alone. There I tremble and shiver and press my eyes shut.

My anger lasts longer into the night. I think of everything bad. Kase calls Barry retard. Kase punched Barry's kidney at a city park a few years ago. Barry peed blood. Every time I close my eyes, I see the face of Kase Kinshaw and I want to crush it. It won't stop. I feel crazy, and I feel like I'm dangerous. This makes me quiet at McDonald's, which is not too bad for Barry Roland, because Barry Roland likes to talk and talk.

"I kicked, like, ten different trees today, so the impact zones would be different," he says.

"Oh," I reply. "Okay," I say. Barry limped badly into McDonald's.

"Because you don't want to just kick the same spot on your shin over and over? Because you might just get a really bad contusion or maybe you might break your shin instead of micro-splinter? The impact has to be spread out."

"Oh," I say.

Maybe it is not so great for Barry that I don't pay attention?

"Are you even listening, dude?" he asks.

I exhale. I look down at the table. "You should use your metal shins to kick Kase Kinshaw in half," I say.

"No," Barry says. "I wouldn't do that."

"Why wouldn't you? He calls you retard. He punched your kidney."

Barry takes a deep breath. "Self-control," he whispers.

"What?" I ask.

"Kase Kinshaw is not a worthy opponent?" Barry says, his voice drifting up into a question that is not a question. His mustache scrunches underneath his nose. "Kase Kinshaw is just a bad jerk?"

"Yeah. Okay," I say. "But . . ."

"You must forget about Kase Kinshaw," Barry says.

"But—" I say.

"Indomitable spirit," Barry says. He puts his right fist into the palm of his left hand. He drops his head like a nun in Poland praying.

"Oh," I say. "Okay."

FIVE

THE INK

Sometimes I have bad nightmares about Poland. My first town, Kulesze Kościelne, was in the east, near Bialystok and not so far from the country called Belarus. There my grandpa ran his dairy farm. It was a good place to be a little boy. I kicked a soccer ball across big meadows.

It was a bad place to be for my mom. She is gone.

It was a bad place to be for my dad. He grew up in Warsaw, in the big city, and he didn't want to pull cow teats (he said this to me many, many times—but I remember the machines, so he never had to milk with his hands—he is a liar). When my mom followed Grandma in cancer, Dad left Grandpa and his farm to die together. Dad took me, age seven, to Warsaw.

My nightmares are in Warsaw in a tall apartment building with a big window and black darkness outside. It is day, but the air has filled with ink from an octopus. The blackness starts to leak in through cracks in the cinder block. I try to plug the cracks with my hands, but there is no chance to stop the ink. My dad isn't there. He can't help me. The ink flows in.

I wake. It is three a.m. Renata is in my room. She sits on my bed. Her hand is on my forehead. "You're screaming, Adam," she whispers. "It's just a dream. It's just a bad dream. You're okay."

"Okay," I say. But I toss and turn for the rest of the night. I am awake. I am asleep. I am both awake and asleep. For much of it I'm not sure where I am. Kulesze with meadows outside? Warsaw with broken cement in my park? Philadelphia in the brownstone apartment? Northrup? Does it matter at all?

There is ink. There is darkness coming for me.

SIX

BUT SOMETIMES . . .

I also dream that my real mom and my real grandpa are wearing red tracksuits, like the Polish Olympic team when I was little, and we are on a nice, big white boat with giant windows overlooking the calm blue ocean. Together we just bob along and eat good food and laugh. This is a good dream, except it is weird. Sometimes there are sheep on the boat, too, and I fall asleep and they lie down next to me. It is comfortable, but I wake up thinking, "Dude, you are a crazy boy."

SEVEN
PASSPORT

"You should teach Tiffany how to cook, Mrs. Renata." Barry Roland now calls his mom by her first name, Tiffany, like I call Renata, Renata (my dead mom is the only mom I have, so . . .).

"Maybe I could teach her?" Renata says, but I know that she doesn't mean it.

"That'd be sweet," Barry says.

"But if she cooks as well as I do, you won't want to come over, and I'd really hate that," Renata says.

Barry's face blushes underneath his thick glasses. "Oh yeah," he mumbles. "I'd still want to come over."

I know Renata tells the truth about wanting Barry here. He talks a lot. In Philadelphia, she had so many friends who were teachers and scholars. In Northrup, she hasn't yet found too many people like her. Everybody at the college where she teaches seems much older. Barry is good entertainment.

"Tiffany doesn't want to cook, so don't worry, okay?" Barry says.

"Deal," Renata says.

At school, Barry disappears to the other side of the building, because he has some classes that are meant to help him get better at reading, except he says the letters get so turned around in his brain he doesn't think that he will ever be able to figure it out. I have no special teachers in Northrup. Philadelphia taught me English well enough. Here there are some Mexican students and two Somali sisters who are brand-new. They receive the special teachers' attention.

I go to my locker. Carli Anderson is standing there propped on her crutches. I stop in place, unable to move. What is she doing?

"Hey. I've been waiting here for ten minutes, dude."

"I didn't know that," I mumble.

She shakes her head. "Yeah, I know. How could you know?"

"I don't know. So?" I say.

"So, I wanted to tell you my dad called some AAU coaches from up in the Cities last night. He doesn't think you should play with the MN Rise."

"Play with who?" I ask. "What about your dad? What coaches?"

She raises her eyebrows and opens her big eyes, which are green, like the spring fields by Grandpa's farm. "Maybe this is a longer conversation?" she says. She looks past me. Her friend, who is short and not as amazing, has stopped and is pouting and waiting and looking crabby. "Gotta run. But, seriously, Dad is pretty pumped about you."

Then she rocks away on her crutches.

I wonder why her dad would spend his time thinking about me. Then I must move fast to make gym on time. As I cross the cafeteria, cheerleaders are hanging a giant banner that says: "Go, Polar Bears, Beat Austin!" There is a depiction of the number-thirty-four player (me) hanging on the rim, and it looks like he is shouting the slogan from his mouth.

My coach in Philadelphia once told me this game, basketball, could be my passport. I already had a passport from coming to America. I didn't understand why I would need another passport, and I never asked anyone what he meant. But as I stare at this banner, I begin to suspect.

A second later, a freshman girl shouts, "Hi, Adam!" Then she blushes and runs away from me.

Passport to a good life.

Basketball is everything.

I go to gym.

E I G H T
SURPRISE RETURN

This game is at a community college very close to the Iowa border. We are on a bus for an hour and a half. Snow swirls all over the road, which makes me nervous about falling off a cliff to our death. Lucky that the land is flat.

I listen to Miles Davis, *Kind of Blue*. Then I listen to Jevetta Mitchell, the only great jazz singer I have ever seen in concert. Jevetta performed at the University of Pennsylvania, where Renata got her doctorate. All these songs keep me steady, like I am just on the couch with a blanket instead of all alone in the back of a dark bus in the middle of the frozen lands.

Then I see lights. The college seems to have no town

attached. It just rises out of a flat emptiness where snow blows fast.

Still, our fans are here. They cheer for us as we make our way to the door. Carli Anderson and her friend give us a big *whoo-whoo*. There are so many. So many. All the people.

Lots of people from Austin, too.

The gym is warm. Both teams have brought pep bands and the drums from each rattle in my heart and ribs.

I survey our opponent. There is no height like mine on the Austin team. Their tallest guy is more like our Greg Day, a big football player wearing gym shorts. I see no one getting to the rim in their layup drill.

But they are slick. The ball movement is like cannons firing. And they are fast. Coach Jenson told us that Austin won many games by going very, very fast. They are run-and-gun. Before the whistle, Coach says what he's told me all week. "Adam, when they get the ball, you sprint back and guard the rim."

It becomes clear from the start they have a big problem. I am just as fast, but I am also tall, and I can see what they are trying to do before they do it.

The Austin Packers cannot run their style of fast-break offense very well, because as soon as they steal from us or get a rebound from us, I explode downcourt. I beat their own players to the other end. I recognize their break and get to the ball before they can score. I slap away layups and jump to block jumpers. Soon they are misfiring all around the bucket.

They start to lose their composure. They start to foul me hard. Greg Day and their center get in a tussle right after half. Both are tossed from the game, and then even our bench players score. Austin has fallen to pieces.

Caleb Olson hits his three-pointers. He scores nineteen.

I have five dunks and three short jumpers, and I go to the free-throw line ten times. I hit seven, which is very good for me. This means I score twenty-three points. The rest of our team scores fifteen points.

We beat those Packers by fourteen.

At the end of the game, our fans are so hyped. I am hyped, too, but I want to get out of there, away from this crowd, because it's hot and people want to talk to me, but I don't like to talk, because I can't talk right. I jump up and down and look over everyone. No. There is no quick route from the gym. No way. To leave, our team must walk through all the fans.

Okay. Okay. Just walk. Smile. Don't worry.

The old men from Northrup all shake my hand, pat my back.

And it is good. It is okay. "Thank you. Thank you," I say when they tell me I am great. They make jokes I don't understand, and Derrick Oppegaard pounds the drum, and the cheerleaders dance. And it is fun. And then I see Carli Anderson with her shiny brown hair. She waves at me.

Her friend, who is another pouty-faced girl like so many in Northrup, also sort of smiles, but not really.

"You need to talk to my dad!" Carli shouts.

"Okay!" I shout back.

And I am okay. I am fine. Maybe I should have stayed in the gym after all our big victories this season? "M-V-P!" a few boys from my grade shout. Nate Arndt jumps down from the stands and slaps me a big high five, as big as Barry Roland ever would.

After we return from Albert Community College, Greg Day drops me off, because Barry had a tae kwon do class. Greg wishes me good night. I am almost unable to respond. Something is strange. It is late on Thursday, but my usually dark house is not dark. There are lights on in every window. Has Renata died before turning off the lights?

"Okay, bye," I say.

Inside, the scene is more strange than I could imagine. There are not dead bodies, but there are bodies. Two little girls are asleep on the floor of the living room. I bend down and stare and I know who they are. I have seen them climbing the college lawn mower shed. I have seen them carrying sticks, chasing a cat across the street. In the fall, I found them halfway up the front yard pine tree spying on me when I was in the driveway completing my dribbling drills. They have messy hair cut at their chins. They look like wild children from anime cartoons.

I stand and smell. Renata has cooked Indian food. She would not do this for herself. I listen. There is quiet conversation in another room. I tiptoe down the hallway. I peek in the door of Renata's study. She wears her black turtleneck sweater. This is what she wears when she wants to look good. She talks to a man, but he is not visible from the crack in the doorway. But I know who he is, because this has been brewing for some time.

I have a hard time breathing. I don't know what to do, so I tiptoe down to my room and I climb into bed, which is gross, because I need to shower, but I'm not going to shower with other people in my house.

NINE

I HIDE ME

I do not ever talk about this.

After me and my dad moved to Warsaw, after my mom succumbed to her ovary cancer, I went to a lyceum, which is a school, but I didn't go all the time, because my dad didn't make me do anything. One morning, though, he was drinking a lot and he threw me out of the apartment door by the top of my shirt. I fell down in the hallway. He told me I was stupid like a dog who followed him around and I had to go to school or he would get in trouble for my stupidity. He locked the door.

I had on only a T-shirt and tan pants. I wore Spider-Man slippers. There was snow all over the ground. I went to school and my feet were wet and I slept in my desk. They made us go outside for fresh air in the midmorning. They made me wear a girl's coat from the lost and found that was too small for my arms.

A boy made shit of me. I grabbed his hand and twisted it behind his back and bent his fingers, and he screamed and screamed. When the teacher got to us we were both crying, but I wouldn't let go. I broke two of his fingers, so I got kicked out of the school.

At home, my dad cried, too. He said it was his fault. He said, "I am walking on my eyelashes. I am making such bad choices for us."

"Walking on my eyelashes" in Poland means you have been knocked down on your face. My dad walked on his eyelashes because he was drunk every day.

I didn't ever tell Renata this story. I tell no one.

TEN

THE PAST LIKE DIRT

Barry Roland comes for breakfast before Renata and me are awake. He is used to just walking in the front door.

"Adam? Hi? Mrs. Renata? What are you guys doing? I'm here?"

I groan and roll from bed. Even though it is an extra-long bed, sometimes it feels like I don't fit right. All night I have been uncomfortable. Maybe because I am still wearing my uniform and my warm-ups and I am very sweaty, itchy, and disgusting?

"Be right there, Barry," I hear Renata call.

Renata has turned on Miles Davis and is already rigging up the coffee maker when I get into the kitchen. Barry sits at the table eating a banana.

"Potassium?" he says, holding the banana up.

"Yes, bro," I say.

"You guys won," Barry says. "By a lot. I heard it on the radio."

"Yes," I say. "Austin could not run their offense against us."

Renata presses go on the machine, then turns to me. "Did you sneak in when you got home? We didn't hear you."

"We?" Barry asks.

"Little girls and some man," I say to him.

"Oh," Barry says. "Okay." He nods and smiles like he understands now.

"You know who he is!" Renata says. "He's Regan and Margery's dad."

"Okay," I say, because she is correct. He is not unknown. Our house is on the corner of a large property owned by the college. The little girls live in a bigger house on the other side of this property. Their dad is the professor who grows plants on the land and in a greenhouse attached to their home.

"His name is Michael," Renata says to Barry. "He's a biology professor."

"He has gray hair," I say.

"He's actually not much older than me," Renata says. She smiles.

And then I worry. Renata last smiled like this in Philadelphia two years before. Six months later, she was

35

crying and crying because the man named Peter drank "craft" beer every night and shouted about how he couldn't handle us, how he couldn't be himself when we were in his space all the time. This was after he played Frisbee with me like a dad and moved his ten thousand smelly books into our apartment and made us watch nothing but public television. For three more months after he left, Renata couldn't act like my mom, because she was too sad. I don't want a repeat. I want Renata happy.

"I give Tiffany gray hair," Barry says. "Because I eat all the groceries?"

Renata stares at Barry for a moment, then says, "I'm going to make you a big breakfast, okay?"

"What about me?" I ask.

Renata gives me a look. "Of course for you. Basketball stars have big appetites."

I slink down at the kitchen table. My big knees slide up and thunk into the table's bottom. "What do you know about basketball?" I ask.

"Nothing. But Michael is good friends with the college coach, and he knows."

I don't want to hear the name Michael again. I don't want to feel so itchy in my clothes, either. "I have to shower," I say.

"I have to shower, too," Barry says. "But I'll wait until after work."

"Seriously?" Renata says. "Now?"

"I couldn't shower with the man in the house," I say.

Renata looks hurt.

"I'm sorry. I'm okay. I will eat breakfast. I'm fine," I say.

"Okay, good," Renata says. She smiles and makes an omelet.

I go to school without having a shower, but it's fine. The day goes by and there is a just a short video session about our scary next opponent and a short basketball practice after. When I get home, I shower for forty-five minutes before the warm water runs out.

ELEVEN

LOSING MY MIND TO THE OWENSES

And then, the next week, things on the basketball court get bad. I have never even heard of the town called Marshall. It sounds to me like a city that should be in the far west of America, where cowboys ride their horses and shoot up banks and saloons. Maybe because I saw a movie with cowboys and a lawman called marshal? Everyone else on the team knows about Marshall basketball, though, because they are a traditional powerhouse in the state.

More bad news. The game is being held at Southwest Minnesota State University in Marshall. "This is a home game for these guys," Coach Jenson says.

The bus rolls for two hours across frozen prairie lands. Our cheerleaders come. Our pep band comes. But not many fans drive on a windy Tuesday night to someplace near the border of South Dakota.

Marshall's crowd dominates the gym.

During the warm-ups, I already know we are in danger.

Greg Day is very good at getting rebounds, but his beef makes him not good at defense. He doesn't swivel his hips quickly or move his feet. To stay with quicker players, he often grabs with his hands and gets into foul trouble.

Marshall has many tall, quick players.

Most of these quick players are named Owens. In practice during the week, Coach Jenson has called them "the Flying Owenses." Caleb Olson nodded. Through the years, many, many Owenses play for Marshall. They are like a dangerous crime family in a gangster movie. When an Owens boy is a senior, Marshall is unstoppable. Coach told me this at practice. He let that statement seep into my mind. Then he said, smiling, "We've got some weaponry of our own, don't we?"

I nodded.

"Just play your game, Adam," he said.

What else would I do?

But this year there are two senior Owenses, a set of twins who are both six foot five. There is also a little brother from the same family who is a sophomore named Joe. He is already six foot two. And then there is Kyle Owens, who is a big-time college recruit, and a junior, and a cousin of the others. He is six foot seven. I will guard him, because he is the best. All these Owens have sandy-brown hair and eyes that seem too close to their noses. Greg Day will guard one of the twins (the really good one named Tyler), except I know he can't do it. He is simply not good enough.

The game begins. The Marshall crowd sings epic fight songs in the stands. The Owenses score around me. They all look the same. Can anybody guard these guys? They are an Owens machine, passing and passing and passing until one Owens is clear for a layup, usually Tyler, because Greg Day is not a real baller.

I can leap up over any Owens boy, though. I am faster than any one Owens out there. So there is me and my drives and Caleb's shooting. Even though we are not an army of Owenses from the Marshall nation, we score and we stay in the game.

But then, the last twenty seconds of the first half, it goes very bad. Greg Day is still on the floor even though he has two fouls (because what is Coach Jenson going to do?). Tyler Owens curls at the key, sprints down the lane, gets to the rim. Another Owens tosses Tyler the ball perfectly. I collapse away from six-foot-seven Kyle Owens to try to help, but it's too late. Greg Day is red in the face. He is so mad about getting beat down the lane. Instead of reaching for the ball, Greg Day tackles Tyler Owens like a football player. Tyler's head bounces off wood. The crowd screams. The ref blows the whistle. Tyler lies on the floor and moans and groans. The crowd boos loudly. The officials bring on medics to treat Tyler, and then they huddle up and start talking about the fate of Greg Day.

The other Owenses all stand and glare at Greg like they will take off his head and shit down his throat.

Coach Jenson calls us to the bench to get us away from possible trouble.

"Just relax. Keep calm. We knew these guys would be good. You can't lose your head again, Greg. We're within striking distance," Coach Jenson says.

But then the officials break and the referee assesses a flagrant foul. Greg Day is thrown from the game, and Coach Jenson loses his own head screaming and the crowd boos and shouts nasty words . . .

Air goes from my sail. I am heavy. Greg Day injured Tyler Owens. The refs were right to throw Greg from the game.

Except then, like a magical elf, Tyler Owens hops up, walks to the free-throw line, and hits two free throws plus a technical foul shot. He was not really hurt. Isn't pretending to be hurt cheating? Then the Marshall Mustangs get the ball again, because of the technical. Tyler Owens scores on Greg Day's replacement, Shane Tinley, who is maybe five foot nine in his mother's high heels.

What can I do against this Owens machine that also cheats?

As the half ends, we are down by eleven points. And there is a bad fire in my belly. I know this is no good. I try to breathe, but I can't.

Coach Jenson talks through halftime, but my fire grows. All I think: the Owenses are cheaters. I barely even hear that we'll play zone defense in the second half. My job is to protect the rim. No dunks, no layups for these Owens cheats. I will crush them first. There is fire.

And my fire burns bright. Most of the Owenses are really only good at layups. Yes, okay, with me not guarding him, Kyle Owens, the big-time college recruit, has space to hit jump shots and he does, but their Owens machine is not running so fast. Now I am underneath the basket and no Owens can throw up weak-kneed crap. Every time they get the ball close, I see what they are up to and steal, swat, smash it back in their cheating Owens faces. The crowd becomes mad. They cry, "Call a foul! Thirty-four is fouling every time, Ref!" But I know I am not. These Owenses are slow!

Kyle Owens becomes more frustrated, and the family play gets worse. He begins to take shots from farther and farther away, without even getting into their family offense. I snarl at him. I get rebounds. I fire outlet passes to Caleb Olson. Caleb streaks down the court. I explode behind him.

He shoots or he lobs the ball to me. Bang. Boom. *Sploosh.* I score many times. Caleb fires up three balls. We are both on fire.

As we hit the middle of the half, we are behind 41–44. I am coming for these Owens boys. Yes, I am getting very tired and have not been subbed out the whole game, and Caleb is red in his face and Shane Tinley looks like he might barf out his dinner, but I am coming for these cheating Owens boys anyway.

And then the sophomore Owens boy, Joe, does something bad. He dribbles at the three-point line in front of Shane. He looks down to me. Then, like lightning, he cross dribbles Shane. Shane, with his weak ankles, almost falls down, and Joe explodes into the lane. Instead of going for a shot, he lowers his head down and crashes into my chest, which is exposed because I am reaching straight up above my head to block his layup. I fall backward so hard, the wind is crushed from my body. My head hits the wood.

My sinuses drain. The lights get bright. Ringing comes in my ears. There are cries from Caleb Olson, shouts from Coach Jenson.

But does the Marshall Mustang crowd boo Joe Owens's dirty play? No. They stand up to see if I am dead.

I'm not. He can't hurt me.

Instead of acting like a man who is dying, I bounce onto

my feet and jump around and shout, "Do it again, bro. Do it! See what happens next!"

Then the ref blows the whistle. He gives me a technical foul for taunting . . .

Me? I was just knocked to the floor. What about justice?

"Are you joking?" I shout.

Coach Jenson shouts, "No!"

But it's too late. The bombs are already going off in my head. If Caleb doesn't restrain me, I might be throwing punches at the ref. He can't stop my mouth, though. My mouth is going on and on. I don't remember what I shout, but Derrick Oppegaard, the pep band drummer who was nearby, later tells me I used every f-word in the book on the ref. I make bad threats.

Just like that, I'm kicked from the game. I deserve it, because I can't control my emotions.

Still, Coach Jenson screams, "You fixed the game! You are stealing this, Ref!"

Coach Jenson receives a technical foul.

I slide onto the bench. My anger drains. My fear rises. What happened? What just happened? What if Renata finds out I am insane?

Joe Owens is given four technical foul shot opportunities. The crowd is silent. He hits one. He hits a second. He misses the third. He hits the fourth. Our few fans boo loudly as

Marshall gets possession of the ball again. They shouldn't boo. I did this.

The bottom falls from our team. Without me, the Owenses reign supreme. Within five minutes, Marshall has gone from their three-point lead to a sixteen-point lead. We only score a single basket the rest of the game.

And this rings in my head like a bell: The season is going away . . .

The season is going away . . .

Basketball is going away . . .

Now what? Now what?

And then it's gone.

As time runs out, Coach Jenson gathers us. "Hold your heads high. You just had the best year in Northrup basketball history. We hung tough against the team that will take our division up at state. I can almost guarantee it. In fact, they could probably beat anyone in any division. That's how good they are. Ten minutes ago, I thought we might take them."

Greg Day cries. Caleb Olson cries. Shane Tinley has a towel over his face. I don't cry, but I don't know how to cry anymore. I am dizzy and drained.

"I love you guys. I love you guys. Heads held high," Caleb Olson says.

I want to play more games with Caleb. I do not want him to be a senior. We hug. "I'm sorry I went crazy," I say.

"That was on the ref, man. You just reacted to the bullshit," he says.

I barely remember the "good game" line when we shake our opponents' hands. I say no words to the Owenses, but I remember Kyle saying, "We'll see you again, Thirty-Four."

TWELVE

I CHOOSE THIS

I get up so early after the loss to Marshall. It has been a bad sleep. I tiptoe down the hall and go into Renata's office. I don't want to wake her up, so I try hard not to bang into anything. This isn't easy, because I have big feet. I turn on her computer.

I have no brothers or sisters. I have no extended family, no aunts and uncles or cousins. In Philadelphia, at the Polish Culture Center Renata took me to each month for a meal and to talk Polish (I don't talk Polish ever, now), everybody said it was crazy for a Polish boy to have no family.

What am I supposed to do with that statement? Pretend I have a hundred cousins so I am okay?

They told me I look Polish, though, because I have dark

blond hair and dark blue eyes and a wide face and full lips and I am very white . . . that also describes many kids in Northrup High School. Do they all look Polish?

An old lady at the center named Magda said I must have lost my Polish part when I came to America, because I'm so quiet and don't smile very much.

But I never smiled when I lived in Poland, either. My dad left me with nuns and only one small suitcase of clothes and two crinkled photographs, one of him giving the finger and one of my mom playing piano that I left in my pants pocket and it got washed and killed.

Was I not Polish when I lived in Poland?

This is who I am: my body wants to fight and basketball is as close as I can get to fighting without being taken by the police. And my heart wants to be warm and safe. Maybe I am not courageous, not loud enough to be really Polish? Having a big bed and a giant couch is more important.

But I feel alone, too. Maybe nobody at Northrup High School really looks Polish. I am awake to google Polish girls in images.

I don't want the sexy poses, but only the regular girls my age who are smiling at festivals or wearing traditional clothes for dancing or maybe taking a walk in the mountains with their families. I stare at one in traditional clothes, with thick brown hair. Green eyes the color of fields.

I think of Carli Anderson . . . Does she look Polish? Anderson does not sound like a Polish name . . . but maybe?

Then I hear footsteps. I hit a bookmark on the browser so it looks like I am just checking assignments at school. The light goes on in the study. Renata stands in the door wearing her nightgown.

"Wow. You're awake already."

I nod.

"What time did you get home last night?" she asks. "It had to have been so late."

"Long bus ride," I say.

Renata stares at me for a moment.

"What?" I ask.

"I listened to some of your game," she says. "Michael had it on in his car."

I stare at her for a moment now. I swallow. "Why in his car?" I ask.

"We went to dinner," she says.

"Okay. Did little girls go?"

"They stayed home," Renata says.

"Here?" I ask.

"No, Adam. At their house."

"Oh. Okay."

Renata blinks at me, like she's trying to read my thoughts. Then she says, "The radio announcer called you a once-in-a-generation talent from southern Minnesota."

I let this sink in for a moment. "Huh," I say, but I think, *I am not from southern Minnesota. I am Polish.*

"I had no idea you were that good," Renata says. "I'm going to have to come to games next year, even if I hate crowds."

Next year. Next year. What can I do with myself without basketball? How can I go to school and see Kase Kinshaw who doesn't see anything but a refugee? How can I make it until next year? This thought almost knocks me out. "Excuse me," I say quietly, "but maybe, because I lost the game and didn't sleep good . . . well. Maybe I can stay home and get rest today?"

"Do you feel sick?" she asks.

"My head."

With her migraines, Renata is sensitive to head pain. She lets me stay home.

I call Barry to tell him I'm sick. He's disappointed he can't come for breakfast.

I lie down. Renata leaves. I eat everything in the house. Then I sleep on the couch while ESPN plays in the background. I have my Warsaw apartment dream two times, black ink flooding through the window. Screaming for my dad. The last time I am engulfed. The last time I choke and begin to die but then wake with a start.

I am so happy to find myself on Renata's couch with

Renata's TV playing NBA highlights. I choose this over being Polish. When people ask me to talk about my life in Poland, I can't say anything at all, because what I think of is dying. I love Renata's couch and her TV.

THIRTEEN
KASE AND CARLI

Thursday and Friday morning, Barry comes for breakfast and that is good, but nothing else is good. I leave the house and am drowning in tired. I don't know what to do with myself at school. I try a little in classes, but when I'm so tired readings make no sense and teachers talking make no sense, and class discussions with other kids make no sense, so what's the sense?

There is no basketball.

I walk down the halls looking at the floor. I become an easy target.

On Friday afternoon, Kase Kinshaw slides up behind me while I walk. He kicks my right foot into the back of my left ankle. I drop the books I am carrying all over the floor and stumble into a girl I don't know. My elbow hits her ear, and she grabs her head and starts to cry.

"I'm sorry," I say. I'm not even sure what has happened.

But then Kase hisses, "Everybody says you're such a great athlete, Duh. But you can't even walk."

I tense. Adrenaline courses in me. I move toward him. The bell rings. I blow out air on his face, which is not much below mine. He is a football player. He is on defense in hockey. He probably weighs more than me by forty pounds. This brawl would be ugly. And I am okay with that, except I can't have a brawl, because . . .

Kase whispers, "Watch out for me, Duh."

The rest of the day, I can't think of anything but Kase Kinshaw. My chemistry teacher, Mr. Burton, asks me to stay after class. He says, "This material is difficult enough when you're paying attention, Adam. If you let your eyes glaze over like that, you're not going to pass. Do you understand?"

I nod, but I am not really understanding. I'm thinking how Kase Kinshaw could be hiding anyplace and I can't fight him.

Barry has gone to his job after school. He isn't waiting for me in the parking lot. I creep through the halls, wary of any movement that might tell of an attack.

When Carli Anderson comes around the bush outside school, I jump and am ready to punch and run.

"Dude, did I scare you?" she asks.

"No," I say.

"Did you talk to Mayberry Cliff?" she asks.

"Who?"

"He called my dad last night."

"Oh," I say. I press myself against the school's wall. I stare at the front door.

Then she raises her arms. She says, "Check it out. No crutches. I can start to shoot next week. We should shoot. You're about the only person in school who could even hope to compete with me. I mean, after I'm all healed, which is going to be soon if I have anything to do with it."

I swivel my head from side to side, scoping for danger.

"What are you doing?" Carli asks.

Greg Day comes out a side door. He waves at Carli. She waves back.

"Hey, man," she says.

I nod at Greg. I have seen him with Kase many times. But Kase doesn't follow.

"Do you have a car?" I ask Carli.

"Yeah?" she says.

"Can I have a ride?" I ask, looking over her shoulder.

"I guess," she says. "What's up?" She looks over her shoulder, too.

In her car, Carli Anderson talks a million miles per hour. It takes me a few seconds to listen, to stop scoping for trouble. When I do listen, I find out many amazing facts. One, Carli was ranked a top-ten state recruit in basketball after her sophomore year. Two, she would try out for the junior national team this summer, except last September, not long after I moved to Northrup, she tore her ACL playing for fun against college boys at the Trinity College gym. Three, she thinks I am the boy version of her, because Northrup girls' basketball sucked until she was a sophomore and then, because of her, they nearly made it all the way to state. "The first time I saw you messing around in the gym in the fall, that's what I thought. *He's going to do for the boys' team what I did for the girls',*" she says. Four, her dad is the men's coach at Trinity College, so that's why he's interested in me. "Seriously, Mayberry Cliff is going to call you, okay?"

"Uh-huh," I say.

I act like none of this is amazing. I take it all in stride. I don't want to show her that she is making my heart leap in my chest. I don't want her to see that I have no clue who Mayberry Cliff is and have no idea why he would call me.

She knows more. Her little sister, Caitlin, is friends with Margery and Regan, so she knows that Renata spends time with Professor Michael. "Do you think they're doing it?" she asks.

"What?" I say.

"Just joking!" She laughs. "He's a great guy. He and my dad are buddies. And, oh man, his ex-wife was a total loon, too. Those girls could use an actual mama figure. Probably a brother. We're all glad you guys are here."

"I think they've been on two dates?" I say.

"Mike and your mom? No, more than that," she says. "She's wasting your inheritance on condoms!"

"Condoms?"

Carli is glowing. Her face is red. Her eyes are teary. "Oh shit. I'm sorry. I'm just joking. It's probably not cool to joke about parent sex, huh?" Even as she drives, she turns to me and her smile is so big across her face.

And I laugh, even though I don't laugh. Not ever. "Yes. Please shut up about condoms."

"I'll try," she says, beaming. She is so pleased with herself.

I am pleased with her, too. We pull in front of my house, and I don't want to get out. But I open the door and step onto the icy pavement, because what else can I do?

Carli leans toward me. She says, "Adam." She doesn't say anything else, but she seems very serious. She stares at me with her green eyes that seem Polish to me.

"What?" I ask when I can't take the pressure anymore.

"Listen," she whispers. "I will beat your ass in one-on-one by the end of this summer." Then she talks very fast and louder. "So you better get in shape, boy! It's not going to be like the weak shit you play in your high school games, either. I'm coming for you!" She points.

Oh boy. Oh man. I like her coming for me. How much

better to have Carli Anderson say this than Kase Kinshaw?

"I'm ready when you are, bro," I say.

"Bro?"

"Dude," I say.

"Okay. You better be ready." She says this softer.

"Okay." I shut the door.

And then she's gone, and I feel a big empty space in the world that she had just filled up.

FOURTEEN

THIS NOISE

It is Saturday afternoon. Some things have happened.

First, Professor Michael (he says call him Mike), Regan, and Margery eat Friday dinner with us. Renata makes kielbasas and potatoes and cucumber salad and sernik (a cheesecake), many of my favorite Polish foods. From Carli I am in a good mood. From the food I am even better. After, while Professor Mike and Renata talk in the kitchen, I play that I am a great dragon and Regan and Margery defeat me with magic and violence. Regan leaps from the back of the couch onto my gut when I am lying on the floor, which does hurt, but is so explosive an act it makes me laugh. Margery cups my head and says I am dying honorably.

Second, Renata, Barry, and I attend the girls' dance

recital on Saturday morning. The floors of the studio, in an old brick building downtown, are wood and shiny. The walls have mirrors. The room is filled with families and many little girls in puffy costumes. An old lady plays bad piano to get things started. The little girls run and jump. I have never been at a dance recital, but this is a fine one. By far the best dancers in the whole show are Margery and Regan. They jump the highest and they mess up the dance and they don't seem to care about anything except for the parts where there are kicks and fast spins. When their part is over, Regan slides on her stomach to leave the dance space. Barry whoops and applauds loud. Professor Mike leans and whispers, "She is too old to behave like that. See what I'm saying?" But I think she is only eight. Is that too old? I don't care what he thinks, because Regan is excellent. Barry agrees with me.

Third, we eat tacos for Saturday lunch. Tacos are now my favorite food, even more than meat pierogi. We all eat too much. Renata and Professor Mike go to the study to talk. Barry falls asleep on the floor of the living room. The girls fall asleep on the couch. I watch basketball all folded up on our love seat (I am too tall). But these kids? And Barry? All the noise they make?

I am happy. Me.

Then the telephone rings. Regan groans. Barry rolls over on the floor. He is drooling. He goes back to sleep. I hear

Renata answer. I hear her say, "I'm sure Adam will want to talk to him."

Who?

But then Renata doesn't come out of the study to tell me who called, to tell me who I will want to talk with.

Who?

I get off the love seat and walk down the hall to the study and walk in on Renata and Professor Mike kissing like they are teenagers.

FIFTEEN
THE FURY

Now it is early Sunday morning.

Mayberry Cliff.

On Friday, Carli had said that Mayberry Cliff would call me. Because I became drunk on Carli, I didn't think again about that name. And he didn't call. But Carli's dad did. Coach Anderson asked Renata for permission to give Mayberry Cliff our phone number.

After she stopped kissing Professor Mike, Renata gave me this information: Mayberry Cliff is the director of operations for the D-I Fury, a basketball team that plays AAU and Nike Elite tournaments. He coaches their 17U team, the oldest and best. The D-I Fury are headquartered in Minneapolis and practice either in the Chaska gym (forty-five minutes from Northrup) or in the Minneapolis Academy gyms (an hour's drive, at least). Renata blushed when she talked, not because of basketball. She told me she didn't know anything more, which was good. I wanted to get out of that room. Overnight, I lay awake, and not just from seeing Renata kissing like a teenager, which reminds me of when she fell in stupid love with Peter the dick man of Philadelphia, but also because Renata and I will speak with Mayberry Cliff today.

I don't know yet what this means to me.

At six a.m., I am at Renata's computer.

The D-I Fury website is good. There are very colorful graphics. There are flashy videos of good basketball plays. In the history section, there are pictures of boys shooting basketballs, holding trophies, and standing in line to eat at a cafeteria, too.

Almost every kid on the D-I Fury is black. From being in southern Minnesota for six months, I thought there were very few black kids in the state, but I am wrong.

I lean back in my chair and think of the boy I fought in Philly the year before. I remember his team. I remember them calling me Forrest Gump and making shit out of my play even as I scored on them again and again. But also in Philadelphia, most of my team were Nigerian and they were good people. I ate dinner at Mobo Bell's house twice, even though I couldn't speak English enough to have a good conversation yet. His parents were kind, and they gave me a delicious stew once and then some chicken on sticks that made my mouth too hot the other time. Mobo was funny. Not like Barry is funny. More like Carli.

I click a tab that contains a schedule for the upcoming season and get a big surprise. The Fury doesn't play much around the state of Minnesota. This team plays against teams from large cities all around America. There are games in Chicago, Kansas City, Las Vegas . . . the Fury travels to all of these places? Last year the team played fifty-seven games between March and August.

Basketball is your passport. Basketball is your passport, I repeat.

But what if I like my warm bed and my couch and my refrigerator? What if I feel at home where I am now?

What if Renata has babies with Professor Mike?

What if Kase Kinshaw punches my face?

I press a tab that contains the list of Fury alumni. Many are now playing in college. They are in universities in Minnesota, Wisconsin, North Carolina, California, New York, Michigan, and all over. Some Fury players now play professional basketball—there are two names in the current NBA, but many names that play professional in Europe.

Europe. *Basketball is your passport. Basketball is your passport,* I repeat.

I spend the next two hours in the basement doing dribble drills.

Then things happen fast. By one p.m., we have spoken to Mayberry Cliff. Renata and I have agreed that I will go to Chaska for the Fury tryouts. Mayberry Cliff says, "Adam is guaranteed a spot. We scouted him at Marshall. We're just not sure which team yet."

At two p.m., Carli's dad, Coach Anderson, has called back to the house to ask if I will work as part of the Trinity College scout team as Trinity prepares for their playoffs. Renata and I agreed that I will.

At six p.m., Barry Roland, Regan, and Margery have eaten pizza. They sit at the table drawing a map to the Dragon's Lair. Regan calls Barry "Shinja." Renata and Professor Mike hold hands on the couch.

I go to my bed, where I hope I will stop being dizzy from change.

SIXTEEN

PIVOT IN THE POST

It is the next Tuesday. It is after school. The Fury tryout is ten days away. For now, I will practice with the college team, because they have some injuries and need good players to act as "warm bodies." I am with them in a conference room high above the gym.

Here's something I should remember, because it's almost always true: with basketball, don't be afraid. Close your eyes and go where you're asked. Basketball makes it all better.

Me and the Trinity players watch a large video screen. On it are highlights of a big black guy making post shots. I am watching closely and listening closely. Coach Anderson, who is tall and skinny with a deep gravelly voice, talks about the player: Lawrence Rivers. Coach Anderson's mouth moves fast like Carli's.

"Lawrence is a transfer from South Dakota. Kid maybe isn't D-I talent, but he's close. He's a heavyset fellow. Big rear end," Coach Anderson says. "Plays in the post every set. Real good footwork, what I'd call refined footwork. Great in isolation. Great one-on-one down there. Reminds me a little of . . . who's that guy, Randy? Used to be on the Timberwolves. Now over at Indiana, I think?"

"Al Jefferson," a younger coach says.

"Right. Al Jefferson. Big butt." Then Coach Anderson looks at me. "See what he's doing, Adam? See how he moves his feet, draws defenders in, shoots or passes?"

"Uh," I say, because I see it but don't understand it.

"This is what we want you to do for the next few days. Give us a look like Lawrence Rivers does."

I squint at the screen. I never play with my back to the basket like that. I don't pivot around like a wheel. "I don't know . . . I don't do that with my feet. He is too spinny for my style," I say.

"Here's your chance to learn how," Coach Anderson says.

"But that's not my game," I say.

There is a long moment of quiet. No coach speaks. The team stares.

"Then make it your dang game," Coach Anderson says.

I nod, but I am worried, because most people don't know

what I know in my heart: I'm not that good. I don't have good ball skills, except dribbling. I don't have good touch on my shots. Other than very fast crossovers (both directions), I don't have many moves.

Maybe Coach Anderson knows all of this? After the players leave, he tells me to watch YouTube highlights of Hakeem "the Dream" Olajuwon. "Watch his hips. Watch his ball fakes. Watch those beautiful big feet. He's so dang crafty down there, guys guarding him nearly fall over."

"I've heard of Hakeem," I say.

"Good. I've watched you, son. You do a lot of running and jumping. Now it's time to hone your craft," Coach Anderson tells me. "We'll work on it together," he says.

After dinner with Renata, I watch highlights of Hakeem "the Dream" Olajuwon. In one way, Hakeem is like me. He is a tall foreigner (Nigerian, like Mobo Bell). In many ways, he is not like me. For instance, he could drop his foot back, shift it forward, pump fake, spin, then drop the ball in the hoop like it floated there on a soft bird, all while double-teamed by six-foot-ten professionals.

I want to do this. Coach Anderson thinks I can do this.

I go to the full-size mirror in Renata's room. She reads in bed and pays no attention. I drop step, spin, pretend to fake, fade away with a jumper . . . and knock over Renata's laundry basket.

"For gosh sake," she says. "What are you doing?"

I go into the basement and do all of this footwork with a basketball in my hands. The ball fake is good. I can show the ball like I am about to shoot, but then not shoot. The dribbling out of a spin is not so good. It is hard to keep the ball under control. The jump and jam I can do all night long (not in my basement, because I have no hoop and the ceiling is low, but in real life). The fadeaway I do not know how to do, because I don't have a soft bird. I have a brick cannon. But I think my practice makes me better. I can feel it. This is a big deal, something I didn't know before. While I am learning, I am smashing the ball into the ceiling, which is the floor below Renata's bed.

"Adam," she shouts. "I will kill you if you don't stop it right now."

Then I pivot all night long in bed. I know because I get wound up in my sheets.

For the next three days I come to the college before their practice begins. Coach Anderson watches what I am doing, plays fake defense, gives me instructions about the angles I should take with my footwork (it makes me think of geometry class), and every day I get better at being like Hakeem. Carli Anderson, who is now off her crutches, takes short shots on another court. She whoops once when I pivot, shot fake, then leap and jam. And even though I don't shoot the ball soft, the Trinity team has a hard time defending me.

On Saturday morning, Coach Anderson yells at his

players for being out of position. But to me he says, "That's amazing work. Just so good, son. My gosh, you're a natural, aren't you?"

"I can't shoot, but my feet can move."

"We can improve that shot. You release at your peak. Carli used to shoot that way, too, and now look at her."

I nod, because she shoots like feathers on a breeze. But then we are done, because the playoff game is the next day.

"We sure appreciate your help," Coach Anderson says.

He does not even know how much I appreciate his help. I hope he invites me back for the next week.

But maybe I didn't help so much. On Sunday, the Trinity College team goes to Moorhead, Minnesota, to play their game. They lose by ten. Lawrence Rivers doesn't score many, but the rest of Concordia does.

So there is no practice the next week.

SEVENTEEN

BARRY'S DOOR

There is too much time on my hands. There are too many people in my house. There is Kase Kinshaw in my school. There is no basketball for a week.

Without basketball, it seems Kase is everywhere. He gives me the evil eye during lunches. He stops across the hall from chemistry to give me the finger and mouth the f-word. He blocks the exit from the commons, and I almost fight him, but breathe and hold back. I can't lose basketball. Worst of all, I see Carli Anderson and her friends walking with him, eating lunch with him, laughing with him, and I get sick deep in my guts. What good person could laugh at his jokes?

At night, I practice my Hakeem "the Dream" post footwork in the basement. Professor Mike and the girls are often upstairs. They are always sitting on my couch.

Monday and Tuesday, Barry Roland comes over for breakfast. He is limping worse every day. On Wednesday, Renata says, "Barry, maybe you should take a break from breaking your shins all the time. I really don't think you're healing."

"Oh, I'm not kicking trees now," he says.

I look up from my omelet. "Why? What about Shinja?"

His face turns red. "I told you yesterday. I have a contusion that turned into an infection and I have to take antibiotics, but Tiffany's insurance is bad, so I have to pay all this money . . ."

"Insurance isn't covering everything?" Renata asks.

"There was a fifty-dollar deductible, and Tiffany says we don't have fifty dollars, so I have to work extra shifts this week."

Renata stares at Barry, then says, "I'll give you fifty dollars."

At first there is silence. Then Barry speaks. "No," he says. "Indomitable spirit," he whispers.

On the way to school, I apologize for not listening the day before, but Barry says it's okay, because he talks too much, so people don't listen. "Tiffany tells me to shut up all the time, so . . . ," Barry says. I can see he is unhappy.

Then on Thursday things get better. Carli Anderson walks up to me in the lunch room and says, "Tonight. Trinity

College gym. You and me shooting a game of H-O-R-S-E. Are we on, dude, or what?"

I look around. No Kase Kinshaw.

"Uh," I say. I smell honey, and I drown in her eyes.

"Uh?" she asks.

"Uh," I say.

"Duh?" she says.

I have no power against her, even if she laughs at Kase Kinshaw's jokes. "You bet, bro," I say.

She destroys me in H-O-R-S-E. Her shot is so much better than mine, even though she's not going through her whole shooting motion yet. She wins four games before her knee begins to get too sore. This makes her worried—she pulls off the brace, rubs her knee, talks to it like it's a child that behaves badly. Then she spends a lot of time stretching on the gym floor. I shoot and shoot and miss, which makes her laugh.

"I will get a better shot and you will be in deep trouble," I say.

"Oh, I am so far out of your league, dude!" she shouts. She is filled with glee.

Barry is not.

On the way to school Friday, Barry asks, "Do you love Carli Anderson, because even if she's really mean, I get it, she's handsome and she's tall, so you match?"

"Handsome?" I say.

"Yes," Barry says, looking at the road, not at me.

"I don't love," I say. "Also, she's not mean."

"Well, she's not very nice," he says. He drives on. His mustache gets small under his nose. "It's okay, Adam. It's okay if you think she's nice."

"Oh, okay. Thanks for that," I say.

We stop at QuikTrip so Barry can buy some wiper fluid. While he is filling the fluid container, I sit in the passenger seat and wonder what exactly his problem is? I can have another friend, right?

Right as I have this thought, the top hinge on the driver-side door, which is hanging open letting cold air in while he fills his wiper fluid, breaks. The corner of the door hits the pavement.

"Uh-oh!" Barry shouts. "Oh crap!"

I get out. We try to lift the door back on, but it will not close. Then Barry says we better just go to school.

"I can hold the door while I drive," he says.

But he's wrong. He drops the door while driving and then the door rips off the car. I turn and watch it spinning on the road behind us. I watch another car swerve so as not to hit it.

"Uh-oh," I say.

"The door caused an accident?" Barry shouts like a question.

"Not yet," I say.

He pulls over. We run behind the car into traffic and pick

up the door from the street. Cars honk at us. I want to give the finger, but I don't. We jam the door in his trunk, but the trunk won't close. Then we get back in the car. It is very cold. Wind blows in where there should be a door.

"What do I do?" Barry asks.

"Do we go to school?" I ask.

A cop car pulls up behind us and puts on his lights.

"Uh-oh," Barry says.

The cop sits for a few moments, then gets out of his car. I remember my dad in our shit car in Poland and how a cop stopped us and Dad jumped out of the car and tried to run down the street. I watched through the windshield. The cop leapt on Dad's back and pounded his head to the ground. Dad kept fighting. I leapt from the car to fight the cop, too. I was eight years old.

The Northrup cop doesn't beat us up, but he won't let Barry drive to school. "You have to get this hunk of crap towed, Barry," he says.

"Where?"

"Wherever you get it fixed."

"Merle fixes it?" Barry says.

"Well, then, get it towed back to your trailer," the cop says. "Let Merle do his magic." Small towns are strange. The cop knows Barry and he knows who Merle is, the boyfriend of Tiffany, the loser man who drinks too much and gets in fights downtown or sleeps on the kitchen floor.

"Okay?" Barry says.

The cop then drives me to school. Before I get out, he tells me I should be more choosy about the people I spend time with.

"No, I don't see Merle ever," I say.

"I'm not talking about Merle."

Only later do I realize the cop means Barry.

What's wrong with Barry? I wonder. But I only think about this for a minute. Carli comes up to me in the hall and says, "Your Fury tryout is tomorrow!"

What if I do love her?

EIGHTEEN

ASKING FOR MYSELF, RECEIVING

Barry's car door is a bigger problem than I thought. It is Saturday morning, and I need to go to Chaska for the D-I Fury tryout in an hour. Renata and I sit in the kitchen. Barry has just called with the bad news. Merle won't help him with the door, and he has no car. I am panicking.

Renata exhales hard. "I can't take you to Chaska, Adam. You know that. We made arrangements," she says.

Renata has duties at the college, because it is Trinity Parents' Weekend, where all the parents of students show up and tour classrooms and go to the chapel and go to big concerts by choirs and bands and donate money to the school. Professors are required to attend.

"Barry's car is dead," I say. "There are no arrangements.

He's going to the horse stable now to work to pay for his door."

Renata shakes her head. She stares down at her steaming cup of coffee on the kitchen table. "He can't drive my car?"

"He has to work!"

"I'm sorry." Renata shuts her eyes. "You'll have to skip today. That coach really wants you involved. I'm sure he'll help you get caught up."

What if I lose this opportunity? What if this ends my passport?

"Do you know anyone else who could drive you?" Renata asks.

I take in a short breath. I think. "Oh," I say. "Yeah, maybe."

Carli. I know where Carli lives. I saw her go into a house with a basketball hoop in front of it two days after we moved to Northrup. This is probably her house. I stand and begin to shove my giant shoes in a bag. I put my water bottle in there.

"What are you doing?" Renata asks.

"I will go ask for a ride."

"Who? Why don't you just call?"

"I don't know her number."

"Her? Do I know this person?" Renata asks.

"No," I say, even though Renata probably does know her dad.

"I think I need to get you a cell phone."

I stand up straight. "Why?" I ask.

"Because you have people to call," she says.

Then I am out the door. I cut across the street and jog across the campus. It is getting mushy, springlike. There is fog in the air. There are puddles from snow melting. I am terrified deep in my heart to knock on Carli's door. But I want to play basketball, basketball is my passport, basketball is my only true desire. I will knock. I will ring.

It takes me perhaps seven minutes to arrive at the house.

I ring the doorbell.

I ring it again.

There is no answer. There is no answer.

I ring the doorbell one more time.

There are creaking noises on the floor and footsteps. Someone is looking through the door's little window! A kid! From inside I hear a little-girl voice say, "Carli?"

There is more creaking. Then Carli looks through the window. "You?" she asks.

"Yes!" I shout. "Me!"

The door swings open. Carli stands in an old wrinkled tank top and giant pajama pants with crocodiles all over them. She is very sleepy. She has some sort of metal brace thing stuck in her mouth. The little girl, her sister, stares at me from a few steps behind Carli.

"What are you doing, dude?" she asks. "You have to go to Chaska this morning."

"Yes," I say.

"So why are you here? Do you want to talk to my dad or something? He's already on campus for Parents' Weekend."

"No. I . . . I . . . Barry Roland's car door fell off."

"What?" she says, and laughs.

"It's not funny," I say.

"Did he karate kick it?"

"No. The car is a piece of shit."

"Yeah, it is!" she says. She looks like she is being tickled by little elves in her insides. "Oh man!" she says. "That is so crazy! Was he driving when it happened?"

I nod. I picture the door spinning on the street behind us. "That's Barry Roland. He's unlucky at life," I say.

"He is," she says. "So?"

"So? He was going to give me a ride to Chaska."

She sniffs and leans toward me. Her eyes become smiling daggers. "So, I'm next man up? You got no one else? No family? No friends? No acquaintances?"

"No," I say. Maybe this is what Barry means when he calls Carli mean? "Nobody."

"That's a sad story, dude."

"Yes."

"Guess I'm your girl, then. Come on in." She smiles big and lets me in her house.

She smells so good.

Ten minutes later she has received permission from her

mom, told her little sister she cannot come along, and we are riding in her SUV, which is much better than Barry's shit show Pontiac (for instance, it has all its doors) and much better than Renata's Toyota (I fit in here without my knees hitting my chest). Like Barry, Carli talks and talks (she asks me once if she talks too much, but I say, "No way. You talk good," which makes me feel dumb). She also sings loudly to pop music.

She is a very bad singer. But I like her singing. It all makes me happy.

NINETEEN

MY REAL HOME

I want to puke like Regan's elementary school friend who puked milk through her nose, which is a gross story Regan told me recently. I am breathing heavy, but no one can know. There is too much noise.

The gym at Chaska High School is large. The whole place is made of glass and metal like a spaceship in the movies. There are three courts with nets that go from the floor to the ceiling separating each. Carli and I have followed the sound of bouncing balls from the building's entrance to here. And now I am glued in place and must seem in love with staring at these tall nets, because I am staring and staring. I am scared of looking at the basketball players who are all on courts across the gym floor, doing drills, shooting, while old men in basketball warm-ups watch and scribble on clipboards.

"Where are you supposed to go?" Carli asks. "Did they tell you which court?"

"I don't know," I mumble.

The oldest team—I believe they are the top team, because they are filled with boys who look like men—is on the court closest to me. I try not to look.

"Hey," Carli shouts. "Hey there, Devin Mitchell!" She waves at a black kid who is easily my height but with many more muscles.

"What's up, Carli?" he shouts back. "What you doing here? Girls don't do tryouts until next week."

She points at me and shrugs. He turns his eyes to me. They land heavy.

I look up and stare at the top of nets. They are some pretty tall nets.

"Devin used to come down to Dad's camp every summer," Carli says. "He's the best player in the state. Plays for the Junior National Team, too. Bet he goes to Duke."

"No," I say quietly.

"No? You don't think Duke?"

"I don't know."

"Are you okay?"

"No," I say.

Basketball is your passport, basketball is your passport, basketball is your passport, I repeat in my head.

An older black guy with a clipboard comes into the gym at that moment. He has big shoulders and wears coaching shorts. He scans the room until his eyes hit me and Carli. A big smile breaks on his face. "Well, hello, Ms. Carli," he says. "You provide some transportation this morning?"

"Yes I did, Coach Cliff," she says, also smiling big. They do a little funny handshake. They act like they are old friends. He turns to me. "So glad you're here, my man. I'm Coach Cliff." He extends his hand. We shake.

"Yes," I say. "Good." My heart is thumping hard from nerves.

"16U is on the middle court," he says. "We think you'll fit there. Coach Kalland is leading the tryouts. They're expecting you."

"Go get 'em, Adam. I'm going to hang with the big boys," Carli says.

"Just have some fun, son," Coach Cliff says.

I nod, then run toward the middle court, into the middle of the net where I poke around, then I have to find my way back to the outside, because there is no hole to get through. The boys on the middle court stop bouncing balls and watch me trying to find my way in.

Basketball is your passport. Basketball is your passport, I think.

It takes me ten seconds that feel more like several days. I look back at Carli, whose face has broken into a giant smile.

This, of course, is funny to her. Then I find my way around the side and the boys start running drills. I stand and watch. I already feel better, my feet on the hardwood, my eyes scanning the competition.

There are two boys at 16U tryouts who are as tall or taller than me. One is a white kid, Sean, who is slow as molasses in January (Coach Jenson used to call Greg Day "slow as molasses in January" back in our practices). Sean can't move his big feet and he can't jump, but he has muscles and is good at shooting the ball. The other is kid is skinny. His name is Mohammed. He is long like he's made of rubber bands that can stretch across the floor. He has a good touch when he shoots. Good for him. He is a better shooter than me. Sadly, I would break him in half if I played against him in a game, because I am explosive. I say this not to brag, but only because it's true.

The other boys are much smaller but are pretty good at basketball.

After some time, Coach Kalland, who is running the drills, points to me. He says, "Adam Reed, right? Come over here. I'd like to test out Sean and Mohammed on defense a little."

I would prefer to stretch, shoot some drills to get ready, but what can I do? I pull off the top part of my warm-up and drop it on the floor. I realize I have not even changed into my new shoes (I only wear basketball shoes, but the ones I have on are kind of worn-out). I still have on my pants.

I jog on the court, and the coach tosses me the ball and points me to go to the right wing. Sean lines up in front of me, spreads his long boy arms, and settles back on his heels. I head fake left. His knees lock. I dribble past him on the right and slam-dunk the ball. He has not even moved.

"Shit," he says.

The smaller boys standing around the baseline all whoop and make a whole bunch of noise.

"Dang, kid," Coach Kalland says. "That's fast."

"Yes," I say. "No. Maybe," I say.

"Yeah, fast," Sean says.

"Mohammed," Coach Kalland says. He motions for the other kid to get out on the court. Very long and skinny Mohammed smiles wide and jogs to the right wing. I run back over there, and Coach Kalland bounces me the ball.

I head fake Mohammed. He smiles. I give him another shake.

"I already saw that move. Don't you got nothing else?"

Before, I didn't, but now Hakeem "the Dream" and Lawrence Rivers have permanently moved into my feet.

I begin dribbling, turn, and back Mohammed down into the post.

"What are you doing?" Coach Kalland asks, like he's speaking to himself.

I pivot on my left foot, ball fake. Mohammed leaps into

the air. I step underneath his arm and leap up hard, jam the ball in the hoop.

The little boys on the baseline go crazy, shouting.

"Cliff!" Coach Kalland cries. "Coach Cliff!"

I stand there staring, not sure what's happening.

Coach Kalland reaches into his pocket and pulls out a whistle. He blows it loud and everyone in the gym stops what they are doing and turns to him. "Coach Cliff, Adam Reed is coming over to you. He's got no use for us," he shouts.

"No! I do! I don't have to play like Lawrence Rivers!" I say.

Coach Kalland looks at me and shakes his head. He laughs. He says, "Boy, that move wasn't any D-III Lawrence Rivers move. That was straight-up D-I, okay?"

"Okay?" I say.

"Now go talk to Coach Cliff. Thanks for stopping by."

Practiced skills are powerful. I learned just a little of the craft from Carli's dad, just a little from studying Hakeem "the Dream."

I don't do too much in the rest of the tryout but watch other boys get schooled by Devin and a smaller point guard. I do play defense on one kid, and he can't score on me. Coach Cliff thanks him and takes him off the court. He does not make the team.

Oh, I love being on the court even if I'm not playing. I

love watching passing lanes develop. I think about how I'd defend, how I'd use that gap. Everything makes sense to me with basketball. I love the squeaking shoes and the sound of the balls being dribbled on wood.

Man, I just want to play.

But I've already done my job. My skills have placed me on the top AAU team in Minnesota.

"Congratulations, son," Coach Cliff tells me. "I thought you might be ready for the bigs."

"Welcome to the show," says an old, heavy man who wears big rings, a University of Minnesota shirt, and a Fury baseball cap.

The only place in the world where I am welcomed is on a basketball court.

TWENTY
MORE SKILLS

Carli drives very fast down Highway 169. Maybe I didn't notice that she is a bad driver before because I was nervous for the tryout? Now I am afraid. In Poland, I saw a fiery crash happen close, near my grandpa's farm. This might be my first memory. Bodies being pulled out of a burning car. Carli zigs and zags through traffic on the highway. She sings. She messes with radio stations. She chatters about a girl from a town we pass who Carli hates and would like to stuff a basketball down her throat. I hold on for my dear life.

After a while she says, "You're from Poland, right? That's what my dad said."

"Uh-huh."

"Was your dad a basketball player? Was he big, too?" she asks.

"He played soccer. Goalie. Those guys are tall, I guess."

"Was he good at soccer?" she asked.

The picture I have of him, he stands in a goal and gives the camera the finger. I don't know if he was good. I shrug.

Carli looks over at me and makes a big show of rolling her eyes. "Dude, why don't you talk?"

"Uh," I say, watching the road. "I talk."

"Not much," she says.

"Don't have anything to say, maybe?" I reply.

"That's bad," she says.

"Why?"

"People like people who talk."

"What people?" I ask.

"Do you know any jokes? That's what I do when I don't have anything to say."

The idea that Carli Anderson would find herself without words makes me laugh. "You always talk."

"Yeah, but I never have anything to actually say! Have you noticed? I'm just making jokes, dude, because it would be pretty boring to sit around staring at the wall saying nothing all the time, like you do! I mean, aren't you bored right now?"

I don't tell her I'm afraid for my life because of her driving.

"No. I am thinking about basketball. My mind is occupied with this task."

"Your what? Your mind is occupied with this task?" She laughs. "See, that's a weird thing to say. You can be funny!"

"Yeah," I say. "Okay. I'm funny because my English isn't good. But I'm not making a joke, so . . ."

"So who cares if you sound funny? Just say what you're going to say and laugh if people laugh. You're not going to get better at English by staring off into space."

"Uh," I say. "But I don't want to get laughed at. Nobody should laugh."

Carli is quiet for a moment. Then she says, "Okay. This is going to sound weird. I mean, I know you're right. Nobody should laugh. But I also know you have no friends and you don't even talk to your own teammates at school and you're about to crash a new team of dudes who have played together for years, so it's not like they're going to want to accept you."

"They don't have to accept. I'll just play."

"Maybe you haven't noticed, but basketball is a team game. If Khalil and Devin don't want you to have the ball, you're not going to get the ball, so you better learn to talk."

"Really?"

"You're an awesome player who belongs with them, right? Mr. Doig wouldn't bring you in if you weren't good enough. So say your weird things in English, dude. Learn a couple jokes, maybe? Don't let it go like it did with Caleb and Greg at our school. They thought you were a stuck-up ass for half the season. They had no idea you were just weird."

"Okay. Maybe," I say.

I am processing so much information. Caleb Olson and Greg Day thought I was an ass? Then they thought I was weird?

Just then she passes another car on a curve, and I feel like we are on two wheels and I might scream like Margery when Regan hit her in the eye with a tennis ball. We make it around without flipping into the ditch.

I catch my breath. "Who is Mr. Doig?"

"The old man in the University of Minnesota turtleneck. He's short. Has a round belly?"

"Big golden rings and a pointy nose?" I ask.

"Yup. He's the man. He and his rich pals fund all the Fury teams. He heads the Fury board of directors. He hires the coaches and helps pick all the players. I'm sure he was at the game in Marshall with Coach Cliff."

"I didn't see nobody at that game."

"Anybody!" Carli shouts at me. "Learn real English, fool!"

Carli is laughing, so I try not to be mad at her. I feel my face go red, though.

"Anyway, Mr. Doig loves to help poor kids." She stops talking for a moment and blinks. "As long as they kick ass in basketball. That's his version of charity."

"Wait. Am I poor?" I ask. If he thinks I'm poor now, he

doesn't know the meaning of poor. Warsaw with my dad and no food was poor.

"I don't mean all the kids on the Fury are poor, just lots of them. I'm not poor. Devin isn't."

Right then a large truck lays on its horn. It is close behind us. Carli screams, pulls into the slow traffic lane, slows way down and laughs and says holy shit and hoots, then talks a million words every second, all the way home.

I am thankful for many things. One, that Carli slowed down and we didn't die. Two, that she has so much information, so many good things for me to think about. Three, that she drops the subject of my problem with talking.

Also, her whole SUV smells like honey. I don't want to get out when she pulls in front of my house.

TWENTY-ONE

GREAT JOKES

Over the next days I look up many jokes on Renata's computer, because Carli is correct. I am boring, and I make people uncomfortable everywhere I go. I am also Polish, and Polish people are known for good humor and for always talking, so what's my problem? I will learn jokes like I learned to play in the post.

I'm not sure I get American jokes, though. On Tuesday Barry's car door has been put back on his car, so he comes to breakfast with me and Renata. While Stan Getz plays in the background and Barry eats his ham and egg sandwich, I break out this joke: "What's the difference between a piano and a fish?" I ask.

He scrunches up his face and blinks behind his big

glasses. "What do you mean?" he asks.

"You can tune a piano, but you can't tuna fish," I say.

"What?" Barry asks.

"Is that a joke?" Renata asks.

Maybe it's not a good joke, I think.

On Wednesday night, Renata and I go to Professor Mike's house, because he has decided to try a Polish recipe. He fries pierogi. When they are made right, they are great. But these don't smell right. He has filled them with mushroom and cabbage, and that is something that would be very fine in a pierogi, but they don't have the same flavor of sweet cabbage pierogi my mom made on Grandpa's farm.

The girls are happy, because they like Chinese food.

"This tastes like Panda Express at Mall of America," Margery says.

She is right. Panda Express is not Polish.

While I chew and swallow big chunks so I don't have to taste too much, Professor Mike says, "Adam, what was your last name in Poland?"

I look over to Renata. She flinches.

"Sobieski?" I say.

Professor Mike has not noticed Renata. He nods. "Oh, isn't that a famous name in Poland? I feel like I know that name."

"It's a famous king's name," Renata says quietly. She is a scholar of Slavic literature and history, so she knows a lot about my country. That's what she was doing when she found me, researching at Warsaw University.

"King?" Regan says.

I nod. "Warrior king. He rode in on horses and saved Vienna from the Ottomans," I say.

"That. Is. Awesome," Margery says.

"You should go back to Sobieski as your name!" Regan says.

I swallow. It's strange to hear my old name. "My mom is Renata now," I say. "Renata Reed."

There is a moment of silence that is awkward. I think about Carli. I bust out this joke: "What did the ghost say to the bee?"

"What?" Renata asks. "Is this another joke?"

"Boo bee," I say.

"What?" Margery says.

"You know, like boobies?" I point at my chest.

"Ha-ha, ha-ha-ha!" Regan cries. She loves my joke. Regan is now my favorite person next to Barry and Carli.

The next morning, Thursday, I stop Barry from talking about his bad mom, Tiffany, and how he has no money to pay for tae kwon do lessons and how he owes Bob for three months of tae kwon do already, even though Bob told him not to worry about it, he has to worry about it, and so he has to work all weekend, but has no money for gas, so how can he drive to work? This is the joke I use to ease his troubles:

"What do you call a cow with no arms and no legs? Ground beef."

"Ha-ha," Barry says. "Good one."

"Cows don't have arms, Adam," Renata says. Then she gives Barry two twenty-dollar bills. "I know you don't want to take this, but you need gas money or you can't earn money."

Barry looks down at the table. "Thank you," Barry says. "I'm sorry. But I will pay this all back, okay? I promise."

"That's a good joke, though, right?" I ask.

"Don't worry about it," Renata says to Barry.

The next morning, I will go to the Fury weekend camp at Minneapolis Academy. Coach Anderson will drive. Carli Anderson will be there, too. Although she can't play, she will hang with her basketball friends and help to coach the 12U girls' team.

I am prepared to tell Carli many, many jokes. I am feeling good.

TWENTY-TWO
TO THE CITY

Friday morning, a Lexus SUV pulls in front of our house. Renata follows me out the front door. The corners of her mouth are down-turned. She says, "You are getting too old, Adam."

"No," I say.

She stares at me like she's expecting more.

"I'm just right," I say. "I'm the age I am."

She laughs a little, more than when I make my new jokes. We are almost to the Lexus. "I've been a good mom to you, right?" she asks.

"Uh," I say. I stop, because Coach Anderson has gotten out of the car and I don't want him to hear this odd conversation. "You are my mom. That's good."

She nods. "I wish we had gotten you that cell phone."

I nod.

"You all ready, buddy?" Coach Anderson says.

Renata hugs me. "Kick butt, or whatever you jocks like to say."

And then I am scared. I've never been away from Renata overnight, not since she finally managed to adopt me in Poland nearly five years ago. I did not let myself think about this moment before.

Coach Anderson stands behind the SUV with the back door open. "Throw your bag in here," he says.

"I call shotgun, dude!" Carli says from up front.

"Shotgun?" I ask.

"Front seat!" she says.

Renata is forgotten.

"I like back seats," I say, smiling big. I throw my bag in back, then climb into the door behind Carli. She twists and gives me a smile.

"I love camp," she says. "It's so fun."

Coach Anderson climbs in the driver-side door. "Don't you even think about playing, Carls. You're here to coach. Your knee is not remotely ready."

"Whatever. I'm just a baller," she says.

"Baller," I repeat.

"My gosh, I hate that word," Coach Anderson says, but he laughs.

He pulls from the curb, and we roll past the college. Maybe Renata stayed in the cold yard and watched me leave? Maybe she waved? I don't know.

We drive through a glowing Minnesota morning. Spring snow that fell earlier is almost gone and the ditches turn green. Carli sings terribly with the radio until Coach Anderson says, "Good lord, Carls. Please put a sock in it."

I don't want her to put in a sock, because I like her bad music so much.

We drive far past the exit for Chaska High School. Soon we are on a road of many lanes, filled with cars, getting closer to Minneapolis. Finally, after going so close to the airport I thought two airplanes would land on the SUV (I ducked, which made Carli laugh, because if a plane really landed on the car my ducking would not help), we take an exit. Then we turn into a neighborhood with nice big houses that overlook a river as big as the Vistula River in Warsaw. I know this must be the Mississippi. What else? It's the biggest river in Minnesota. Actually, it's the biggest river in all of America.

"We could live here, Dad, if you'd get a job at one of the Twin Cities colleges," Carli says.

"No way. I'm happy where I am," Coach Anderson says.

"Blah. Northrup," Carli says. "I want the city, man!"

TWENTY-THREE

YOUNG BLOODY BOY

Two minutes later, we are in the parking lot of a very fancy school. Buildings are made of blond bricks and glass or red bricks with ivy growing up the sides. It reminds me of an old place in my memory, the center I lived in in Warsaw with the nuns after my dad dumped me off. I have a hard time leaving my seat.

Carli Anderson puts on her backpack, and slides from the front. "You coming?" she asks.

I sit.

Coach Anderson leans back in the SUV. "Ready, buddy?" he asks.

"Adam?" Carli says.

"Yeah. Okay." I open the door and climb from the SUV.

I gather my bag from the back seat and pull it over my shoulder.

Carli leans on the SUV. "They're a bunch of ballers, just like me and you," she says quietly. "Don't worry."

But I'm not worried about basketball. Basketball is a dream come true. The rest of life is the nightmare.

Carli smiles big. "Time for me to go be a girl," she says. She turns and walks slowly away, stiff on her leg.

"You coach. You don't play," Coach Anderson shouts after her.

I am sad the boys and girls aren't together.

Coach Anderson heads toward another building. I follow him to the redbrick boys' dormitory.

In the lobby area, two ladies sit behind a folding table. They have a stack of folders piled up and a paper with a list of names in front of them.

"This is Adam Reed," Coach Anderson says, before I have a chance to say my name.

"Yes, Reed," I say.

"What team?" one woman asks, looking down her list.

"17U," I say.

"You'll be on the third floor," the other woman says, a nice smile spreading across her face. "Do you have your permissions and your Conduct Contract?"

I unzip my bag and pull out the permission slips Renata signed and also a long contract that lists all kinds of bad behavior on it that I promise not to do. I can't take drugs or smoke cigarettes or drink liquor or beer or get arrested by the police. I don't want to do any of those things, so I am okay. I hand the papers to her.

Then the first woman says, "Oh no."

"Oh no?" Coach Anderson asks.

"Adam's on floor one. You're with a 14U boy for some reason," she says.

"Wonder why?" Coach asks.

"Don't much matter. You'll be with your team plenty, Mr. Reed."

They give me a towel (I brought my own), sheet, and pillow (I have my own), a folder with a map, rules, offensive diagrams, and a schedule. They give me a little envelope with the key to my room.

Coach Anderson then says bye to me. I go to find the room and my fourteen-or-under roommate. His name is Jesse, the lady at the desk tells me.

The dorm at Minneapolis Academy is very pretty on its outside, but its inside is smelly and dark and the room I will stay in looks like a hospital room in an old Polish horror movie.

My roommate is only thirteen. Jesse is so white he is like a sickly ghost. He is also as tall as me, but he weighs maybe a hundred and twenty pounds. This boy has the biggest feet I have ever seen—big, floppy dolphin flippers—and he has a nosebleed for the whole first hour we are in the room together.

"Sorry," he says with his voice that sounds like a sad goose honking. "I have a bad nose." He bleeds on his pillow, on the floor, on his own chin, on ten thousand Kleenex, which he drops on the floor after he fills our whole garbage can.

"Excuse me," I say, making my bed. "But are you dying?"

"No. Ha-ha. This happens a lot," he says, tipping his head way back to stop the blood. "Especially with stress."

"But maybe you need to see a doctor?" I ask.

"Nobody wants to room with me because they think I'm gross," he says.

I look at blood on Kleenex everywhere. "Oh really?" I say.

"How come you got stuck with me?" he asks.

It doesn't matter. I will soon be playing basketball and everything will be good. That's what I think.

TWENTY-FOUR

BAD REACTIONS

Very soon we are due to the first practice. My gut's nervous, but I am ready. I will be a good teammate. No one will think I'm an ass. I have a joke ready about a lonely cookie and his mom, who has been "a wafer so long." Get it, a wafer? Away for?

My bleeding roommate and I head to the boys' gym together. Girls are practicing in the academy's nice gymnasium. We are in the ice arena, which is made back to a basketball and tennis court area after the first week of March and the end of the high school hockey season. Jesse has twenty-five Kleenex jammed in the left side of his nose.

We enter and are the last boys to arrive. There are basketballs bouncing everywhere. I love the sound. Cement arches of the arena echo with this beautiful noise. Then the whistle blows. All motion stops. "Over here, Adam," Coach Cliff shouts from the court farthest from door. I jog to Coach Cliff, and the basketballs begin their bouncing once more.

But not at 17U. No basketballs bouncing.

Eleven other boys await me. All of them have crossed arms. I wave, which is my stupid nervousness, like saying, "Duh." And in return, they glare harder, like I am not welcome among them. This is not the right time for my cookie joke.

I slow down my jog. I swallow hard.

Coach Cliff slaps me on the back, then says, "Glad you're here, buddy." He turns to another boy, the one who has muscles like a big man. "Devin. You lead warm-ups. Paired with Adam."

"Come on, Coach," he says. "I'm with Khalil."

"Not today." Coach Cliff turns to me. "Adam. You remember Devin from last week?"

I nod.

"He's your partner. Just do what he does."

I nod again.

Devin shakes his head.

Why? I'm good at basketball. Why would he not want to be paired with me? Heat grows in my heart. Devin dribbles the ball away from me. I follow him to a spot on the floor. Other boys get paired and line up near us.

Then Devin fires passes at me. Hard. Chest, bounce, overhead chucks that hurt my hands to catch them. He doesn't even look like he's trying. The ball pops from his hands. I copy what he does. I can throw hard, too.

After a minute, Devin shouts, "Read and react." The smaller, guard-like boys go to the top of the key. Me, Devin, and few others—taller ones—stay down under the basket. "Just make a move," Devin says without looking at me, because I'm nobody to him. "Like you're committing to defending one side or the other. Like this." The guard dribbles down. Devin leaps to his left. The guard reacts to Devin and drops in a layup. "Then rebound," Devin says. He grabs the ball and dribbles up to the top of the key. The shooter remains below the basket waiting to pretend to play defense. I get it (except maybe I don't).

A boy with the ball is coming up to me. I slide left, and the boy makes his move to shoot a layup. But I can't help it. Defense is fun. I leap back and hit the ball out of the air. "No, dude," the kid says. "Come on. Let me warm up."

"Don't block him, Adam," Coach Cliff shouts. "Not now."

"Oh," I say. "Okay." I chase the ball and go to the top of the key behind Devin. He shakes his head at me like I'm an idiot. The heat grows more.

Does he think I care if he is happy to play with me? I am used to all the bad people. I have lived with my dad. I have fought boys in Poland and Philly. I exist with Kase Kinshaw always trying to be in my head. I don't care about this muscle guy!

We repeat the drill for some time. No defense. The defender rebounds and soon gets a chance to shoot. Teammates keep stopping and popping shots from farther out from the hoop. At the elbow by the side of the free-throw line, I have hit the end of my range. My shots look dumb and dumber, like I am whipping the ball. But Devin, who is big as I am in height and more of a man in muscles, keeps moving backward, farther and farther, beyond the three-point line.

And he does not miss. The ball takes wing from his hand and slides through the net silent and perfect.

And I see, for the first time since my growth spurt and my arrival in Minnesota, a boy about my age who is far better at this game than me.

My stomach tightens.

He doesn't like me? Screw him. I don't like him.

But, shit, he is too good. He is better. He is bigger. He jumps high easily. He runs light on his feet—I am not even faster. He shoots the ball better than the best of the guys I saw in the playoffs.

Devin Mitchell fires from five feet beyond the three-point line. The ball slides through the net. I fire a brick into the front of the rim. He is not just a tiny bit better than me. Devin Mitchell belongs on a different planet.

He doesn't like me?

The heat in my heart grows stronger. I feel it burn down my arms and legs. I am different everywhere. I stick out like a sore thumb. I am the sore thumb. In Northrup, at least I am the best. But here, I am not even the best. I am just different. Weird. Awkward. Fumbling.

The team moves to a passing drill where the dribbler reacts to a defender by passing to another guy, who crashes to the rim for a layup, and I am a head case, confused. I throw the ball out of bounds. All of these boys laugh and shake their heads like I am stupid. They all hate me, huh? Then we move to what Devin calls back-door cuts and I am lost again, but I end up with Devin slam-dunking over me, bouncing the ball off my shoulder. The whole Fury team shouts and woots.

I burn in every part of my body. This makes me focus.

On my next back-door cut (I run to the right wing, then quick turn back to basket, fly in), the boy who handles the ball gives me a lob. I leap, take it from the air well above the rim, and smash it through the hole. Then, before I am thinking, I hang on the rim and shout loudly.

When I drop to the floor, I am surrounded by the Fury team. They are shouting, not good things.

Coach Cliff blows his whistle.

Devin shoves me. "You want to show us up, Farmer?" he spits. "You get on our team for a minute and you front?"

Coach Cliff blows his whistle louder and longer.

I know Devin could destroy me. It takes everything I have not to punch his big face. I lean toward him. I remember that I could lose everything if I act . . .

Then Devin shoves me so hard I fall back onto the floor.

There are suddenly many loud whistles blowing from everywhere. Five coaches come in and surround us.

"Devin Mitchell, what in the hell are you doing, son?" Coach Cliff shouts.

"D-Mitch, you get off my court right now," another man yells. It is the short old white man in his Fury baseball cap. Mr. Doig is what Carli called him. "No brawlers, no thugs!"

Devin stands over me, swears under his breath, shakes his head, and walks off the court.

"Everybody go clean yourselves up," Coach Cliff says. "No more practice until we have this issue sorted out. Shower, then a meeting in forty-five at the fourth-floor lounge."

I push myself off the floor. Everyone stares at Coach Cliff.

"Adam Reed, you stay behind. The rest of you, get out of here," Coach Cliff says.

As they leave, Coach Cliff says, "Now you listen up, son. These guys don't think you belong here. You're not doing yourself any favors by showboating."

"That's right. Show you belong with your play," Mr. Doig says.

I nod. But it wasn't my fault. Devin is the ass.

All the way back to the dorm room, I grumble and mumble. So many people are shit. I don't like bad people in Warsaw or Philadelphia. I don't like them in Northrup. And I don't like these stupid Minneapolis ballers.

I stop walking for a second. That's every place I've lived since I was little.

Maybe I don't like people? Is there something wrong with me?

Then I imagine big Devin busting a dunk on my face and terrible Kase tripping me as I walk by. Why do they all do it?

I don't care about people. I hate people.

I walk fast.

TWENTY-FIVE

GUIDANCE, PART I

Forty minutes later, I sit on my bed in the dorm room. I have punched the bed many times and am exhausted. It's good that Jesse has not yet returned from his practice to see me crazy. At the end of the punching, it occurs to me once again that I have problems and maybe I myself am one of them.

Why did I get angry that Devin is better at basketball? Isn't it just a fact, not something he did to me? I can be angry about him being nasty, but what made me slam-dunk the basketball and hang on the rim is that he is better.

Just then, a knock lands on my door. I expect it is Coach Cliff, but it is Carli Anderson.

I am not wearing a shirt.

She pauses and looks down at my chest. She says, "Oh. Whoa." I fold my arms because I am embarrassed. Her face blushes. Her eyes come back up to mine.

"Uh?" I say.

"Okay. I have to concentrate," she whispers.

"What?" I say.

She shuts her eyes for a moment, takes a deep breath, then opens her eyes wide. "Uh, holy shit, dumbass. You already got in a fight?"

"Yes," I say. "Okay."

"Well, great job."

"No. Not good."

She shakes her head, and I can smell her shampoo. I become a little drunk in my brain. "Listen," she says, "I know you only have, like, two minutes before you have to meet with the team, or whatever, but you need to know a couple of things, okay?"

I nod, still drunk. "Yeah?"

"I'm coming in, which breaks team rules, by the way, so don't let me do it again."

I step out of her way. She looks at my chest as she passes, but then she finds many bloody Kleenexes on the floor. "What's with this mess? Did you get punched?"

"The Kleenex is from my bleeding roommate," I say.

"Did you punch him?" she asks.

"He bleeds all by himself."

"Good." Carli nods. Then she crinkles up her eyes. "Adam, my dad thinks you have huge potential."

"I know," I say.

"But you aren't that good yet."

"But . . ."

"Shut up! You're not that good yet, okay? And Dad thinks you should be on the 16U team. He couldn't believe they moved you up. No way you belong on the same court with Khalil Williams."

"Who?" I ask.

"That point guard? He's awesome."

I know who she is talking about. "He's pretty good," I say.

"No, he's really, really good. And Devin Mitchell? Why would you fight him?"

"Because," I say.

"Have you watched him at all? Have you looked him up on YouTube? There's, like, hours of Devin Mitchell highlights out there," Carli says.

I nod. "I know. I saw today. Devin is a hundred percent better than me, okay? He jumps as good. He shoots way better. I do not belong on court with him."

"Then why'd you fight him?" Carli asks.

"I didn't really fight," I say. "He shoved me."

"Because you tried to show him up."

"I don't know."

Carli nods slowly. "Adam . . . I know you're smart."

"I don't think so."

"You are. You're actually cool."

"No," I say.

She nods more. "But you are not easy, okay?"

"I know," I say. "But I'm trying. Listen, I learned some jokes."

Carli laughs a little. "Really?" she asks.

"Yeah."

She takes another deep breath, then says quietly, "Man, nobody knows you, but everyone thinks they know you."

"Why do they think that?"

"Because you let them make up who you are."

"I don't understand."

"Everybody in Northrup thinks you're some kind of mute, basketball-playing freak show."

"Not everybody. Kase Kinshaw, yes. But not everybody."

"Yeah, Kase Kinshaw."

"He's a bad jerk."

"He's not. He's my friend." Carli pauses for a moment. Then she says, "Let's just talk about these dudes here."

"What about them?"

"They think you're something you're not, too. They think they know exactly who you are. And if you act weird or angry or if you stay silent, they will keep thinking you're just some stuck-up, rich blond kid from southern Minnesota."

"I am not that," I say.

"No," she says. "So you have to speak."

I stand back up. "But I don't speak right when I try."

"You speak fine."

"I got jokes. Should I tell jokes?"

Carli shakes her head. "Try this, please. Try, okay?" She looks at the ceiling for a moment, then back at me. "In the meeting, tell them you're from a different country. Tell them you're really stressed out about getting moved up to 17U and the dunk was a release. Tell them you cannot believe you're playing with such giants of Minnesota basketball . . . well, you don't have to say that exactly, but let them know that you know they're really, really good and it's a privilege to play with them. And you really want to be a part of their team."

"Then my jokes?" I ask.

"No, dude. Jesus!" Carli says.

"I was joking about that," I say. "I'm not dumb."

"I know," she says.

"I'm not a mute freak show," I say.

"Dude, I know," she says.

There's a knock on the door.

"Is it really against the rules for you to be here?" I say.

"Coach Cliff sent me to talk to you. It's okay this time," she says.

TWENTY-SIX
GIANTS OF BASKETBALL

I have seen rooms like this at colleges where Renata has worked. We lived for two months in a graduate student apartment when I first came to America. There are chairs of faded red color that are low to the ground and they look cushy and comfy, but don't be fooled. They are not comfortable. These chairs are strewn about on dirty gray carpet. There is an old TV in the corner and a crusty fridge. This place is a student lounge.

All the D-I Fury 17U team has once again beaten me to the spot. I enter right before Coach Cliff. All the players are very low in those chairs. No talking. They all glare at me as I enter, and I feel sick and I want to give them the middle finger, but I want to play basketball with them more.

Remember they are giants of basketball.

Mr. Doig leans on a table at the front of the room. "Sit down, Adam," he says.

There is one open chair in the front row. I go and sink into it.

Mr. Doig begins walking back and forth in front of us. "Do you know why I started this organization?" he asks.

No one says a word.

"Because," he says, looking at the ceiling, "I love this game and I believe kids are the future. And so I wanted to merge these loves, basketball and kids, with my personal understanding of what makes an individual successful." He stops and looks to me. "Have you had a chance to read the materials in your folder yet, Adam?"

"Not too much," I say.

He shakes his head at me. Glares. "*No, sir.* That is the appropriate response to my question, son. Show respect."

I am confused for a moment, but in Poland there is more respect shown for old guys than there is here usually. I think I understand. "Okay," I say. "No, sir."

Then Mr. Doig looks to Devin Mitchell, who is also in the front row.

"Stand up," Mr. Doig says.

Devin Mitchell pushes himself up from his chair. He makes Mr. Doig look like a little toy fat man.

"What do we learn on the Fury? What are the six factors

of success?" Mr. Doig asks.

Devin takes in a deep breath, then says in a quiet voice, "One, work hard. Two, dream big. Three, prep particularly. Four, respect your coaches. Five, no excuses. Six, never give up."

"Good. Now, who brought Adam Reed onto this team?" Mr. Doig asks.

"You and Coach Cliff," Devin says.

Mr. Doig's face turns a shade of red. His voice gets low and gravelly. "How are you to refer to me, son?"

"Sorry, sir. You brought Adam Reed onto this team. Sir."

Mr. Doig nods. "And who am I?"

"You are a coach. You also lead this organization, sir," Devin says.

Mr. Doig nods again and returns to his walking. "Now, if I see any one of you treat Adam Reed in a fashion that is anything but respectful, I'll call it like I see it. And that is that you are disrespecting the wishes of your organization's CEO and the wishes of your coach. Does that violate team rules, Devin?" Mr. Doig asks.

"Yes, sir," Devin says.

"And what happens to boys who violate team rules?"

"They are dismissed, sir," Devin says.

"That's right. Terminated. I don't care if your dunks are ESPN highlights, if you can't follow the rules, you are out of here," Mr. Doig says. "But maybe you don't care anymore?

Maybe you're too big for this team? Have you talked to your father about how big you've become?"

"No, I'm not so big, sir. I love this team," Devin says.

Then Mr. Doig turns to me. "I believe you disrespected your teammates this afternoon, too, didn't you, Mr. Reed?"

Without a thought, without a duh, I speak. "Yes, I did, sir," I say.

"Do you have anything to say for yourself?"

There is a short pause. I am thinking he knows what Carli Anderson said to me before in the dorm room. Should I confess I am a poor, troubled Polish boy now? Even if I don't want to talk about Poland to these guys? Mr. Doig lifts an eyebrow. So I stand. I say the thing Carli told me to say, but nothing about Poland.

"Fury team. I am sorry I dunked and shouted like that. This day gives me a lot of stress, and so I dunked and let out the stress. You boys are giants of basketball in Minnesota, and I am respectful. Please forgive me." I sit back down.

From the back, someone speaks. "Giants of basketball?"

"Khalil, do you have something to add?" Coach Cliff asks.

Khalil is the special point guard Carli discussed before.

He stands. "Yeah. Yes, sir. I do," Khalil says. "Me and Devin talked through this over the week. We aren't trying to disrespect our leaders or even Adam Reed. Not really. We're just confused, okay? Between the two of us, we know at least five dudes who have skills that exceed this . . ." He points at me. "They exceed what Adam Reed can do on the basketball court."

The other players all nod their heads.

"At least five," Devin says from his chair. "Probably more like six or eight, sir."

Khalil nods at him, then turns back to the rest of us. "So the only reason we can come up with that you, sir, and Mr. Doig, chose him is that he's a farmer boy."

"No, I'm not farmer," I say.

Devin stands up again. I look up at him from my chair. He is very unhappy and very nervous. I don't understand what's going on. He talks fast about me. "Now why we grabbing this farmer boy? Why would coaches go outstate to pick up this farmer? It's not like he's one of those big blond fives you sometimes see around here. He's not six foot ten. He's just blond, right?"

I begin to understand something that Carli told me. That they see me only as a boy who is blond and blue-eyed from a small town. They don't see my life.

"Why him, sir?" Devin asks, pointing at me.

"Yeah, why?" Khalil says.

Devin waits for no answers. "Maybe because it looks better to the press if you can put a token white boy on the team? Was it bad the 17Us were all black last year? Maybe it looks better to the dudes my dad and Mr. Doig hit up for cash to help fund this program? Is that it . . . sir?" Devin again does not wait for answers. "But I have to ask this: who is going to benefit more from this program? A farmer who probably lives in a nice house, with a nice old mom and dad, who can afford college no matter what . . ."

He doesn't know me. "No," I say.

"Or maybe Shawn Carter, up at Columbia Heights, who averaged twelve a game this season and has three sisters in that little house of his?"

"Hold on, son," Coach Cliff says, raising his hand.

Mr. Doig makes a fake spit sound. "First, it is not your role to wonder about my leadership. You do your job. I'll do mine. Do you understand?"

Devin stares hard at him for a second, then nods. "Yes."

"Yes?" Mr. Doig asks.

"Yes, sir," Devin says.

"Second, I don't give a rat's ass what color hair my players have. What do I care about? Shawn Carter has a juvenile record. Isn't that true?"

"Um. Yes, sir," Devin says. "But, come on, it's not real. It's from a stupid fight in seventh grade . . ."

"No thugs on this team," Mr. Doig spits.

"He is not a thug, sir," Devin almost whispers.

"'Thug' is not the right word," Coach Cliff says. "But Shawn Carter does not meet eligibility requirements for the

Fury. That's the truth."

"The board agrees unanimously on this count," Mr. Doig says. "You must be a good citizen, and you must be the best or have the potential to be the best. That's all we care about. And it is offensive for one of my boys to tell me that black and white matters after all I have done. Race isn't a factor here. Not in my organization. Do you understand, Devin Mitchell?"

Devin doesn't say anything for moment. Then says, "Yes, sir."

Khalil sits down slowly. Devin stays standing. He gets an odd look on his face, like maybe he swallowed a bad piece of fish.

There is a long silence. Awkward. I think of Carli. I think how they don't know me and that is causing problems.

"Listen, please. I'm not a farmer," I say.

Coach Cliff shakes his head, says quietly, "That's just what these boys call any white kid from outstate, isn't that right, Devin?"

"Yes, sir," Devin says.

"But, okay. My grandpa used to be a farmer, but he's dead. Also, I'm not from outstate," I say.

"Dude, of course you are. That's anyplace outside the city," Devin says.

I shake my head. "No. No way. I'm not from this state

at all. I'm from Poland. I just have one adopted mom, who is American, who found me when I was homeless. No 'good old dad,' because he was so poor that he left me with nuns. No 'good old mom,' because my real mom is dead . . ." All the boys are staring at me with their mouths hanging open. "Also, I'm just pleased to be here with giants of basketball, and I'm sorry I slam-dunked and shouted, because I have a lot of stresses and I just want to be part of the team," I say.

Khalil stands up fast. "Damn, dude. That's it? You speak so jacked up."

Coach Cliff growls, "Khalil."

"We heard about you from the Owenses. They were like, *who the f* . . . who the heck is that dude? There was one newspaper article just about how you're some badass dunker. I mean a *very fine* dunker. But then when we tried to find you on Twitter, Facebook, Instagram? You got nothing!" Khalil says to me.

"Nope. Not anything. I got no phone," I say.

"Khalil. Sit down," Coach Cliff says.

"But? I just . . . ," Khalil says.

"Sit."

Then Khalil does sit, slowly again, like he's scared.

Coach Cliff turns to me. "Adam, how tall are you?"

"Six foot, six inches, maybe six foot seven."

"What is your vertical jump?"

"I hit thirty-nine inches."

"Damn," another kid says.

"How many points did you score a game this year, your sophomore year?"

"About fifteen," I say. "But a lot more the last half of the season."

"And how long have you been playing basketball?"

"Since eighth," I say.

"Since what?" Devin asks.

"Eighth grade," I say. "Began two and a half years ago, when I was in Philadelphia."

Devin exhales slowly. He sits down.

Mr. Doig points at me. "Now that is what I call potential. You fellas understand me?"

"Yes, sir," Khalil says.

"Anybody else?" Coach Cliff asks. There is total quiet. "Then how about we talk basketball? Any of you have any problems with that?" There is more silence. "Okay. Well then. Listen up. We're going to run motion this year."

A round kid behind me groans from his gut. "Oh man, no."

"Charlie, you got something to add, son?" Coach Cliff asks.

"No, sir," the kid says.

"Good," Coach Cliff says.

Everybody seems sad about "motion." I don't care what offense we play. They talk more. I don't care about our schedule (we will have three warm-up games in Minnesota in the next month, then start traveling for tournaments). I don't even care that we will eat pizza donated from a fancy restaurant for dinner.

I am so tired from speaking.

TWENTY-SEVEN
GUIDANCE, PART II

It is 5:30 in the morning. I am still in bed, although I am awake. My worry is that I will sleep through practice. There can be no more mess-ups.

I've spent much time examining handouts about the motion offense. It is team passing, constant cuts and picks, and a requirement that I not just post or drive, but also stop and pop if the defense sags and takes away scoring lanes. Jump shooting is not good for me.

During the meeting, Coach Cliff said the motion offense is the same one the Marshall Mustangs, the Owens family, used to win the state tournament. All these Fury teammates know about the Owenses, know how good they are, but they think the Owenses play like farmers. Even though I was exhausted during the meeting, I heard that.

"We've run isolation for the last three years, sir," Khalil had said. "Why are we doing this?"

"We have no Kenny this year. We don't have height. We have athletes. The motion gets our opponents' bigs out of position. We'll make them run. We'll strand them out on the three-point line if they try to man up on us," Coach Cliff said. "We'll get bad switches. Imagine Devin down there posting up point guards?"

I would like to post up point guards.

I turn over in my bed.

Jesse sleeps. He is not bleeding now, but he snores loudly.

I will not sleep anymore . . .

Then there is a tapping sound. I sit up fast. I listen. For a moment, there is nothing. Then the tapping comes again.

"Uh-oh," I say in a whisper.

I roll from bed. My heart pumps hard. I slide across the tile floor to the door in one giant step. What am I thinking? That I am late for practice and don't know it or, maybe, Renata is dead from a car crash and this is the police coming to tell me.

I crack the door open. "What?" I whisper.

Carli Anderson is standing in the hall.

"Can I come in?"

"What about the rules?" I say. "Mr. Doig will terminate us."

"Just let me," she says.

I pause.

"Now!" She pushes past me into the room.

Jesse sits up, blinking, looking scared.

"Hey, dude. Don't tell anyone I'm here," Carli says to Jesse.

"Okay," he says.

"Cover your ears," she says.

He lies back and covers his face with his pillow.

Then she leans in really close and whispers in my ear, "Last night I hung out with Tasha Tolliver and Katy Vargas, and Tasha said that Rashid told her at dinner that he was going to mess you up on the post, because Kyle Owens called you a head case."

"Who is Rashid?" I ask. "Who are Tasha and Katy?"

"Dude, ballers. Fury players? Do you even know where you are?"

"Okay," I say.

"Listen. Khalil said it was stupid, that you seem like a good dude, but Devin still doesn't want you around and Rashid definitely doesn't."

This news hurt me. "But I said I'm Polish and not a farmer."

"In the meeting Coach Cliff named you the starter at the five, right?"

I nod.

"Rashid is taller than you, and he's waited for his turn to start. I mean, it's his turn, dude! Why can't you come off the bench?"

"I didn't ask to start."

"But Rashid blames you anyway."

"Shit," I whisper.

"Anyway, because the Owenses got you to flip out in their game . . ."

"I didn't."

"I was there, dude. You lost your mind," Carli says.

"No one got hurt," I say. Usually there is more damage when I lose my mind.

Carli raises her eyebrows. Then she says quietly, "Rashid and Devin are going to rattle your cage. Don't lose your shit. Even if you catch elbows, okay? Mr. Doig will give you the boot if you lose your shit. He's famous for doing stuff like that."

I sigh. "Okay. Okay."

Carli reaches her long arm out and puts her hand on the side of my face. It is soft. It makes warm blood fire all over my body. "I want you to stay on the team. You and I are really good for Northrup basketball," she says. "I don't want to lose you."

I nod again.

A half second later, she is gone.

"Is she your girlfriend?" Jesse asks.

"No," I say, still standing on the spot where she touched my face.

"She's pretty hot," he says. "Like, she walks like she's hot."

"Please shut up," I say.

TWENTY-EIGHT

MR. CALMNESS

Morning practice. I have spent time being calm. I am ready, thanks to Carli Anderson.

Rashid throws his elbows into me as he establishes space on offense. He is very strong and rough and pointy, and those elbows hurt my ribs and shoulders and even my neck one time.

When he plays defense, he shoves me and slaps at my face and scratches my arms with his long fingers. I am bleeding from a cut on my right arm, which a trainer has to dab and put a pad and tape on. "Keep it clean, fellas," Coach Cliff shouts.

On rebounds, one hand of Rashid's goes into the air to tip the ball away from me, the other makes a fist and drives into my kidneys, and I am hurting from this big-time, and I have a desire to kill everyone, but instead I just keep smiling at Rashid and telling him that he is a fine player and that he is doing a dope job.

The other players slowly believe I'm a crazy man. They make faces at me. They make faces at each other. Rashid says, "Owens doesn't know what he's talking about."

Then Devin runs over me to get a loose ball, even though he is on my scrimmaging team. I would like to punch through his head, but I get up and offer my hand for a high five. "Good hustling, Mr. Basketball!" I say. This is goofy shit I'd say to Barry, but no one else. I don't mean it, but they will not push me out.

Trey bounces a pass off my face from very close range.

Khalil actually shouts, "Come on, man," at him. Khalil is my favorite.

Then Devin bounces the ball off my face. My sinus passages drain from the pounding. "Sorry I got in the way," I say to him. "Don't understand this offense yet."

"Okay," he mumbles.

Finally, Coach Cliff screams at us, "What in the hell are you boys doing out here? You call this basketball? Run the damn offense. Make good passes. Keep your bodies under control or I'll send you all home!"

"Yeah, Coach," Devin says. He then gathers us together and says, "Let's just really play."

"That's what we should've been doing, you fools," Khalil says.

"Kyle Owens is a big shit bag," I whisper.

They hear me. All the boys laugh a bit. "What?" Khalil says. "I thought you weren't on Twitter?"

"He wrote tweets about me?" I ask.

"Ha-ha. Farmer knows more than he lets on," Khalil says.

I shrug because I don't know shit, but I keep smiling.

And soon I am smiling for real, because when Devin decides to play real basketball instead of spending his time making me Farmer the Fool, this offense begins to work. Khalil is so good. As he moves, I can feel this offense. I know where to go as defenders hedge. I swing underneath and set picks and pop to the three-point line and take passes that open space for flying Devin, who I hit with lobs, and he jams the basketball like an NBA superstar. "Good look," Devin tells me two times.

Rashid soon must work just to keep up with my flow, my fast running. He is not like me, and he gets tired. Devin picks him, and I back-cut to rim. Khalil lobs the ball in the air for me. I leap, grab, smash the ball through the hole. It bounces off Rashid's shoulder.

"Kyle Owens!" I shout.

Khalil laughs. Devin smiles a little.

Khalil gives me a high five on the way back for defense. "You paid Rashid back for all that scratching."

"What scratches?" I ask, like nothing ever bad happened. Khalil laughs. "Oh, no scratching, dude."

"I bleed from my arms all the time," I say. "It's natural."

He nods. He smiles. He fist-bumps me.

A few minutes later, Coach Cliff blows his whistle after I dunk once more. He says, "Boys. That's it! That's what I'm talking about!"

At lunch no one talks much, because we have run very hard all morning. Khalil does say, "We play the Minne-Kota Stars in our third warm-up game. You can pay Kyle Owens back in person."

"That's his team?" I ask.

"Minne-Kota Stars. That's the Owenses' AAU."

That is good. Payback in person. I will do that, I think.

After lunch there is a break and more practice and then we will get on a bus to go to dinner at Devin's home, which is also in Minneapolis. I am a little bit scared of this for a few reasons. But the morning was great. I am back where I belong, excelling on the court.

Before I go to my room to take the post-lunch break, I walk all over the Minneapolis Academy campus looking for Carli's dormitory, because I need to thank her. She is my basketball guardian. She is the best girl. I need to tell her I get to play Kyle Owens again. I find her dorm. I try to go in. A large woman stops me. "Oh no you don't, child," she says.

I go and rest in my room.

The afternoon practice I am very sore from the beating of the morning, but the balling is so dope. We all work on post moves and dribble drills between little orange cones.

I am not the super king at post, but I am better than all the Fury players other than Devin. He is a real Hakeem "the Dream" Olajuwon, patient and baiting the defense like an animal trainer who makes seals stand on their tails. Then, when the defense gets too close, he spins, shoots, scores so easy. I learn from watching how he goes slow and then very fast.

But I am truly excellent at dribbling, as good as Khalil, maybe. Many dribble drills are the ones I did for hours and hours in the ice and snow of Philadelphia's sidewalks and in the basement of Renata's house, where the floors are a little uneven. These are Steph Curry dribble drills.

"Farmer! Man!" Khalil says. "You got a handle!"

"Yeah?" I say, without stopping my dribble, two basketballs that I make go between my legs one after the other.

Then coach fires passes at us, and we dribble quick between our legs, back and forth, and then fire the ball back out. This drill is like a baby game to me.

"Farmer has ball skills," Rashid says almost so I can't hear.

"Yes, but I am not a farmer," I say.

"You're a Polish farmer," Rashid says. He smiles.

It's good, I think.

TWENTY-NINE
THE F-W-B

There is a small bus built for twenty people that waits at the entrance of the Minneapolis Academy main door. I'm outside first after I showered fast. These showers remind me of my time with the nuns. The floors had puddles where you soaked your socks, and there was no privacy. Also, Jesse began his nosebleeding once more in the dorm room. I don't want to watch Kleenex making more piles.

Jesse does a weird thing before I leave the room. He says, "If I let you take my phone, will you take a couple pictures inside Devin's house? I want to be an architect."

"Can I watch some videos on the phone?" I ask.

"Sure! As long as you take pictures."

I agree. And so I carry the phone in my hand as I leave the

building. I watch Hakeem highlights while standing outside the bus, waiting for the other 17U Fury players to come out from their rooms. Hakeem is number thirty-four, like I am in my school.

By the time the other boys have come out, I have watched videos of Steph Curry and Michael Jordan and LeBron James. I think of all of these players, I am more like LeBron James in my speed and my jumping. I do not shoot as good as he does, but I think he had to learn to make jump shots as he got older and that part of his game did not come as easy as his driving and jamming. His jump shots are not as soft as Curry's or even Jordan's.

James is three inches taller than me, though. He is also one of the greatest of all time, so maybe I am not so good?

But I am only sixteen. Maybe I can be the greatest? Devin walks past me and goes on the bus. *No, not me*, I think. Maybe Devin Mitchell can be the greatest.

"Farmer, why you staring off in space? You getting on the bus?" Khalil asks. He has come outside and is dressed better than me in my warm-ups. He is wearing black jeans and a shirt buttoned up to the top button.

"I have a phone," I say, and show it to him.

He shakes his head. "Okay, dude," he says.

"It's a nice phone, right?" I say. "I didn't steal it."

"Good." Khalil laughs.

This is a joke. I made it. During this night Khalil begins

to laugh when he looks at me, because I make more dumb jokes. I think I was meant to be funny. I think I remember that I was funny before my mom died. I remember her laughing at me with tears in her eyes. I remember her gathering me in her arms and laughing.

The neighborhoods we drive through are nice and then they get much nicer and then much more. This is not what I expected to see, but Jesse did give me his phone because of architecture, so maybe.

Soon we drive by a lake with giant homes nestled on tree-lined bluffs. The bus stops in front of one.

"This is it?" I ask.

"Devin's pops is so rich, bro," Khalil whispers.

I stare at the white, modern expanse of this house. So many giant windows. So many old, big trees surrounding it. Now I understand why Jesse wants pictures.

We all leave the bus in a single line. Out in the driveway, Mr. Doig says to us, "Be on your best behavior. Show Devin's father that you understand what it means to be a member of the Fury."

"Yes, sir," Khalil and a few others say.

Devin shakes his head and closes his eyes.

We walk up the drive and then onto stone steps that rise through steep white walls and planters with bushes.

"How'd his dad get so much money?" I ask Khalil.

"He's an inventor or something and owns a business."

Devin heard me. "My grandmother had money. It's not all my father. She built something real by herself."

"What did she do?" I ask.

"Famous jazz singer," Khalil says. "For old people."

"Jazz singer?" I say. They don't know I listen to jazz every morning. They don't know how Renata loves it. "She sings jazz? Your grandma?" I ask. Nobody answers me. Devin's father stands at the front door.

"Come on in, come on in!" he shouts. "Welcome D-I Fury basketball! Welcome Coach Cliff. We're so happy to see you boys here."

"I like jazz. Me and Renata listen to it all the time," I whisper to Khalil.

"You're a weird-ass farmer," Khalil replies quietly.

We walk into the front door. I follow Khalil, and Mr. Doig walks in right behind me. Mr. Mitchell pats all the boys on the shoulder and smiles wide. When we get nearby, he looks past me to Mr. Doig and says, "Hello, Karl! How these boys treating you? They staying in line?"

Mr. Doig glances at Devin. Then he says, "They're a fine team. We've never had so many athletes, so much speed."

The first room I enter is very big with tall white walls and warm yellow light coming from lamps. I pull out Jesse's phone and take a pic. Then I realize that the black-and-white photos on the wall are the people I eat breakfast with each day. All are famous jazz people. Oh boy. I lose my mind.

"Dizzy!" I shout.

Yes, I mean very much shout.

"Are you dizzy, Adam?" Mr. Doig asks.

"Dizzy Gillespie!" I point at the big photo on the wall of a puffy-cheek guy playing a bent trumpet. "Thelonious!" I point at another of a man leaning over the keyboard. "Mahalia!" I point at a picture of a woman raising her hand, singing. "Coltrane!" I shout at a man with a sax.

"Really?" Devin says to me. "You know these people?"

"Kid knows his music!" Mr. Mitchell says.

"Jevetta!" I say, pointing at a picture of a very young Jevetta Mitchell with arms spread, singing big. "I saw her in Philadelphia with Renata. She's so good."

"That's my grandma," Devin says.

I turn to Devin. "What?"

"Jevetta Mitchell. She's my dad's mom, man," Devin says.

"Jevetta?" It's like I have been hit on the head and stunned. I stare at Devin. "She is grandma?" I say. I drop the *a* like I used to when I just learned English.

"What's that accent?" Mr. Mitchell asks me.

"Polish," I say.

"Polish? No kidding? You eat at my table, son. You've got me curious."

As we walk from the big living room with beautiful

photos down a long hall, Khalil talks over my shoulder. "You just made yourself favorite white boy, Farmer."

"FWB?" I ask.

"The F-W-B!" Khalil says. Everyone looks at me.

"Maybe Farmer is better," I say.

THIRTY

TELLING NO JOKES

All of us sit in a dining room that looks out onto a nice, grassy backyard. Ten of the players sit at a big table, and they laugh and eat many lasagnas and breadsticks. Devin and I sit with his parents, Devin's sister, named Saundra, Mr. Doig, and Coach Cliff. I have only had lasagna a few times, but this is as good as anything I have put in my mouth. It's as good as my real mom's bigos, which is lots of meat in cabbage and honey that tastes like heaven. I have four full servings, which makes Devin's mom think I am crazy, but in a good way.

Devin's dad says, "If you love Caroline's cooking, Caroline will love you right back. Isn't that true?"

"I know you have good taste, that's all," Mrs. Mitchell says.

"I do. Also, I am so hungry every day, so this is extra good," I say.

"Devin, bring this child back here anytime. He needs nourishment."

"Yeah," Devin says quietly.

Maybe it's because I'm drunk on food? I keep talking free, like I'm a real Polish kid who likes parties and people.

There are speakers hung in the corners of the dining area. All the meal, they play songs that I love, songs that Renata and I have listened to throughout our life together.

"This is a good song. Miles Davis. He's a smart man," I say.

We hear Modern Jazz Quartet and Brubeck and Mingus and Stan Getz and Charlie Parker. Each one I can name and I can hum along. The boys at the other table have their conversations and talk basketball and girls and other sports, too. But I get more from this meal. By dessert, Mr. Mitchell tells me the whole story of Jevetta, how she was born in Chicago in 1939 and got to study opera in New York, but only loved jazz music, and how she toured all over the world, and how she was old enough to be in the South of the United States, performing back when she couldn't drink from white people's water fountains and had to use separate doors to get into concert halls, and all this crazy stuff I have seen on TV but thought was ancient history, not from people who are just grandmas now.

Devin doesn't say a word through any of this talk. He looks down at the table.

Mr. Doig does not say anything, either, until the story of Jevetta is complete. Then he talks to Devin, who still does not look up. "None of that trouble got in the way of your grandmother's success, did it, Devin? She kept working to achieve her goals. Climbed to the top of the ladder. I wish our culture valued those stories instead of focusing on how this country fails your people."

There is a moment of silence.

"Come on now, Karl. Our culture loves those stories," Mr. Mitchell says. "How much TV time every fall Sunday morning is dedicated to retelling some NFL player's rise against all odds?"

Then Mrs. Mitchell says, "Jevetta has a magical talent, Karl. That voice opened doors that would not open for most people of her generation."

"All hard work pays off in some fashion," Mr. Doig says.

"I do think most hard work pays off," Mr. Mitchell says. "The other story happens, though. There is hopelessness, poverty that is too great to overcome without the benefit of great talent, great luck, or more likely both."

This I understand right away. "Yeah! If I couldn't dunk, I would be eating at McDonald's in Northrup right now," I say. "Just a dumb Polish kid with only one friend who has a fluffy mustache. No one wants to hear this story."

Devin turns and looks at me. A small smile creeps on his face.

"Now how in the world did you get to Minnesota?" Mr. Mitchell asks me. I think he's happy to change the subject.

"I'm adopted."

"Don't hear much about Polish adoptees, not like Russian or Ukrainian kids."

"No. Maybe not? Polish people have big families usually, I think. So maybe kids get taken care of? But I saw plenty of orphans when I lived with the nuns. Maybe those kids are from families like my family? Death caught us by surprise, and we fell to pieces."

There is silence for a moment.

Nobody wants to say anything. I am in shock these words have fallen from my mouth, and I don't want to say anything more. I think of the black ink coming into the apartment in my dream. But some kids can't stop themselves. It's Devin's twelve-year-old sister, Saundra, who speaks.

"What do you mean, death caught you by surprise?"

Carli says I must talk. Okay. I take a heavy breath. I speak slowly. "My mom—her name is Malwina—got cancer. She probably had it for a long time, because I remember her going from strong to weak when I was smaller, but I don't know, except I know she died."

Everyone looks at me wide-eyed, like they are sad, or maybe want more information?

"My dad was so upset about my mom. We lived on a farm with my grandpa, who was my mom's father. Dad and Grandpa got in a big fight. Dad pushed my grandpa down on the floor of the kitchen and he kicked him and then I tried to fight my dad, but I was seven years old, and we left that night. We went to Warsaw. It's the biggest city in Poland."

"Yes, we know it. We've been there," Mr. Mitchell says.

"You?" I say. This is surprising. I can't picture the Mitchells in Poland. Also, just saying "Warsaw" makes me sick to my stomach. I exhale to get rid of the black ink. Then words fall out of my mouth that have never fallen out. Why here? Why in this home sitting next to a big basketball kid who doesn't seem to like me?

Because Carli.

"I don't like Warsaw. My dad said we belong there in the big city, because we're Sobieskis, and Sobieskis are important to Poland. We're supposed to be the greatest Polish family, kings, except at school nobody treated me nice, maybe because my dad drank all our money and I missed so many days when he was angry or asleep and none of my clothes were clean and none fit and then he started hitting me so much I felt ill and then he would feel so sad about hitting me he began to cry all the time, and then he'd get mad about crying and he'd do it all over again and again, and I got kicked out of my school, and I should've gone to another, but I didn't go to it. Then Dad knocked out three of my teeth all at once and he lost his mind and hugged me and cried and soon after took me to a Catholic home, a nun school—it was an orphanage, I guess—and he cried and cried and said sorry, but he just left me standing there. The nun held me, and I watched him walk across the street, light a cigarette, then get in a car driven by a man I never saw before. I don't know what happened to him. They couldn't even find him when Renata adopted me."

By this point, all the players are silent, even the ones at the other table, and they're staring at me.

"Oh, honey, I'm so sorry," Mrs. Mitchell says.

"Were they baby teeth?" Saundra asks. "The ones your dad knocked out?"

"What kind of question is that, Saundra?" Mr. Mitchell asks.

"If they're baby teeth it's not so bad!" Saundra says.

"No. Not baby. Renata got me some new teeth. A bridge?" I point into the side of my mouth.

"Who is Renata?" Devin asks. Even he is looking at me now, maybe for the first time.

"She's my adopted mom. She teaches college in Northrup at Trinity."

Mr. Doig nods. "That's how we found Adam. Ted Anderson down there."

"Well, how did Renata even find you? Is she American?" Saundra asks.

I sigh. Because I have said more words in a row than maybe I ever have in my entire life, I am already exhausted. But everyone leans toward me. I have to tell the rest or I will seem like a weird kid, right? I take a big breath. I nod.

"Yeah. Renata is American. She is a Slavic scholar, so . . . I was living with some other kids with the nuns for a couple of years and it was okay, but then I did something. I was ten years old and I had begun to be hungry all the time, because I think I was beginning to grow fast, so I stole some candy bars from the store across the street from the nuns. The store clerk saw me and tried to chase, but I was too fast. I knew he recognized me, because I was in there all the time. I got scared and didn't want to go back to the nuns. I was in trouble with them a lot already and this seemed much worse, so I ran to Lazienki Park. This park is as big as the whole town of Northrup, and it was summer, so I could hide in there, in bushes and trees, and sleep okay on newspapers against this stone wall behind bushes, and there is plenty of water to drink. I just had to stay away from cops, you know? But by the fourth day I was hungry, even though I ate some trash."

"Trash?" Khalil shouts.

"What do you mean, trash?" Mrs. Mitchell says. She has tears in her eyes.

"It was food, but in the trash, yeah," I say. "I think maybe I began dreaming while I was awake, because I didn't have enough food."

"That's called hallucinating, dude," Khalil says.

"You could've been poisoned from eating trash," Saundra says.

"Let Adam talk," Devin says.

"Okay. Maybe I was hallucinating? It was a hot summer day, and I was lying along the stone wall behind bushes to rest and I heard this music begin to flow from a piano. They have concerts in this park, so that is not weird, except it was Chopin music."

"I play Chopin!" Saundra says. "I'm practicing a nocturne for my piano competition."

"Oh. Yeah. The nocturnes. My mom played those. She played piano well, and Chopin was her favorite because he is a Polish guy . . . and because I was a little crazy, maybe, I thought she was the one playing the music in the park."

"Like, her ghost?" Rashid asks.

"Yeah. I think so. I left my wall and wandered across a field, right through a soccer match and then to the concert. I sat down in an open chair and saw that the piano player was an old man in a tuxedo, not my mom, and then I just lost it bad. I started crying like a baby."

"Didn't you say you were ten? You were a baby, practically," Mrs. Mitchell says.

"I cried when I couldn't find Mom in the Mall of America two weeks ago. My phone ran out of battery," Saundra says.

"She disappeared for all of five minutes," Mrs. Mitchell says.

"I was lost!"

"We know. Could you be quiet?" Devin says.

"What happened?" Khalil asks me.

"This woman, who was young, who was sitting next to me, leaned over and said in the ugliest foreign-sounding Polish I ever heard, 'What is wrong with you?' It was Renata. She asked, 'Can I help you?' I wanted help pretty bad then, so I said, "'Yeah, please.'"

"It's like the ghost of your mom led you to your new mom," Saundra says.

I just nod, because I thought of that many times, and I don't want to think too hard about it now. It might make me cry like a baby again. "Renata was studying Adam Mickiewicz, a Polish poet, for her PhD dissertation. My name is Adam, which she thought was a sign she was meant to find me. It took her almost two years to get through bureaucracy, but she adopted me and brought me to live with her in Philadelphia."

"Was your grandpa sad?" Saundra asks.

"I found out he is dead also. I have nobody, except basketball."

"Except your adopted mother, who sounds like a remarkable woman," Mrs. Mitchell says.

"Yeah," I say. "I have Renata and basketball."

"Man," Devin says quietly, shaking his head, "we didn't know what we were doing when we messed with you."

"Messed with him?" Mr. Mitchell asks.

"Not really messed," I say. "Just playing basketball."

Devin laughs, but it is not a happy laugh. Maybe it's more like a sigh.

"Well, Adam Sobieski, you have an incredible story," Mrs. Mitchell says.

She says my name that is not my name, and my chest aches. "I'm Adam Reed. Renata's last name is Reed."

"Dude, Sobieski is fearsome, though," Khalil says.

"Reed's not," Rashid says.

"You don't remember Willis Reed, then," Mr. Mitchell says. "Great NBA player. Hell of a business executive, too."

But I am not listening. I know Sobieski is badass. I miss my name so much. Renata took it, but she also gave me a life. I miss my real mom. I could fall onto the floor of the Mitchell's house.

It doesn't help when Saundra plays a recording of the Chopin nocturne I heard in the park that day Renata found me. I have a hard time holding myself together. It's good that Mr. Doig has his sixty-fourth birthday. It's good that we eat cake and ice cream and everybody stops looking at me.

I go and take a few more pics of the big house for Jesse. Then I hide in the bathroom and press my fists into my eyes.

Jesse loves the pictures when I get back to the dorm.

I have not thought much about my name in a couple of years. But then Professor Mike brings it up when he cooks for us. Then Regan says it's a better name than Reed. Then Khalil says it's a better name. It is a better name, because it's my name.

I am Adam Sobieski. I am not Adam Reed.

What if I didn't sit down next to Renata in the park that day?

I would be dead, maybe.

THIRTY-ONE

WE ARE A TEAM

The next morning, there is a final practice before camp breaks. We spend most of the time scrimmaging and our motion offense looks good. The only time the offense grinds to a halt is when I catch the ball outside the block and the defense gets time to sag away to let me take a jumper. Rashid just smiles and nods, because he knows I hate jumpers. I dribble and look. Dribble and look. Someone must get open.

"Pull the dang trigger, Adam!" Coach Cliff shouts.

Then I do, with great hesitance, and the rock is more like a brick crashing against the rim and bouncing away.

It is rare, though, that I hang on to the ball, that I don't find a good passing lane or drive to the basket very fast.

During the final five minutes, all the Fury teams from all

the ages, from girls' side and dudes' side, all come to watch us. The presence of this audience makes us all play harder, and I am sad to say that Rashid scores two buckets against me.

He has long arms, and although I jump higher, it seems he is able to jump sometimes twice when I only jump once, so he is good at tipping the ball out from me on rebounds and then scoring the ball before I can do my second jump to block him. He is so good.

But I score, too. On the final play, with only a few seconds left on the clock, Khalil drives, then finds Devin swinging to the three-point line on the far left. Rashid hedges and jumps out to defend, and I think Devin will shoot, so I dive behind Rashid to collect the rebound if necessary. Instead of shooting, Devin sees I am wide open and he lofts the ball sweetly into the air. I leap, catch the ball, and slam it home. Rashid, who cannot stop me after overplaying on defense, screams, "Noooo, Farmer! No way! How do you get so many lobs, dude?"

I shrug. I smile. We high-five.

Mr. Doig uses the air horn to show our game is over, and then Khalil and Rashid come in and hug me tight like I am their long-lost brother. Devin hangs back but fist-bumps me.

"Warm-up games two and three weeks out, boys. Just a month until the Hampton, Virginia Nike Elite Tournament. And you know what?"

"What?" everybody shouts.

"I'm feeling good!" Coach Cliff says. "Real good! We got ourselves more than a showcase for talent. We got ourselves a team. I bet we hand those Owens boys their butts, isn't that right, Farmer?"

Yes. We are a team.

Carli Anderson is watching. I think she has tears in her eyes. Maybe the beauty of my basketball game has made her cry? Maybe she likes the girls she hangs with here better than the pouty-face girls at home. Those girls seem boring and mean, so I understand. Carli spends a long time hugging these girls here.

Then it is me who wants to cry. The Minneapolis Academy camp was the best. Not just for basketball. Am I Polish? I have been sociable. I have spoken like a Polish guy speaks. I am being me.

THIRTY-TWO

I AM KING

Carli is sad on the car ride home. She disobeyed doctor's orders and played a scrimmage with her friends. It was not good. She is weak. She is slow. She was fine shooting when no one guarded her, but she has no lift, no shot when someone has a hand in her face.

"I suck. It's like I'm broken," she says.

"You are broken. That's what an injury is," Coach Anderson says.

"I know."

We stop so she can get ice. Her knee has swollen up.

I can tell Coach Anderson is not happy with her, so it's good when he changes the subject and talks about motion offense.

"Motion works best if you're like a close-knit family. You want to know exactly where each of you are going to go."

"Khalil and Devin act like brothers already," Carli says. "You'll be good."

I hope they will be my brothers.

When the Andersons drop me off at my house, I am deflated like a balloon. I don't want this weekend to be over. I don't want to be home in tiny Northrup. I am not in any mood to tell Renata everything that has happened to me.

I get inside. She asks so many questions. I feel tired. I feel not happy to see her. Maybe because she has taken my name and made me Reed? I answer with yes, no, shrugs.

But then we go to Professor Mike's for dinner. I don't know why, but I am very happy to see Regan and Margery. There I talk more than I ever do. I review the whole weekend, tell all about the basketball and about Devin's house and Jesse's bleeding nose and even how Carli snuck to my dorm room to give me information to help me survive.

Regan and Margery think Carli would make a good assassin. I agree.

It's when I report that Devin's grandma is Jevetta Mitchell, famous jazz singer, that Renata finally reacts.

"What? Are you kidding? Why didn't you tell me that when you got home? I asked you for . . . you said nothing, Adam! I grew up listening to Jevetta! Papa loves her! I took you to see her perform, and you don't tell me that you went to her house?"

"Yes, but it wasn't really her house, so I forgot," I say.

Renata stands up, looks at me hard, then walks out of the kitchen.

I don't say I'm sorry, even though I feel wounded in my chest.

I maybe don't understand myself at all? The next morning at breakfast, I don't want to talk to Barry, either. He has not taken my name, so what is my problem? I don't know.

His shin has healed enough that he can go back to his regular workouts in tae kwon do. "My second-degree black belt test is next month? Will you guys come and see it? It's a pretty big deal. There's a grand master coming over from Mankato to do the judging."

Renata smiles. "Of course. Second-degree? That is a very big deal!"

Renata doesn't know anything about black belts. I roll my eyes at her.

"Yeah," Barry says. "I've thought a lot about being Shinja, and it's not a good idea, you know?"

"Yeah, I agree," Renata says. Then she stares hard at me again. "Do you have something to say, Adam?" she asks.

"Hardening your shins was stupid," I say.

"Well, yeah, I know?" Barry says.

On the car ride to school, Barry won't talk to me, which

makes me feel bad. "Renata is pissing me off," I say. "I am in a bad mood with her."

"She's the best mom I ever met," Barry says.

But the truth is, I don't want to hang out with Barry either, and I feel pissed at him for being around so much. I want to be with the Fury. And I want to be with Carli, who knows basketball.

On Tuesday, I see her in the hall. Even though she is talking to her friends, girls who don't like to look at me, I walk up and say, "Can we hit the college gym, dude? You have to show me how to shoot a jump shot better."

"Yeah, man," she says. "I'll check with my dad tonight. Maybe tomorrow?" She looks at her friend. This girl is rolling her eyes in her head. This girl is mad? Why doesn't she like me? I don't know why. Here I am speaking, not acting like a basketball-playing freak show!

"Dope," I say.

"Yup," Carli says. "Okay."

Her other friend looks away from me.

I don't care. I am Adam Sobieski in my heart. I can handle their faces.

But I am also aware that Carli was not so happy I approached her.

The next morning, Barry doesn't show up for breakfast. He doesn't call, either. That puts Renata in a bad mood, because she's made food for him. I leave early to walk to school. It's drizzling. I am mad.

But just as I get to the sidewalk in front of school, Carli pulls into the parking lot. "Farmer!" she calls out. "Wait up!"

Farmer? I am beginning to like the name Farmer.

She jogs across the lot, dodges cars, waves at a couple of people.

"Good jogging," I say.

"Yeah, my knee feels good today!"

"No swelling?"

"Some swelling. But that's to be expected. Anyway, Dad says we're cool tonight. The gym will be empty with spring break. So you in? Do a little ballin'?"

Of course I am in.

After school, I run all the way home and put on warm-ups. I'm about to leave the house when Renata arrives with groceries.

"What are you doing?" she asks.

"Going to the Trinity gym."

"It's open?"

"Coach Anderson is letting me and his daughter in for a workout."

Renata takes a deep breath. "Michael and the girls are coming over for dinner," she says. "I'm cooking. I could use some help."

"Um. No. I have to work out. For the Fury, okay? Because you want me to play for them, right?"

"Could you have told me this morning?" she asks. Her face is red.

"I didn't know this morning. But I have to go."

"Fine. Okay. Go," Renata says.

Carli and I meet outside the gym, and she talks and talks about nothing at all and I am happy. Inside we take warm-up shots.

"I lifted hard yesterday. I can feel my knee getting stronger underneath me, dude. That crap scrimmage up in Minneapolis is no big deal. I'm going to be fine, okay? I'm totally going to be a beast next year!" she shouts. "I'm going to be me again!"

I don't know what she means by "beast." She is too beautiful. But I do know how basketball can give you back yourself. And it's so good to see her take real shots. She jumps more today. A little, at least. A week ago she shot more from the balls of her feet.

"I don't feel pain!" she says. "This is awesome!" She tosses another shot from beyond the three-point line. It swishes. She shoots and shoots. Six straight, one after the other, without missing. Finally one bounces off the back of the cylinder. "Oh my God, I feel good." She's not talking to me, just saying the words into the air.

"My turn?" I ask.

"It's going to be over fast, dude. Shoot till you miss."

I take a few shots then. Each one rattles off the rim.

"Shoot till you make?" She laughs.

"What's my problem, okay? That I shoot from the top of my jump, right? But I tried shooting from just after, like when I'm coming down, like double pumping? Made me much worse."

Carli nods. "You're so messed up, dude."

"I know. I can feel it. I am unnatural."

"Yes." She laughs. "Very unnatural."

"Uh-huh."

"But I can fix you," she says, like she is a mad scientist. Carli moves to me. She puts her hands on my shoulders. "First, square up, man. You're leading with your right side too much." She straightens me. "You do this weird hop thing, too, when you shoot. Just step forward a little bit with your shot-side leg." She grabs the back of my right leg, above my knee, and pulls it a few inches toward her. I am naturally lowered to her height. We are so close, and I have stopped breathing. Then she lifts my arms up. The ball is in my hand. "Your elbow should be shoulder level, ninety-degree angle over your leg." She bends my elbow. "Balance the ball in your right hand. You shoot kind of two-handed now, which doesn't help." I put all the ball's weight on my right hand.

She is wearing a large T-shirt with the sleeves rolled. I am staring at her muscular shoulder. I can smell her deodorant, maybe? It's very fresh. "Are you paying attention?" she asks. Then I am staring in her eyes. She is staring in my eyes.

She swallows. She blushes. She says quietly, "Now, without jumping, just extend and follow through. Put the ball in the net." I shoot without my eyes leaving hers. The ball arches up and down. It goes through the net soft. I know it has happened, but she doesn't.

Except she does. "That sounded like a swish," she whispers.

I nod. We stare. We breathe. She swallows.

Then she shoves me away. "See? I can teach you, dude!"

I think I am going to fall over on the floor.

She turns and gets the ball and begins talking in Carli speed. "Okay. I'm going to feed you the ball. Visualize this. You are going to be square to the basket, have your legs under you, your elbow cocked, and you are going to pull the trigger right before you get to the top of your jump. Not at the top. Not after the top. Before. Dad taught me to do it by bending my knees, lifting, shooting, then hopping with your follow-through. Like all in slow motion. Want to try that?"

But I have only half listened. Because I want to try something else. I want to put my arms around Carli and put my face into her neck. I want to breathe her in and then I want to take her for meals and buy her cars and a house and a nice couch and get married and then watch TV and eat some good food on our couch after we come back from our jobs. Then we'll go to sleep together.

A shock of fear goes through me. Is it good for me to like her so much?

"Hey?" she says. "Okay?"

"Okay," I say. *Just play basketball.*

She tosses me a bounce pass. I take a deep breath. She instructs. I do what she says, and in forty-five minutes my jump shot has improved by maybe fifty percent. No, I don't make a bunch from behind the three-point line. Not even close. But nearer, midrange, the ball goes in more, and if not in, it arches and bounces so much softer than ever before on the rim.

"You're getting it! You'll get good at this, dude," Carli tells me. "Now rebound for me. I'm going to hit marks."

For the next twenty minutes, she moves from one *X* to another *X*, all of them taped on the floor. She doesn't go fast because she can't cut. But she is light on her feet. I send her a pass and she catches, lifts, and shoots. Oh boy, Carli is a baller.

No. Baller is too tiny a word. Carli is more than a baller. She is great with the ball and she has swagger, but also she is so much more. She has taken all of this time to help me, even while she needs to be helping herself. She is generous? She is good in her heart? She is a baller plus something.

She takes a shot from ten feet behind the three-point line. It is a heave, but the ball goes through the air in a perfect arc. It slides onto the side of the rim and rolls around it, like water going down the drain. Hoop. Hoop. Circle. Hooper. Maybe hooper is a better word? The ball drops through.

"You're a great hooper, okay?" I say.

"Yeah?" Carli stops. The ball bounces on the floor behind me. Her face is red. She glistens with sweat. There are dark patches on her T-shirt.

"Yes. Great hooper."

Carli flexes her knee. "I'm a very sore hooper, dude. Better go home and ice."

"I don't want you to go home," I say.

"That sounds a little psycho, boy."

"I'm having a good time," I say.

"Yeah." She smiles, and her eyes crinkle. "Me too."

When I get home, Professor Mike and Renata are slow dancing in one spot in the living room to the song "Blue Moon" playing on our record turntable. Renata waves at me, then puts her head on Professor Mike's chest. Professor Mike smiles at me, too.

Okay. Okay. This is fine. But my stomach twists at the sight of them.

Margery and Regan roll dice on the dining room table. They are writing down numbers on a piece of notebook paper.

"What do you want your cleric to be named?" Margery asks me.

"I don't know what you mean," I say.

"For Dungeons and Dragons. Dad and Renata said you'd play," Regan says.

"No, uh-uh. I got homework," I say.

"Well, then for later. What is your name?" Margery asks.

"Hooper," I say.

"Bad," Margery says.

"Hooper the Cleric?" Regan says. "Boo."

"That's a dragon name," Margery says.

"Fine, I'm a dragon. I don't care about no cleric. I don't even know what one is."

"*No cleric* is not proper English," Margery says.

"I don't give a shit about English," I say.

I go to shower and to think about jump shots and Carli, because that's what matters. I hear Professor Mike and the girls leave before I towel off and get on my Philadelphia 76er pajamas.

I look in the mirror. I wish I was nicer to those girls.

THIRTY-THREE

AT PATRICK'S

It is Saturday morning. The first day of my spring break. I have gone to the Trinity athletic facility with Carli Anderson on Thursday and Friday after school. My jump shot is better still. When you start with bad, improvement can happen so fast. Carli hasn't gotten close to me like she did on Wednesday. If I wasn't afraid of destroying my new form, I may have tried bad form so she would come and adjust my body again. It's okay, though. We're so comfortable together. I am happy.

But Renata is not so happy. She knocks on my bedroom door, because it's past nine and I'm not a guy who sleeps in. "Adam?" she asks through the door. "Are you in there?"

"Yeah. Where else would I be?" I ask.

"Can I come in?" she asks.

I don't want her to, but, "Okay," I say.

She comes in. "Sleepy, huh?" she says.

I'm actually achy, because Carli and I lifted weights after shooting. Although I love to drill, for some reason I've never lifted weights before. Nobody has told me to, or showed me how. Carli warned me I would hurt. I feel like the muscles of my chest and arms are going to pop and fall off my bones. "I'm sore."

"Maybe you're playing too much . . . sports?" she asks.

"No," I say.

Although I did go and eat dinner with her and Professor Mike's family at their house the night before, I didn't talk much to them, and I left right after eating to come home and lie down.

"I feel like I haven't seen much of you for the last few weeks. I'm going to run some errands now. Do you want to go?" Renata asks. "Like we used to in Philadelphia?"

"No thank you," I say.

"Okay," she says. "Well. How about I take you to Patrick's for dinner tonight?"

Carli is gone for the rest of the weekend for her grandma's birthday in South Dakota. There will be no basketball. I have no excuse to say no. "Just you and me?" I ask.

"Yes. Unless you want to invite Barry, too?" she asks.

"Uh. No, maybe not," I say. "Just us."

While Renata is gone, I dribble in the basement and

my body loosens a little. Then I watch NBA games—New York Knicks against Washington and Houston against San Antonio—and I spend time thinking about Carli. Barry calls, but I don't pick up the phone. He leaves a message to see if I want to jog on the Red Jacket Trail, like we did when it was warmer back in the fall, and then to go to Seven Mile Creek to throw rocks at trees.

Throw rocks? I am not a little kid anymore!

Patrick's is in downtown Northrup. It has so many foods I love: pizzas, Reuben sandwiches, onion rings, and seasoned french fries with many kinds of sauces for dipping. Usually it's filled with college kids, but as this is the end of their spring break, it is a bit empty for a Saturday night. This is good, because Renata doesn't enjoy seeing her students, and she doesn't like sitting in big crowds of what she calls *townies*. We sit in a corner booth.

Renata gets her salad. She orders a glass of wine, which surprises me. She knows I get worried when people drink. This fear is not very Polish of me. Magda back in Philly said so during a Constitution Day celebration where all the people got really drunk and I cried and Renata had to take me home. Magda didn't live with my dad, who could drink a whole bottle of vodka in an hour and went from too happy to sad to powerfully angry and violent. I want to be Polish now, a Sobieski, so I don't ask Renata not to drink her wine. I get a patty melt, a hamburger sandwich with some good onions, and also fries and an order of battered cheese curds, something they didn't have in Poland or Philly, but I love.

I eat half my sandwich fast.

Renata barely eats. She sips her wine.

"Can we talk?" she says.

I am chewing. "I don't know."

That makes her smile for some reason. "You've always been quiet," she says.

I nod. I bite my other sandwich half. I chew.

"But you're more quiet with me than ever," she says.

I swallow. "No. I'm not quiet anymore," I say.

She stares at me for a moment. "I know you're going through some changes. I get that."

"Yeah," I say.

"You're meeting new people."

"Uh-huh," I say.

"Maybe getting angry, too?" she asks. "About what you've been through?"

"No," I say fast, but I'm not sure if this is true.

"Really?" she asks. She waits for me to reply.

The server comes up and asks if I want a refill on my Coke. I'm relieved this takes the focus off the question. "Yes. Please," I say. She asks if Renata wants another glass of wine.

Renata looks at me for a moment, then says, "Yes, thanks."

"Why do you need to drink so much wine?" I ask when the server leaves.

"It's something I enjoy. I haven't had wine because it makes you uncomfortable, but maybe we're getting to a point that we can start being our normal selves with each other. You've been my son for years, Adam."

"Maybe you drink wine because Professor Mike likes wine and you want to be like him," I say.

"Okay . . . okay," Renata says. "Are you upset with me about Michael?"

"No. He's good. He's fine," I say.

"Are we spending too much time with him and the girls?" she asks.

"No," I say. "I like Regan and Margery."

"Then what's going on, Adam?"

I am holding my half sandwich in my hand. I put it down on the plate. I look down into my lap. It is true that I am in a bad mood with Renata, that I have a bad feeling. I have fear about Professor Mike, because of stupid Peter in Philly. I don't want to say that to her. I say the other thing instead. "Maybe I can be Adam Sobieski and not Adam Reed anymore?"

Renata nods quickly. Tears come into her eyes. She swallows hard.

Behind her I see a very big man in a baseball cap come in. Behind him is Kase Kinshaw and what must be his two little brothers and a little sister who is preschool age. My heart starts to beat hard. The sight of Kase pumps adrenaline through my body. But Kase doesn't see me. The family begins to slide into a booth nearby. Kase lifts the girl in before he goes. She wriggles. He does a raspberry sound on her cheek. She screams and laughs. I am struck. Maybe Kase is not as bad as I think? Then the big man, who must be Kase's dad, looks directly at me. He pauses for a moment, then walks to our booth.

My adrenaline grows.

"Adam Reed?" he says.

"Yeah?" I say, almost unable to breathe.

He smiles and nods. "Just wanted to tell you how much me and my wife loved watching you play this past season." He turns to Renata, who has just mopped her eyes with a napkin. "You must be so proud of your boy." He extends his hand to her. "Rick Kinshaw."

She shakes hands. "Renata," she says. "Renata Reed."

"Sorry to bust in on you. Just wanted to say I've watched a lot of games over the years, and I can tell you we haven't had basketball like that here before you showed up. It's fun, isn't it?"

"Yeah. Fun," I say.

He smiles. Turns and walks to their booth.

Kase is looking down and shaking his head.

"Shit," I whisper.

"You're a local hero," Renata says.

"Uh-huh," I say.

Then she reaches into her purse, I think maybe to get Kleenex for her eyes, but she pulls out an iPhone instead. "I got this for you," she says. "It's all set and ready to go. You can text your new friends and . . . and do whatever and let me know where you are, okay?" She hands it to me.

"Ah. Okay. Thank you. Thank you so much," I say.

"I want everything to be okay," she says. "I'm going to work on it."

"Okay," I say. I don't know what she has to work on, but what can I do? I look down at this phone. I love it. I can call Carli. I can watch videos of basketball drills out in the driveway.

Renata doesn't eat any of her salad before we leave.

Kase Kinshaw doesn't look at me, as far as I know.

THIRTY-FOUR
CHASING THE OCEAN

On Monday morning, Barry calls to say he won't be at breakfast because he had a bad night and couldn't wake up. It's okay. The college is back in session, and Renata has an early morning faculty meeting, so she hasn't made any food. Still, she says, "Have you and Barry had a falling-out?"

I don't know about that.

After she leaves, I work on dribbles and post footwork in the basement. Then the day spreads out in front of me. The week. The first Fury exhibition game, played in Minneapolis against a team from far in the north of Minnesota, is coming on Saturday, but nothing until then? Can I go and knock on Carli's door? I have my phone, which I used to watch YouTube videos all weekend while Regan and Margery jumped on top of me because I'm the right size for a dragon, but there are no phone numbers yet. I set up a Twitter account, because everyone on the Fury has Twitter. @PolishHooper. I tweet *Kyle Owens is not so great at basketball. He is slow.* It goes to nobody, because there is no one who is following me. Should I follow people? Should I go to Carli's house?

Am I lonely?

Should I go play with Regan and Margery?

I don't want to be a dragon.

The house is empty. It feels like time is a terrible forest all around me.

Should I go walk on the college campus to see people?

Then the landline rings and it is Barry Roland again. I answer.

"I was thinking, since I missed breakfast, that maybe it would taste good to go to Mankato and eat at Perkins?" he says.

"Will your car make it to Mankato?" I ask.

"Yeah. I gave Merle all my money and he gave the Pontiac a tune-up. It purrs like a cat now?"

"Really?" I say.

"Kind of?" he says.

"Come get me," I say.

"I have to drop off my sister at work, so it'll be a little bit? But I'll be there pretty soon."

I shower, then jump into pants and am about to pull

my Joel Embiid Philadelphia 76ers jersey over a T-shirt when the doorbell rings. "That's fast, Barry," I shout. "What about your sister's job, huh?"

I go down the hall pulling on the jersey and swing open the door.

Carli Anderson stands outside. "What's up, man?" she asks.

"What's up?" I ask. "Why are you here?"

"I'm going up to the Y in Minnie to work out with Tasha Tolliver. She was hanging with Khalil last night, and he asked if I'd drive you up, too, because Rashid is in Florida with his dad until Friday and they need a third for three-on-three and it would be cool if it was you—Kyle Owens plays with these giant South Dakota dudes, so you're going to want to be ready!"

"What? South Dakota? Owens?"

"Do I talk too fast for you, Polish boy?"

"Yes. Maybe."

She talks very slowly then. "Do you want to go play basketball in Minneapolis with Khalil and Devin?"

"Shit. Yes. Now?"

"Now. I would've called, but you have no phone."

"I have a phone!" I pull it out of my pocket and show her.

"That will make things easier in the future. Get your stuff, dude. Let's go."

In two minutes we are out the door and rolling toward

the highway. Carli talks about scholarship offers and good fits and different college divisions and all of it seems too far away for me. Even though she missed the whole season with her knee, she has just received a Division I scholarship offer from University of Wisconsin–Green Bay. She is worried. "It's fine for them to give me a scholarship and everything, but what if I never can run like I used to? What if I end up in Green Bay and I can't even really play ball?"

I remember Magda saying that in Minnesota I'd be close to Chicago and Green Bay and there would be plenty of Polish people, except it turns out Green Bay is pretty far from Northrup—maybe a five-hour drive—and Chicago is even farther. "You know, there are lots of Polish people in Green Bay, so there might be dudes that look like me," I say.

She turns, takes her eyes far off the road, and says, "I would like that."

I have trouble thinking for the next twenty minutes. Carli likes how I look. This has now been confirmed.

We drive into the suburbs and then into the city, into a neighborhood that looks more like Philadelphia than any I've seen so far. There, next to a trolley station built on a platform above the streets, we come to a beautiful Y facility.

Khalil, Tasha, and Devin greet us in the lobby.

"Farmer in the hood!" Khalil shouts.

"This isn't the hood," Devin says.

Khalil is happy.

Devin is not ever happy.

"We're going to drill with some Augsburg College girls upstairs," Tasha says.

"Courts are this way, Farmer," Khalil says.

I sign in at the front desk as Devin's guest and then follow the two of them down a long hall.

Many people maybe don't like the smell of a gym, because it contains a lot of sweat from human beings. But it also smells like the rubber of shoes and basketballs and the heat of the large lights that hang from its ceiling. It smells like the ointment Coach Jenson gave me for my quad when I had a strain near the beginning of season. These smells are sacred. They are the smells of hooping, which is the most important aspect of my life.

There are not quite the normal smells in this Y, though, because the floor in the main area is not made of wood, but is hard rubber. The sounds are different, too. No shoe squeaks. I miss some squeaks. Also, there are so many lines for other kinds of games on this floor, it's hard to tell what is in and what is to be considered out of bounds. At first I am nervous and too aware of how different the space feels, and how Devin doesn't smile or look at me, but then, guess what?

Basketball.

After warming up a little, we play three-on-three in the half-court.

The first team we play are men older than us, and not

just a little bit. These guys are probably in their thirties and maybe in their forties? They don't look very quick. They look mostly like old man versions of Lawrence Rivers with their big butts.

We begin, and in three seconds the fellow Devin is guarding shoots a three-pointer like blowing sawdust off a table. So easy.

Then the shorter old guy strips Khalil, and the first old guy shoots another one from the three-point line.

"Damn, dudes!" Khalil shouts.

Devin has had enough. He checks the ball, fakes a pass to me, then from the top of the key rips off five steps, explodes, and dunks.

"Oh, is that how it's going to be?" One of the old men laughs.

"Just so you know," Devin says, not smiling.

I will say this: if you haven't played basketball before, this game against the old guys would not be a good place to start. The old farts (Khalil calls them that) are so crafty. The first time I touch the ball, I get picked clean by Mr. Three-Point Shooter Man, who doesn't even seem like he's playing defense on me, but then bump, he has the ball.

That guy is named Nathaniel. He mostly keeps track of Devin, thankfully. Or maybe not.

The dude I am supposed to be guarding is named Dwight. He is big and a couple inches taller than I am, and he is bald and he has his T-shirt tucked into gray shorts, even though he has a big basketball-size gut. When I first looked at him, I thought, *Go easy.* But I was wrong, because he has me jumping out of my socks with post moves. He taunts me with jabbering, too. "Oh, here it goes, white boy! Here it goes, vanilla cream! You ready to slap my weak-ass shit out of here? You ready?" I keep telling him I'm ready, but I'm not ready. The ball seems on its way up, but then is not. I don't understand how he doesn't let go of the ball on shot fakes, because I swear the ball is leaving his hands, but then it stays.

After he gets my undies all tied in bundles, he easily makes layups without even jumping more than an inch off the ground.

He messes with me in this way twice in a row, saying funny stuff and twisting my undies. Next possession for us, I am a little pissed, so Devin nods and I run, leap up to the perfect lob Devin throws, and bam, boom!

"Alley-oop," I say. "Lob city."

"Oh, vanilla!" Dwight shouts at me. "You got the hops, boy! Would you look at that?"

"How about you stop messing with our farmer, Dwight?" Khalil laughs.

"No. It's okay. I will learn your ninja moves," I say.

"That's my boy," Dwight says.

But then he makes me look like a clown on ice skates two more times in a row. I don't get it. It is not just his feet and it is not just his hands. Every time there's something new, unexpected. Dwight is a creative genius like Miles or Coltrane.

What is lucky for us young men with young legs and young lungs: we can keep going for a long time. I don't mind my legs burning. They will be better in a minute. I don't mind when I bend over to catch my breath. It will come back in a second. I don't even care when my feet get hot and I get blisters. They will heal tomorrow.

But the old fart men start their huffing and puffing after only ten or fifteen minutes. They go slower and slower and then stop playing defense. They keep laughing, though. And in the game we play, they beat us 11–8, mostly because I can't stop Dwight. The effort does them in, and even though they could keep the court, they don't want to.

"All yours. You all-stars wore us out," Dwight says.

Funny that these old men are the hardest team we play in next two hours. We go against other crews of African-American dudes and some Asian kids and Somali kids and three guys from Mexico who are pretty good, but not like the old guys. Each team, we destroy by more and more points. By the end, Khalil seems to know where I will always be. I know that Devin will run his back cut off his screens for me (a very fast pick-and-roll kind of play). Devin attracts so much attention when he gets near the basket, he can always locate an open Khalil at the three-point line. I take and make a few jump shots. And I see how much better and quicker Khalil is than Caleb Olson. Khalil can bounce with the basketball two steps under the three-point line, leap back in a half breath, then fire it up or pass it before you even know what has happened.

Devin Mitchell is the best player I have ever seen in person.

And the three of us? We reach what Khalil calls the flow. I've never had this with other players. I'm not me, but part of a larger animal. We're like the Owens family of Marshall, Minnesota. We're like a three-headed Dwight playing jazz in the post. But I like what a Somali boy says after we beat him and his friends, 11–2. "You dudes never stop. It's like chasing the ocean!"

Like chasing the ocean. That's good to imagine.

Also impossible to do.

THIRTY-FIVE
COOKED IN A HOT TUB

We sit on benches in the lobby area. Khalil packs up his bag. He has to go babysit his little brother, Lonnie, so his mom can go to work. "Man, we are going to kill the Pride Saturday. We could take them, just the three of us," Khalil says.

Devin leans back against the wall, dabbing his face with a towel. "I think I'm going to stay, Farmer," Devin says. "Not ready to go home yet. Want to hit the weights?" Devin has said so few words directly to me. He still doesn't look at me.

"I'm not a good lifter. Only did it once with Carli," I say.

"Man, you are so raw!" Khalil says.

"Like a little baby," Devin says. "I can show you some stuff, though."

Before he leaves, Khalil finds me on Twitter. "I'm your first follower, bro!" He says this like he's shocked.

"I'm a little baby," I say.

Then Devin and I go to the weights area upstairs.

Upstairs we find people of every color on the earth. It's like my neighborhood back in Philly. Here there are black grandmas next to Mexican dudes next to white moms in yoga pants, like Renata wears, next to Vietnamese teen boys next to girls with Muslim scarves on their heads and dudes who must be speaking Arabic. Devin and I go to the free-weight section, and I have a big knot stuck in my throat. I love this. All of us up here are striving to improve.

"What are you doing, dude?" Devin asks.

I realize I am stuck in one spot, staring out into the treadmills and weight machines. "I like all these people," I say.

Devin giggles. This is not the deep laugh of a giant man, but more like a little kid. "What?"

"They're good people," I say. "They're trying hard."

He smiles and shakes his head. "You are odd," he says.

I nod. "It's hard to be me."

He giggles again and puts his hand on his forehead. "I'm trying not to like you," he says.

"What? Why?" I ask.

"It's not about you, man . . ." He takes a big breath. "Let's just do some lunges, all right?"

"Okay," I say, but I would like to know why he shouldn't like me. Instead, I follow him to a place where we put weight on a bar. I copy what he does, load plates.

For the next forty-five minutes we do more than lunging. We pull and squat and clean and jerk (this sounds disgusting, but is really more painful) and curl and press. Pretty soon I feel like my whole body has become soft rubber. I am sweating and dizzy.

Devin is able to lift almost twice as much weight as I can for every exercise. How do I compete with that? If he doesn't like me, he can break me in half. But during the workout, he has been nice. He has given me good instructions. He has laughed at my jokes and kept me from dropping a weight on my head.

During my last set of bench presses, Tasha Tolliver and Carli come up. Devin helps me guide the bar back onto the rack. I sit up and I think I might die. I am so tired, really.

"How about the hot tub, y'all?" Tasha asks.

"I gotta ice," Devin says.

"Come on, they don't got ice baths here, boy," Tasha says.

"Unless you dudes get something we don't," Carli says.

"Nah. I'd have to go home to do it," Devin says.

"Well, we don't want that!" Tasha says.

I borrow a pair of shorts from Devin. They are big on my butt. Carli and Tasha have both brought swimsuits. We are the only people in a large bubbling hot tub that sits in the shadow of a two-story water slide and next to a kids' wading pool.

I don't like sitting in hot tubs very much. I've only been in one before. When we moved to Minnesota last summer, we stayed in a hotel in Northrup for two days. There was a hot tub. I thought I was being cooked in a soup. How is that relaxing?

But Tasha and Carli are big, powerful, beautiful girls and I want Devin to like me, so I decide, even if I feel like I'm being made into soup, there is no place in the world I would rather be.

They all talk Minnesota basketball and about people I don't know and then they talk about recruiting. Tasha has made official visits to Iowa, Iowa State, and someplace called Butler. Devin has visited only Duke and Kentucky, because they're the only schools he thought he was interested in. "I'm going to check out Howard and Harvard now, though."

"Dude, you are not going to go to one of those schools," Tasha says.

"Why?" I ask.

"Harvard doesn't even give athletic scholarships."

"They play good basketball and the coach is black," Devin says. "And I could get the best education in the country."

"So you going to play that system they do at Harvard?" Tasha says.

"Sure. Why not?"

"You can play tough D, limit possessions? Maybe you average nine points a game?"

"Why is that bad if the team wins?" I ask.

"Duh, because," Carli says.

"What?" I ask.

"Because Devin could be a top-ten NBA pick in two years," Carli says.

"There's more to life than basketball," Devin says.

"No," I say.

"So much more. Why do I want to go to some school that just wants to use me up for basketball?" Devin asks. "You think Kentucky cares about my education?"

"Go get your Harvard degree after you leave the NBA, dude!" Tasha shouts.

There is a moment when no one says anything, but we all just look at the water.

Then Tasha talks. "Just like Khalil always says, you too rich to even see what you got."

Devin shakes his head. He glares at Tasha, then climbs out of the hot tub.

"Aw, come on, man," Tasha says.

"I'm out," Devin says. "Keep the shorts, Farmer." He wraps in a towel and walks away.

I'm not sure what to do, so I stay in my spot. Nobody says anything for a couple of minutes. Carli pulls out her ponytail and shakes her head, so her shiny hair falls on her muscular shoulders. I try not to stare, but I do. She smiles at me and sinks down deep into the tub.

"Shit," Tasha whispers. Then she turns the bubbles up high. "Devin Mitchell gets on my last nerve," she says.

When there are a lot of bubbles, Carli puts her foot in my lap.

"Just need to straighten out my knee," she says.

I nod. I hold on to her foot with my hand. I am happier than ever. There is nothing else, not basketball, not Devin . . .

But Tasha's brain is still with Devin. "You know what? He might really go to, like, Howard University, right?"

"No way," Carli says.

"His dad wanted him at Duke since he was in middle school. Devin has to do everything his dad says or else, okay? He gets grounded, stuck in that house by himself weeks at a time, just for being home late from school. But when he's eighteen, he's free. He can go where he wants. If Howard pays, why shouldn't he go where he wants to be? His daddy can suck it."

"I like his dad," I say.

"You wouldn't if you were his kid," Carli says. "Devin can barely have friends. Definitely no girlfriend. He can't go anywhere after dark by himself, right, Tash?"

"Uh-huh." Tasha nods. "And he had to stop playing baseball, because his dad said he messed around too much in the dugout and practice got in the way of his basketball development. Devin loves baseball!"

"Why?" I ask. "Why is his dad so mean?"

"Well, I don't think he's mean," Carli says.

"No way. Daddy's scared!" Tasha says.

"Of what? Devin is the toughest-looking boy I ever saw," I say.

"Yeah. Exactly, dude. You got it," Tasha says. "Devin looks like a big man, even if he just a kid. People are scared of him, and these cops don't play. He could end up shot."

"Jesus. Really?" Carli says. "I mean, I thought his dad was strict just to keep Devin out of trouble."

"Devin Mitchell wouldn't get in no trouble," Tasha says. "But trouble is looking for him. Trouble is out looking for all black kids right now."

"I'm glad I'm not black," I say.

Both the girls' mouths drop open. They stare at me. "You still can't say shit like that," Tasha says.

"Seriously, Adam. That sounded terrible."

"Why? I don't want trouble looking for me," I say. "I have enough trouble, okay? Trouble finds me a lot. I don't want to get shot, too."

"Well, you think Devin does?" Tasha says.

"He probably wishes he was white," I say.

"That he does not, dude. Not at all." Tasha stands and climbs out of the hot tub. She grabs her towel and dries.

"Farmer's Polish. He doesn't know what he's saying," Carli says.

"I do, too," I say, because what does me being Polish have to do with it?

"See, he do," Tasha says. She walks out of the pool area.

Carli leans back and shuts her eyes.

"I didn't mean to make her pissed," I say.

"Just shut up for a few seconds, okay?" Carli says. She presses her toes into the inside of my thigh, and I do shut up.

THIRTY-SIX
BAD VERSION OF ME

I wasn't trying to be racist or anything. As I dress, I replace black with Polish. "I'm glad I'm not Polish," somebody could say because Poles are unlucky, or maybe they think Poles are dumb, or Poles are poor, or drunk, or whatever the reason. The thing is, whatever the reason, they'd be wrong, because Poles are not one thing, but many different things, so it's a stereotype. I can imagine if I heard someone say those things, I would get mad. But those things are simply opinions. Isn't it a fact that black guys get shot by the cops? I see the news Renata has on. That's not a stereotype, is it? Black guys get shot.

"That's why I'm glad I'm not black," I say to Carli when we meet in the lobby. "Black is nothing wrong. My favorite basketball players are all black. I just don't want to get shot."

There is a black kid in the lobby, probably waiting for his mom, maybe ten years old, staring at me when I say this.

Carli rolls her eyes at me. She rolls up her swimsuit in a towel. Then she says, "I think the response Tasha and other actual human beings look for in this situation is more about how Devin walking around worried he's going to get shot just because he's a black guy is totally unacceptable . . ."

That makes me think. "Oh," I say. "Okay. I see."

The kid is still staring at me.

"It's like you're lost in your own world," Carli says.

"I have problems." I nod. "Will you text Tasha that I am stupid but understand?"

"I saw her in the locker room. She's not going to hold it against you, dude, because she's nice and knows you're just trying to figure shit out. But I would think, since you know that an apology is needed, that you'd be the one to do it yourself, right?"

"Yes," I say.

"Good," Carli says.

"Yes, Mother," I say.

"Ha-ha," Carli says.

The kid is still staring like I am from outer space. "You're good at basketball," he finally says. "I watched you play."

"Thank you. Okay," I say. I don't say anything more. We leave the Y.

But I'm thinking. Even before we are out of the Minneapolis suburbs, I turn to Carli, who has been quiet, just listening to the pop music on the radio, not even singing along, and I say, "It's like how Kase Kinshaw makes shit of me just because I'm from a different country. That's totally unacceptable."

"Kase doesn't care that you're from a different country. He just doesn't like it that you're better at sports than him."

"No. He calls me a refugee."

"He makes dumb jokes, that's all."

"No, he doesn't make jokes."

"I know he can be a dick, but he's not a bad guy, I swear. I've known him my whole life. We're buddies."

"He punched Barry Roland."

"What? Is Barry Roland Polish, too?"

"No."

"So I guess Kase doesn't pick on him because he's Polish?"

"Are you joking?" I ask.

"No."

"Of course Barry isn't Polish. Barry is just another victim of Kase Kinshaw."

"Barry is not the best example to use here. Sorry."

"Why?" I ask.

"You don't even know the story of the dog," she says.

"What dog?" I say.

"God. Can we not talk about this?" she asks. "I'm not a

spokesperson for Kase Kinshaw, okay?"

"I'm not a spokesperson for Barry, either . . ." And then I think for a moment and get a shock of lightning in my veins. Oh shit, Barry Roland. He was on his way over to my house this morning! "Oh shit, oh shit!" I say.

I reach down and pull my phone out of my pocket. It never rings. It never buzzes. I am not used to it, so I never look at it. There, on the front screen, are several notifications:

First, two texts, Khalil sending over his number and Devin's number.

Second, a notification from Twitter that I have forty-one new followers. Khalil has retweeted out my only message, *Kyle Owens is not so great . . .*

Third, and worst, a Renata voice mail. When I tap in my code, I find there are a bunch of older texts and voice mails from her. They are asking again and again, *WHERE ARE YOU? BARRY CAN'T FIND YOU.*

"Uh-oh," I say. "I was supposed to hang out with Barry Roland, but I just left with you and didn't tell anyone."

"This morning? You didn't tell your mom?" Carli asks.

"She wasn't home."

"That's why you have a phone. For texting!" she says.

"Oh no," I say. "No."

"Sorry, dude," Carli says.

I fall into despair.

THIRTY-SEVEN

HOOPER THE DRAGON

Renata is waiting for me when I come in the door. She is standing, not sitting. Her arms are folded over her chest. "What are you doing?" she asks.

"I went to Minneapolis with Carli Anderson to play basketball."

"I know," she says. "I spoke to Ted Anderson, because I thought you might be with her."

"I made the problem," I say. "I got excited and forgot to tell anyone. That's not Carli's fault."

"I'm not upset with Carli Anderson, Adam, I'm upset with you."

"I should have told you what was happening."

Renata closes her eyes tight. She walks across the living

room and plunges backward on the couch. "Yes. You should've told me, but I'm not the injured party here. I would've been fine. I would've told you yes, go to Minneapolis. I would've been happy for you to pursue what you love with people who are as passionate about basketball as you are."

"Okay?" I say. "We're okay? I made a mistake and you forgive me?"

Renata sighs. "What about Barry?" she asks. "What are you going to do about Barry?"

"I'll call him and apologize, because it was just . . . it was an accident."

"Your priorities are changing, Adam. Maybe you better tell him that you won't be available to spend time with him like before. Basketball is more important."

"Basketball is more important than Barry? He's a . . . he's a person."

Renata sits forward. "Think about this, okay? Would you choose practicing basketball over spending time with Barry?" she asks.

I don't say anything, but of course I know the answer.

Barry left so many messages on the home answering machine. I only listen to a few.

10:32 a.m. *"Did you fall down in the house, dude?"*

10:44 a.m. *"Are you dead, because you're not answering the door or the phone?"*

11:33 a.m. *"I found out you just left without telling me, so*

197

that's not a good friend thing to do, Adam? I wouldn't do that to you?"

It is too sad. I lie down on the floor and fall asleep.

Maybe a half hour later, Regan and Margery come busting in from outside. There is no knocking anymore. My home is now their home, it seems. Margery holds on to a large poster-size piece of paper, which is rolled up into a tube.

"Want to see what we made at art camp?" Regan asks.

I do not. But they unroll it on the living room floor next to me.

Hooper the Dragon. Giant. Green covered in glitter. Shooting out flames from its mouth. Wearing a number thirty-four jersey. A basketball in one claw. Hugging a little brown-haired child in the other arm.

"This is my favorite picture of all time," I say.

@PolishHooper suddenly has 112 followers. @KyOw23 has written: *@PolishHooper is a bad head case with no true skills. Runs and jumps. That is all.*

Hooper the Dragon will burn you, Owens!

That's what I think.

I am okay with my new life.

THIRTY-EIGHT
I LIKE BARRY

It is Wednesday morning of spring break.

Tuesday Barry didn't show up for breakfast. He didn't answer the phone at his house, either. The whole day, I did nothing but worry about Barry. I called him again and again. Then I sent texts to Khalil, and he sent me YouTube highlights of Kyle Owens being great because Khalil thinks that is funny. I got a text from Carli, who took a picture of Andrew Wiggins's Minnesota Timberwolves jersey at the mall in Mankato, where she was with her pouty friends. She said Wiggins should be my favorite player and not Joel Embiid, since I live in Minnesota and am not a big-butt center.

It was nice to be in contact with Khalil and Carli on Tuesday, but my mind and heart were with Barry.

There is no Barry again this morning. Renata gave me a very sad look at breakfast to mark the occasion. After Renata leaves, instead of going to the basement to do my dribbles, I decide to go for a run through cold and foggy Northrup.

I run down the street alongside the college, then take a right and run across the neighborhoods to the downtown area. This is not where I want to be—nobody wants to run in the downtown—but I must cross Highway 169 and then a bridge over the Minnesota River if I am to get on the Red Jacket Trail. Before I had played any basketball in Northrup, back in the fall when I'd just arrived in town, I ran on this trail all the time. It is peaceful. Actually, it's how I met Barry. I found him out running barefoot in his karate uniform. He stopped me and said, "Hey, you're the big guy? The new one from a different country?"

"Uh," I answered.

"You like to run in the woods, too?"

"Uh-huh," I said.

We ran together for a half hour. He talked and talked, and he made me laugh by saying strange things. Then we ran to his trailer and he took me to McDonald's. The rest is history.

But I am not at the trail yet.

I get to the highway crossing downtown just as the don't walk light begins to flash. I jog in place, right near the natural food co-op and Taco John's restaurant. Just then a very big pickup truck pulls in next to me. Small towns make it hard to avoid your enemies. The truck has a white sign on its side that says Kinshaw Construction. Kase Kinshaw sits in the passenger seat. His father, Rick, is driving. Kase squints at me, glares, then turns and looks forward.

The light turns green. "See you later, dick," I say under my breath.

The truck is gone.

Then I take off sprinting and run all the way to the Red Jacket Trail, too fast. When I get to the access, I suck for air. Fog curls over the bank of the Minnesota River. It looks like there are clouds that blow across the trail.

I watch this amazing thing. Fog tumbles like a movie of waves of the ocean slowed way down. It goes and goes and goes.

Like chasing the ocean.

Okay. Yes.

I am a different kid now. Not the same as when I met Barry with his bare feet.

Barry is still the same kid. He still has Kase Kinshaw to make shit of him. He's back to having no friends.

I take off and run. Barry has no friends. I have abandoned him. I know what that feels like. Instead of running the whole way down to the Highway 14 bridge, as I would usually do, I cross back to the Northrup side of the river on County Road 13. I run right down Main Street past QuikTrip and Taco

John's and past the co-op. I turn on the big, curving Linden Street and go up the river bluff, not toward the college, but toward the big trailer park where Barry lives. I have only been to this place two times, but I think I can remember where his trailer is.

I will not abandon Barry.

I turn on the access road. Shady Crest, the place is called. I run past a boy and a girl in their winter coats who are throwing a spongy football back and forth. The boy lets a pass drop and shouts, "It's that guy! That basketball guy!" when he sees me.

Barry's trailer is near the back of the neighborhood, on the edge of a ravine. The second time I visited him, me and Barry found a washing machine crushed at the bottom. On the other side of the ravine are farm fields that smell like pig shit sometimes and other times like cat pee, Barry says.

I see his car first, parked outside the gray-and-white trailer. I slow and begin to walk. I don't want to see Tiffany or Merle. I take big breaths, because I will knock on his door even though I am scared.

I will not abandon my friend.

Turns out there will be no knocking. I come around the car and find Barry sitting in a lawn chair in the muddy yard. He has a short whip made from leather in his hand, and he is, over and over, whipping another lawn chair nearby him.

"Barry," I say.

He will not look up.

"Bro, I am sorry," I say.

He shrugs and keeps his whip going, *whack, whack.*

"I made a bad mistake. It was accident, though. Carli Anderson came to my house when I expected it would be you and . . . she is pretty hot, right? She's good at basketball, too. So I lost my brain, okay?" I say.

Then Barry looks at me. He says his tae kwon do thing. "Courtesy, integrity, self-control, indomitable spirit."

"Those are words," I say.

"Courtesy, integrity, self-control, indomitable spirit?" he says again.

"Okay, but . . . I'm sorry about what happened."

"Courtesy, integrity, self-control, indomitable spirit!" he shouts. "These are the tenets I live by, because I am a warrior, and so I will not kick you or call you curse words, because I am strong!" Barry shouts. "Okay?"

"Okay," I say. "That's good. You know what else is good? I promise I will not abandon you."

"You already have," he says.

"No. I made a mistake, but I will not abandon you."

"No?" he says.

"No," I say.

"Why should I believe you?"

"Because I am very serious," I say.

Barry takes in a big breath. "Have you thought about this

decision, or are you just saying it to make me feel better?" Barry asks.

"I ran on the Red Jacket Trail just now and thought long and hard about our friendship."

Barry nods. "Okay?" Barry says.

I nod back. "Yes. Now I would like to buy you some McDonald's to show you I am sorry."

Barry stands up. He places his whip on the chair he has been whipping. "Really?" he asks.

"Yes," I say.

"I am hungry," he says.

"Then let's do this, bro," I say.

"Okay. I will go with you to McDonald's, to accept your meal, and to accept your apology," he says. Then he puts his hands together like a fist into palm prayer and bends at his waist to honor my offer.

I do the same back to him.

We have to stop by Renata's office so I can borrow money. She is happy to have the opportunity to fund our meal.

At McDonald's, while he puts a lot of french fries in his mouth, I say more to Barry, because Renata is right. My priorities are changing and I owe Barry the truth. "You need to know something important."

"Okay?" he says through his french fries.

I talk again in the weird way we talked outside his trailer.

"Because I am pursuing greatness in the sport, I will spend more time than ever practicing basketball. It is true that I am also interested in spending time with Carli Anderson, and not only because of basketball, but because she smells like honey and she's funny and she is interested in the things I love. Even though I won't be around as often, none of this will stop me from being your homeboy. Please come over for breakfast every day. I miss you, and so does Renata when you don't. And nothing will stop us from being friends. Nothing ever. I am always your friend, and I will do a good job telling you if I won't be available and will not break plans we already have together once they are made."

"Okay," Barry says. "Sounds good." He smiles. He eats more french fries.

We are good now. I know.

Barry comes to breakfast Thursday and Friday. He eats pancakes and egg sandwiches. Both mornings after breakfast we play dragon catcher with Margery and Regan. After dragon catcher, we all eat lunch in the Trinity dining hall with Renata and Professor Mike.

The afternoons of spring break belong to Carli Anderson, though.

THIRTY-NINE
MAKING OUT WITH A HOT GIRL

It is Friday afternoon. Because the main gym at Trinity is being used by the college softball and baseball teams, Carli and I go to the recreation center, where her dad is teaching a gym class that is full of his freshmen players from the men's basketball team. The whole floor is reserved for Coach Anderson, but he doesn't need it.

Coach Anderson's boys warm up on one side of a net. Carli and I grab two balls off a rolling rack and begin to fire shots on the other. This is our third day doing the same thing. So far Carli's knee is holding up well. We have gotten into a rhythm of practice together.

Carli doesn't even need to warm up. She starts popping

three-pointers from the men's college three line like it's no problem.

I know it's a problem. I know how hard it is to do what she's doing.

It takes me longer to get a feel. I don't go out to the three-pointer line but practice my jumper at the elbows of the lane. I imagine giving Kyle Owens a head fake, like I'm going to drive, but then rising up and dropping a soft shot into the net, except in reality I miss. I do it again. I miss. I do it again. I make. I do it again. Soon, I hit three in a row from the same spot. That's our cue to move on.

We lose one of the balls and do a stop-and-pop drill. Carli kills. She only misses one shot. I do the same drill and hit from six of the twelve spots. Usually we do this shooting progression three times before moving on.

But when I pass the ball over to her, instead of shooting, she throws it back. I hold on to the ball. "What?" I ask.

"Do you know I chose to be here with you instead of going to the Mall of America with my friends?"

"You did? What friends?"

"All of them," she says.

"That's nice. I'm happy," I say.

"They're super pissed at me. But I don't care."

"Basketball is important, right?" I throw the ball back to her.

She throws it back to me. "I'm not here just for basketball, okay?"

I stand holding on to to the ball.

She walks slowly up to me and grabs the ball from my hands. She stands very close. "Do you know the other reason?" she asks.

"No?" I say, like a question.

"I'm ready for you."

"Oh?" I say.

"Guard me in the post." She dribbles toward the basket and beckons me to follow with her left hand. I do. "Come on, man. Guard me," she says.

"Okay."

She dribbles. I guard her but also sort of don't. I place my hand on her hip. She backs into me. She pushes in very close until her shiny ponytail is almost in my face, and then she spins and lays the ball up over the top of me. I raise my arms straight up to act like I am blocking. When she lands we are body to body, chest to chest, legs to legs. We both freeze solid.

"Hello," I say.

"Hey," she says.

We are stuck together, and my heart explodes.

Then there is a whistle. We jump apart. Her dad shouts from the other court, "How's your knee feeling, Carls?"

"Okay! Great!"

"You two want to get in some scrimmaging?"

And then we are jogging toward the other court.

Okay. Here I am. We are here to play basketball?

I follow Carli around the net to where the dudes are, and I'm trying not to look at her legs, because Coach Anderson is standing next to the dudes and they want to play basketball. That's what we're doing here, right? Yeah, but . . . were we about to kiss right on the court?

Basketball. Basketball.

"Let's do full five-on-five," Coach Anderson says. "But you take it easy, Carls. No hard cuts, soft D for now."

"Uh-huh," she says. Her face is bright red.

Then we play. We use the offense I learned when I pretended to be Lawrence Rivers, so I am in the post. I spin and dunk several times. I'm better than the Division III freshmen ballers. Carli jacks two threes and hits them. They give her too much space because of her knee, but what she does is incredible, even if she's not guarded closely. I watch the ball leave her hand. Her follow-through is like the neck of a swan.

She's so beautiful I want to drink her from a glass.

After fifteen minutes, Coach Anderson blows his whistle. He says, "Thanks, Adam. Thanks, Carls. Great to have you two out here."

Carli and I jog off the court, both of us are sweating. We drink at the drinking fountain—so cold and good in the corner. Carli picks up our warm-up tops from the floor. "Let's go," she says. I follow her. For some reason Carli doesn't head for the main doors, the ones we came in through. She goes to a single door in the corner of the gym. We exit into a dark hallway. Carli throws our warm-ups on the ground, backs me into a wall, and kisses me with her cold, drinking-fountain mouth, but I can taste her sweat, too, salty and it tastes so good and it makes my feet feel like they are coming off the ground, like my head is a balloon filled with helium, like my chest is following my head into the clouds.

I almost say to her I love her and we should be married. I don't, because as soon as I think it, I get so terrified that she will leave me. We slide onto the floor. Stop kissing. Sit next to each other. Hold hands. We breathe really hard.

"Sorry," she whispers. "I had to get that over with right now. I'm ready for you. I made my decision."

"It's a good decision?" I whisper back.

Carli says, "Yeah, right? It is, isn't it?"

I want to ask her if she's going to leave me, but I know that sounds so crazy. Instead I lean and kiss her neck. She breathes in deep.

"Okay. My dad could come walking through here any second."

But we kiss again. Then we hear the boys running sprints in the gym. Could they come running through this hall? We leap up and sprint out of our spot into the main hall in the building. It is filled with college students.

Ten minutes later, I enter the living room at home through the front door. I don't even know where I am. Margery and Regan are watching a movie about a sea monster on my TV. Regan turns and looks at me. She crinkles her brow. "What's wrong with your face?" she asks.

Carli, is what I think.

"I'm a happy boy," I whisper.

"Do you have the flu?" Margery asks.

I go into my bedroom. I tweet to my 236 @PolishHooper followers: *@KyOw23 throws bricks when pressure is high. #weakballer*

Bring it, Kyle Owens. @PolishHoops, the team Twitter of the Polish National Team follows me. I follow back. I am feeling so good!

I made out with a hot girl!

I am Adam Sobieski!

I am Hooper the Dragon!

FORTY

EATING TWIN PORTS PRIDE FOR LUNCH

Then it is Saturday. The D-I Fury has our first of three local games. Something special is coming after this game, too. Friday evening Devin called to ask if I would stay overnight at his house. His sister, Saundra, is playing the Polish Chopin music in a recital. "My pops and Saundra both want you to be there," he said.

Renata agreed that I can stay.

Carli will drive me, go to the 17U girls' game in Saint Paul, go to Saundra's concert, then stay overnight at Tasha Tolliver's house.

I am excited about what's coming after the game, although I am a little scared to stay overnight at Devin's house. I have never stayed overnight at anyone's house, and Devin is not quite a friendly guy.

On the drive up, Carli pulls her SUV off the highway in Belle Plaine. She parks in the parking lot of a restaurant that sells pies. We make out. Then an old grandpa knocks on the driver-side window with his cane and waves and laughs at us.

"Oh shit, dude," Carli says. She blinks. Her lips are so red, and her green eyes are wet.

"Who is that?" I ask. I am dizzy on another planet.

"We better drive," she says.

We go to the University of Saint Thomas then. Carli drops me off at a giant building in the middle of a very pretty campus. The building is called the Anderson Athletic and Recreation Center. "They named it after me," Carli says.

"Really?" I ask, because I believe her.

"Duh!" she shouts. "No, you fool! Now go have a good game."

I watch her drive away to Saint Catherine University, where Tasha Tolliver and the 17U girls' Fury will go.

The team we play is called the Twin Ports Pride. They are made up of the best players in Northeastern Minnesota and Northwestern Wisconsin. I recognize some of these guys, because I watched them play in the state tournament on TV. They are mostly all farmers, like me.

"Run that motion," Coach Cliff tells us.

Mr. Doig nods.

"You know what you need to do," Coach Cliff says.

The game begins. Their center, Joe Hunter, outjumps me to start it. I timed my jump badly, or it wouldn't have happened. A fine guard, Evan Pingatore, streaks down the court with the ball. He stops and pops. The Twin Ports Pride is up three to nothing.

This is the last lead they will have. In fact, it is the last minor victory they have for the whole afternoon.

Khalil and Devin are better than everybody by maybe 50 percent. They run pick and roll that is not really part of our offense, but how can you say no to these guys? They are incredible. Even though Khalil is only five foot eleven, he attacks the rim. He lays it in or dishes to Devin, who doesn't just attack the rim, but destroys it.

Rashid gets the start at the four. He and I are better than everybody except Devin and Khalil by maybe 25 percent. Our motion causes many switches. I end up posting guards. Rashid does the same. In the middle of motion, if the defense sags, I put up jump shots. I make two of three.

"You looking smoother all the time, man," Devin says during a time-out.

But it's not my jump shots that win this game.

By the next day, there is a highlight video on YouTube, because we dunk so many basketballs. Most are of Devin, but I am in one highlight as well. That's how good this game goes.

Coach Cliff sits down and smiles. Mr. Doig looks very smug, with his arms crossed, leaning back on a folding chair next to the court.

I don't play the last ten minutes. Neither does Khalil or Devin. We win this exhibition by thirty-six points. When the horn blows, I lean over to Khalil and say, "We are going to kill the Owenses."

"The Owenses are a lot better than these dudes, you know that," Khalil says.

"Still, though," I say.

Khalil smiles. "Yeah, we kill 'em. We kill 'em."

FORTY-ONE

THE PERFECT LIFE

There is only an hour for us to clean up. Devin, Khalil, and I all shower at the Anderson Athletic Center. This is not great for me, but what can I do? If I will play more basketball, I will have to shower in places where there are other naked people. I will have to keep in mind that this is not a sign I've been abandoned to nuns by my drunk dad, but is rather a sign that I am pursuing my dream.

Devin, when he called, told me to bring nicer clothes for the concert. That is difficult, because I refuse to wear anything but shorts or warm-ups, usually. In fact, I only have one pair of regular pants and a shirt that is maybe okay. Renata made me wear khakis and a check button-up shirt for my picture day in the fall. This is what I put on after showering in the locker room. The pants are too short by an inch or two, and I only have basketball shoes and white socks and the shirt won't button across my chest, so I have to wear a Philadelphia 76ers T-shirt under it and leave it unbuttoned. When I walk out from behind the locker where I dressed, a big smile explodes on Khalil's face.

"What?" I ask.

"You look like a big-ass third grader," he says. "I like it."

"Okay, thanks," I say.

"Aw, don't be sad, Farmer. How could you know about fashion when you live out on the frozen prairie where you probably got no internet."

"I don't need nice clothes too much."

Then Devin walks around the corner. He is wearing blue jeans, but also a black jacket, like he's a professor on TV. He just stops in his tracks when he sees me. His eyes get watery, and he looks happier than I have ever seen him look.

"You like my clothes?" I ask.

"Mmm." This sound is very high-pitched.

"Yeah?" I ask.

"Bah-ha!" he shouts. Then he falls onto the bench, and he and Khalil hoot and laugh and handshake each other, like they were the guys who dressed me up as a joke. This does not make me feel bad, because they are so happy, I am getting happy, too. A few minutes later, Carli and Tasha pick us up.

Carli looks very nice. Tasha looks very nice.

Khalil says, "You gotta show this young man the way. He's lost!"

"Not my responsibility," Carli says. Her face also looks like it might break open. "But, yeah, I think I'll help next time."

The joke is now getting old to me.

The church we come to for Saundra's recital is more like a cathedral than a little Northrup church. In fact, it reminds me of the Warsaw Cathedral on its inside. This church has giant wood arches the color of chocolate holding up a very high, beautiful ceiling. Warsaw Cathedral is not such a good memory. I sat with a nun who pinched me a lot, because I had a difficult time sitting still. There was also music. The arches were not chocolate wood, but made of stone, and the sound echoed around the place, like ghosts were carrying it on their backs.

How long has this memory been tucked in my brain without once coming out to remind me it exists? I would like no more memories of Warsaw.

There is a big difference between then and now. There is no nun. There is Carli, who smells like honey. She doesn't pinch me, but she does put her hand on my leg. On the other side of me is Khalil. He is the one who can't sit still, but it is not due to feeling hungry or sick, like I did in Warsaw, but because he recognizes and wants to greet so many of Devin's family in the audience. "Hey, Ms. Mitchell! Hey, Mr.

Fitzgerald! How you doing, Mr. Phelps?" He is twisting and waving and standing and shaking hands. I sit calmly in one spot.

Saundra's piano recital is with a group of ten student piano players who are all taught by the same teacher. Of the ten, only one other is black, but maybe half the people in the audience are black. This doesn't make sense to me. "Who are all these black people?" I whisper to Khalil.

He smiles. "What? You scared of black people?"

"No. There's just so many and only one Saundra and one other girl."

"They are the Mitchell entourage, dude," Khalil says.

"If you're part of this family, you better be ready to go to some event just about every night, because that's what everybody expects: full support," Devin says.

"They're all here for Saundra?"

"That's why Devin's got no time for friends," Khalil says. "Has to pay all these people back when their kids have something to do. Isn't that right, Devin?"

Devin nods.

Then Khalil whispers, "But you think he's ever been up to Brooklyn Center to see one of my little brother's band concerts? His dad wouldn't allow that, would he?"

The concert begins. These young kids, none of them any older than me, are so good. They play music I remember from when I was a child. It goes into me, through my heart, into my lungs, and it makes me tremble, not just from being sad, but from the joy of having the tunes reentered into my mind. As much as Renata loves jazz music, my Polish mom must've loved classical. I read in the program that this music comes from Bach and Brahms and Debussy and from my own Polish man, Chopin. When Saundra plays her nocturne, and the music swirls through the church and into me, I find myself in Adam Sobieski heaven.

It is only later that I recognize Jevetta Mitchell, Renata's favorite jazz singer. I get a picture with her. I send it to Renata, because Renata is my family and family is important.

This is all I want. It's so simple. Basketball, family, good concerts.

Life is not so simple, though.

FORTY-TWO

HERE IT COMES AGAIN

Somehow everything turns upside down. It happens so fast. I should have been ready, because I have lived long enough to know how bad things go. When I feared Carli leaving me, I should have listened to myself. Gotten prepared in my head.

I am at lunch in the cafeteria. Barry chomps on chicken nuggets across from me. It is Wednesday. I can't even make myself eat.

Saturday night was so good. I stayed over with Devin. We watched a documentary film about Larry Bird and Magic Johnson. Khalil also stayed. He cracked good jokes. We tweeted insults about the Owens boys. They tweeted insults back to us. We ate enchiladas. I passed out happy on a soft couch.

But my mind knew the truth. Happiness does not last.

During the night, for the first time in weeks, I dreamed of Warsaw and the apartment. The black ink of an octopus flowed in, choked me, no one there to save me. In the morning Khalil said I cried out in the night as if I were dying.

"It's because I was dying," I said.

And I couldn't shake the bad feeling.

The Mitchells and Khalil left the house before I did, because they went to church. Carli was supposed to pick me up early. She had plans with her pouty friends in the afternoon. But she was late to get me. We were supposed to go at nine a.m. She didn't answer texts. I paced. I worried. I texted Tasha. Tasha did not reply. Finally, Carli showed up at just before eleven.

Her face was pale. "Sorry," she said when I got in the SUV.

"What happened?" I asked.

"I had a hard time sleeping," she said.

"Couch at Tasha's no good?" I asked.

"No. It was fine."

"What's wrong?" I asked.

"I don't want to talk about it."

"What?"

"Nothing, okay?"

"I don't understand . . . nothing?"

Carli turned to me, her face red. "Well, first of all, I tweaked my knee playing Nerf with Tasha's little brother. I can barely walk this morning!" Her eyes filled with tears.

"Oh shit. I'm sorry."

"That's not even it. Not at all."

"What is?" I asked.

She bit her lower lip. Shook her head. "It's nothing. How can you not understand nothing?" Her chin quivered. "Could you just be quiet?"

My heart sank so hard. I am good at being quiet. We said nothing all the way home. She said nothing to me as she dropped me at my house.

I texted her later to ask her what I did so wrong. She didn't respond.

I texted Tasha after that to get more information on what might have happened. This time Tasha did respond. She wrote:

Dude. She got all weird and freaked out. Think her school friends got nasty on her on Snapchat. But she wouldn't talk about it.

School friends? The pouty girls? No. Not just the pouty girls.

When I dream about the apartment, it's because I have been abandoned.

I sit and feel sick at the lunch table. Carli hasn't talked to me all week. She won't even look at me. This is abandonment.

Barry is happy as can be.

"I think I have my second-degree form down?" Barry

says, mouth full of chicken. "But I have to get it so it's, like, part of my body? Otherwise my ego might get in the way and make me fail?"

I look up. Carli walks past our table with her pouty friends. She limps like her knee won't bend. She hangs her head down. Kase Kinshaw is close behind them. He is with Greg Day, who doesn't acknowledge me, even though we were good teammates. Kase slows down. "What are you losers looking at?" he asks.

"Indomitable spirit," Barry says.

"Man," Kase says. "So messed up."

I shake my head and stare at my milk carton.

Kase follows Carli, the pouty girls, and Greg to a table. He sits down next to Carli. He puts his arm on the back of her chair.

I get up and go to the bathroom so I won't do anything crazy.

FORTY-THREE

NOT OKAY

I lie in bed. It is Wednesday night.

Khalil texts me:

Dude you can't hope to understand these girls. Carli's ok. She will be fine. Focus on the game.

I don't think Khalil knows about life. I know about life.

I fall asleep and dream of the Warsaw apartment. I am choked by ink. My dad will not save me. He has left me to die. I wake up sweating, cramps in my gut.

This I remember. The few days before my dad took me to the nuns were the best we had together. We ate in a restaurant and we ate a big dessert, and he ordered no beers and he made good jokes and talked about when he and my mom first met at a music festival outside Warsaw. We played soccer two days, kicking a ball across a field. We went to a movie about a kung fu bear. Then one morning he smoked a thousand cigarettes. He put my few clothes in a small suitcase and put two pictures in there, and then a man drove up in a car. We got in the car. I asked him where we were going. He didn't answer, like Carli doesn't answer my texts. He said good-bye to his son and never said hello again.

Carli is not okay.

Thursday, I sit in a chemistry test and I can't do nothing. Anything. The desk is too small. My body doesn't fit in it. I flunk this test, because my mind hurts.

I try to be normal. I tweet about Kyle Owens after school. *Nine days to your defeat @KyOw23.*

Khalil does not retweet. I text Khalil. Khalil does not text back. By the time I fall asleep in my bed, I am sure that Khalil has spoken to Carli and found out that he shouldn't be my friend and that he has abandoned me, too.

I text Devin. *What's up?*

He texts back. *Nothing. Golden State game on.*

I don't even want to watch NBA.

I don't even want to sit with Renata and Barry at the breakfast table in the morning. Together they make plans for how I'm going to get to my game the next day. Renata and Professor Mike are meeting with local people who want to garden on the big plot of land next to us.

"You promise to be careful?" Renata asks Barry, because

she has just suggested that he could drive me in her car.

"I'm a good driver? I never take my eyes off the road. Right, Adam?"

I stare at my egg sandwich but won't eat it.

"Are you okay?" Renata asks me.

"I'm very sick. I have to stay home from school," I say.

Renata puts her hand on my forehead. "You might be a little warm."

FORTY-FOUR
TRYING TO HANDLE

Basketballs are bouncing. Coach Cliff and Mr. Doig stand to the side, arms crossed, talking quietly. We are in the gyms at Normandale Community College. Not very fancy or new, but bright. There are six teams here. Three on each court. There are plastic chairs surrounding each, with a few spectators sitting here and there, but not many. Barry is one. He gives me a big thumbs-up. He is wearing his karate headband. I dribble the ball with one hand and thumbs-up him back, very quickly. Devin stretches on the floor on the other side of the court. His mom and sister sit very close to Barry. Somehow this makes me nervous.

Speaking of nervous, there was a moment the night before when I thought I couldn't come to this game, because

I had my dream again and again and my stomach was too upset. But two things happened.

First, at nearly two a.m., the phone buzzed in my hand. I was only half-asleep, still wearing the clothes I had worn all day. The text was from Carli.

Good luck tomorrow, dude. You'll do great.

I had two responses at once to this text: I wanted to tell her I love her. I wanted to tell her she can drive her SUV off a cliff and I don't care.

I didn't text back at all. I won't be fooled again, but I'm sorry to say her text makes me feel a little better.

Second, at seven a.m., Devin texted me.

Have you heard from Khalil? Can't get a hold of him.

Right away, my anger at Khalil—because I thought he was joining Carli in abandoning me—turned to worry. Khalil and Devin are brothers. There is no way Khalil would ignore him. Has something bad happened to Khalil?

And here we are on the court. He has not made it to the game. The coaches have said nothing about his absence.

"Passing. Passing. Right now," Coach Cliff shouts.

The Fury, without our point guard, move into serious warming up.

Rashid and I are together. He looks nervous. As we pass the ball, he says, "Where's Khalil?"

"I don't know," I say.

"We got no other real points. These dudes are quick, too.

Titus Lartey busts ankles."

The team we will play, the TC Tigers, are all boys from northern suburbs. Some big white boys and African kids from Africa. "Like Liberia and shit," Khalil had told me after our first game. I eyeball this team. One of them looks a little like my old friend Mobo Bell. At least he has the same haircut and dribble posture. The team has a couple bigger boys than me and Rashid. They have some small, fast kids, too.

We run through our shooting progressions. We do our layups.

Coach Cliff blows the whistle. "Come on in here, fellas. We have to make some lineup changes."

We gather around him and Mr. Doig.

Before Coach Cliff has a chance to say anything, Devin speaks up. "Where's Khalil? Do you know?" he asks.

Coach Cliff takes in a big breath. Mr. Doig makes a big frown with his face.

"Khalil got into a little hot water on Thursday afternoon. We don't know the particulars, but there are charges pending."

"There's no damn way," Devin says.

Mr. Doig glares.

"For now, we have to consider Khalil to be in breach of the team contract. Until we know something more, that's all we have," Coach Cliff says.

"No way," Devin says, shaking his head.

"Show some respect," Mr. Doig hisses.

Devin leans in, opens his eyes wide, and says, "No. Damn. Way. Sir."

"Just cool it," Coach Cliff says. "This will all get figured out. Right now we got a game to play, and we have no point guard. Devin, you're going to be bringing the ball up."

Devin doesn't say anything. The ref blows the whistle. Other games begin in other parts of the gym.

"Once we get into the half-court, we'll just go motion. Don't matter what spot you're playing. Just do motion. Marques, you're at the four. Rashid, you're starting at the five. Farmer, you're our third-best handle. You'll move to two."

"I never played guard."

"Just do the motion," Coach Cliff says.

The ref blows the whistle again. The TC Tigers are waiting at center court.

"Do I jump?" I ask as I jog on.

"Rashid. You," Coach Cliff shouts back.

The game begins with Rashid outjumping a giant fellow for the tip. I see there is nothing to be intimidated about with our opponents' size, because they are very slow. The rest of the TC Tigers are not like those Owens boys, either. They have no team game at all. They run isolation. Although I go to the wrong spot two times in the first minute and Devin has to point me where to stop, I score one basket at the post, Devin scores on a dunk, and Trey, our small forward, hits a three-pointer. We are up 7–0.

I relax. I am on a basketball court and nothing else matters.

Except, as soon as I relax, the boy named Titus Lartey goes crazy. He does not pass. He only drives for layups or he only stops and shoots. He does not miss. The boy is maybe five foot nine, and he is chili peppers on fire. While Devin makes two more baskets and I miss my stupid jump shot and Rashid misses, Titus flies downcourt, drives to the hoop, scores and scores. The TC Tigers pull within one point just five minutes in.

There is a time-out, and Coach Cliff yells at Trey, who is supposed to guard Titus, to stay in Titus's face.

"I'm trying!" Trey shouts back. "Dude is a half foot shorter than me!"

Mr. Doig nearly jumps out of his fat man shorts. He shouts, "You do not talk back to your coach!"

"Yes, sir. Sorry, sir," Trey says.

I do not think Trey was being salty, only telling the truth. We are wrong without Khalil. We are all between six foot three and six foot seven. Titus is too quick. But Rashid knows something. As we jog back on the court, Rashid says to Trey, "We've seen this before, dude. Titus can't miss until he does, and then he'll miss everything the rest of the game."

"Shut up, man," Titus says. He's heard Rashid.

"I'm just saying," Rashid says. He shrugs and smiles.

And what he says is true. Titus misses his next shot. He glares at Rashid and shakes his head. Then he misses three more. "Sorry, little man," Rashid says to him.

We go on a super-fast ten-to-nothing run, rolling through our motion, almost turning into a Khalil-less ocean, except Devin stops shooting. He gets the ball with lanes but won't drive. He gets the ball with open three-pointers but won't pull the trigger. Coach Cliff yells at him, but he doesn't look over at Coach.

It's okay. We are much better than the TC Tigers. Near the end of the half, Coach Cliff calls time-out and takes Devin from the lineup.

"Sit down at the end of that bench, son," Coach Cliff snarls.

During halftime, Coach Cliff asks Devin if he's going to play the game.

Devin shakes his head and looks down. "I don't feel good," he says.

"What's that, boy?" Mr. Doig spits.

Devin looks up from his hands. "I don't feel good. And don't you call me boy, sir."

There is a shocked silence that falls on everybody. Mr. Doig's face turns the color of a plum.

Coach Cliff puts his hands in the air, as if he's an orchestra director asking for calmer music. "Okay, okay. I understand some of you might be feeling anxious about Khalil. We will address that issue, understand? But not now. Now we focus." Coach Cliff turns to Mr. Doig when he says this. Mr. Doig takes a deep breath, shuts his eyes, and nods like he agrees. "Devin, if you are feeling sick, I won't send you back in. Are you sick?"

Devin looks at his hands again. "Yes, sir."

"Then next man up. Farmer, you're handling."

I'm stunned. I don't understand for a moment. "Wait? Handling? Bringing up the ball? I don't know how, sir."

"Just do it. You'll learn. Charlie, you get ready to run, because we're thin now."

Charlie, who only played five minutes during the Twin Ports Pride game and hasn't yet gotten in this game, nods. He's a good shot but is a little chubby.

I look at Devin, who is folding in on himself. I look to his mom, who is now standing and staring at him.

Okay. Okay. Focus. When I am on the court, I just play.

At the beginning of the second half, when they see that I am now bringing the ball up, the TC Tigers do much more trapping. I am not sure how to deal with this at first. I pick up my dribble, and Titus and the other guard are both scrappy. They rip the ball right out of my hands. Titus scores on a layup.

"Farmer, don't seize up!" Coach Cliff shouts. "You gotta stay moving, look for an outlet if they close up. Trey, make sure you hang close. Shid, you pay attention, too."

"Yeah, Coach," Rashid says.

Like Coach Cliff said, I learn to handle by doing it.

Rashid stands out of bounds. He winks at me. "I'll hang out a second," he says. He throws the ball into me and right away back come Titus and the other guard. They surround me. I toss it over the top back to Rashid. They collapse over on him, and I take off. Rashid lobs me the rock over their trap and then it is like the waters part. I explode downcourt, away from Titus and his pal, and the slow bigs cannot react. I leap and jam the ball home.

"That's how you break the pressure!" Mr. Doig shouts. "Great job, my boy! Great job!"

"Yes, sir, yes, sir," Coach Cliff says, clapping.

The game goes very well—we break the pressure so hard, the Tigers stop. I can sense what the Tigers are going to do on defense right before they do it. I see them hedging, getting out of position, before my own teammate has even made any move. When Charlie, Trey, Rashid, or Marques cuts, I am already delivering the ball. Our motion offense moves so fast, we score so quick, because I can see my teammates' way to the hole, not just my own. I reverse rotation in a blink. I drive when the red sea opens. I am like old man Dwight from the Y playing jazz on the basketball court.

Everyone is excited as the ref blows his whistle to end the game. We have destroyed the TC Tigers. "They're the best metro AAU team other than us, and check that shit out, dude." Rashid points at the scoreboard.

"Pretty good, pretty good," I say.

Off court Coach Cliff gathers us around. "Fellas," he says. "We may not be as big as we've been in past years, but even with two of our best players out"—he looks over at Devin— "don't we have something going on right here? I mean, don't we?"

"Yes, we do!" Trey and others shout.

"But next week it gets real. We got the Minne-Kota Stars up at Saint Cloud State. That team is filled with those Owenses. They play together the moment they drop out of their mamas. So get ready." Coach Cliff turns to Devin. "You going to be ready, son?"

Devin stares straight forward. "I'm going to see about Khalil," he says.

"We all will," Coach Cliff says. Then he addresses the rest of us. "Do some running. Keep yourselves in shape. Keep handling the ball. You especially, Farmer, because no matter what, you'll be playing some point from now on. See you next Saturday, nine a.m. in the Chaska High School lot. We'll take a bus up to the game together."

Devin stands quickly. He doesn't look at me. He walks over to his mother and sister. They leave fast.

As we drive home, Barry says, "You're even better than you were before? You look like a guy on TV playing basketball?"

"Uh-huh," I say. But I'm not on the court, and the peace that comes with playing is gone. I text Khalil. Ask him what's happening.

There's no reply.

"Hey. Let's go to this roast beef place in Mankato? I ate there once with my sister. It was tasty? We can celebrate your victory!" Barry says.

"Uh-huh," I say. "Okay." I'm hungry. Food is a fine idea. "You're a good friend, Barry Roland."

"Yeah? Good!" he says. "That's my goal!"

FORTY-FIVE
BAD BEEF

We stop at my house. I shower and change into my favorite 76ers shirt. Renata, who is covered in dirt, because she helped people dig gardens on Professor Mike's land, gives us forty dollars to celebrate my basketball victory. I believe she is celebrating the fact me and Barry are friends. She asks us not to take her car, though.

Then we are off, back driving in Barry's shit Pontiac that smells like french fries. We get on the highway and head south, along the steep Minnesota River bluffs. Cold wind blows in through the holes. I begin to get achy, maybe from playing a game and not stretching after, maybe from the cold wind, maybe because Khalil doesn't respond to my text, maybe because I thought, just one week before this moment,

I had a beautiful hooper girlfriend who loved me?

We get to Mankato and drive up the opposite bluff, out of the river valley to this mall across the street from the state university. There we find the restaurant Barry loves. It is called Jonny B's. It has a big sign on the window that says "All Roast Beef" and "Great New Menu Items" and "Student Discounts."

"We're students," Barry says. "Discounts?"

"Do you think they have cheeseburgers?" I ask.

"I'd be willing to bet for sure?" he says.

Once inside this restaurant, we get seated at a big window that stares out at the grimy parking lot. College kids drink beers in booths all around us. It is only five p.m., but they are loud, drunk, and not nice, shouting shit at each other, and I feel jumpy in my skin. I don't like drinking. I don't like them shouting shit. Worst of all, the restaurant menu only contains various styles of roast beef sandwich.

"The *B* in Jonny B's stands for beef," the waitress tells us.

"Cheeseburger is beef," I say.

"Should I come back in a moment?" the waitress asks.

"Yes. Maybe," I say.

She leaves, and Barry leans in. "Beef is what makes burgers. You said it yourself, right? So, you should try a sandwich, because they're so good?"

"I know what is roast beef," I spit at him.

"What roast beef is?" he asks. "You can get cheese on lots of these sandwiches."

I am more and more agitated, like maybe I know what is about to happen deep in my soul. "Roast beef is hard to chew, and my teeth don't like it," I spit.

But at this point, he is not listening to me. He is turned to his left and is staring out the window. I turn to look. An SUV pulls in. I know this SUV. The driver turns it off. A girl climbs out of the back seat and then another. "Carli?" I say.

"No, that's Sara what's-her-name and Darci," Barry says. Then he sucks in air, because a big dude climbs out of the passenger-side door. "Uh-oh. Do you think we should hide?" Barry whispers.

Kase Kinshaw. Carli has driven with those girls, Kase Kinshaw, and Greg Day. She gets out of the driver's door and laughs, because someone has made a joke. She comes around the front of the van and takes a playful punch at Kase's shoulder. He grabs her and puts her in a headlock, squeezes her head to his chest. She wraps her arms around his middle and lifts him off the ground.

"Carli is strong?" Barry says.

"Uh," I say. "No limp."

She drops Kase on his feet, and he lets go of her head and they laugh.

I know now. I get it. Kase Kinshaw texted her while she was at Tasha Tolliver's house last weekend. Kase Kinshaw wants to be her boyfriend. Carli was just waiting for him. She is ready for him.

I am frozen. And if I get unfrozen I might lose my mind, break the window, scream like a crazy man. I cannot breathe. I cannot see. The five of them all laugh. Kase Kinshaw talks more. The girls laugh and laugh. Carli, of course, is the biggest laugher of all.

Are they coming in Jonny B's? Will I break this booth in half? At the last second they steer right, toward the entrance of the movie theater, which is next door.

"Oh shit. Oh shit, man," I whisper.

"It's cool. They didn't come in here?" Barry says.

Our waitress comes over to see if we're ready to order.

"I'll have the french dip?" Barry says. "Does that come with some cheese?"

"We can put cheese on it. Cheddar okay?" she asks.

"Okay?" he says. "That's good cheese?"

She shrugs. Then the waitress turns to me, but I don't want a french dip or any other beef. I want the blood of my enemies.

"I have to go," I say.

"You what?" Barry asks.

I exhale. I think of the boy's fingers. I broke them. I got kicked from school. I think of the team in Philly, the boy who called me Forrest Gump and his dislocated shoulder. *Stop,* I think. *You have basketball.* I breathe deep. "Okay?" I say. "No. It's okay. Just some fries, please?" But then Carli runs out into the parking lot with Kase chasing her. He grabs

her again, and then she spins away and runs back out of sight.
"Okay," I say. "I will come back."

I stand up.

"What's happening?" Barry asks.

My head pounds. How could she do this? All she could do was kiss me a week ago. Me. Adam.

"Adam?" Barry says.

"I have to go speak to Carli Anderson," I say.

"Now?"

I am out the door of Jonny B's.

And they are there, all five of them. There is a line to buy movie tickets of maybe ten people. Carli and her friends stand against a wall, not yet in line. Kase, Darci, and Greg now all stare at his phone, big stupid smiles on their stupid faces.

My heart pounds so hard in my throat, in my forehead, in my chest. Carli sees me and I can see the color rise in her, lit by theater lights above. She takes five steps toward me, then stops.

"Dude," she whispers. "What are you doing here?"

"No." I can barely talk.

"What?"

I point at Kase Kinshaw, who is still on his phone. "He was touching you."

She grabs my arm. "Be quiet. Don't talk so loud. This . . . this is no big deal." Her breath is heavy.

"No," I say.

Carli's face turns very red. Her eyes water. She shakes her head. "I'm going to see a movie now. We'll talk tomorrow. We'll play . . ."

"No, we won't."

"Just stop, Adam."

"No," I say.

"Please," Carli says.

"No."

And then . . .

"Holy shit!" Kase Kinshaw spits. "Look who's here." He walks toward us. "You stalking Carli, Duh?"

Carli spins around. "Shut up, dude. Come on!" She is trying to sound light and funny.

"Aw, Jesus, seriously? Just leave it alone, Kase," Greg says from where he is standing. "Adam can talk to whoever he wants."

Kase doesn't listen. "What's up, buddy?" he says. He pushes past Carli, and his face is right in my face.

I back up, away from him. My body wants to fight. I don't want to lose my mind. I don't want to lose. I want to break him, but I can't break him or I am lost again.

"Not so cocky outside of school, are you?"

He keeps pressing closer into me. His face is so big. I can feel his breath. "Get away from me," I say.

"I don't think so, pussy. I'm tired of bowing down to you foreign re—"

I shove him hard in his chest before he can finish his sentence. For a moment he is shocked. He exhales like a horse. His eyes water. He swallows hard. He is back in my face in one second.

"Do it again. Please. Shove me again," he hisses.

"Stop it," Carli cries.

Kase looks at her. "Why do you care about him?" he shouts.

"Because he's cool," Carli shouts. "Why won't you listen to me? Why can't I hang out with who I want?"

Kase's eyes water. His chin trembles. "Everything's been shit since you moved to town," he whispers. He grabs the collar of my 76ers shirt with his left hand and pulls on it. It rips. He swings his right fist into my ribs. I twist, pop him in the head with my elbow. He keeps coming.

Then Sara cries, "Watch out, Kase!"

There is a sound, like a whip cutting the air, then a crack. Kase screams out in pain and lets go of me at the same moment. He crumples to the ground. My eyes are filled with tears and I am shaking, trying to regain balance, trying to see what is happening. I blink my eyes clear in time to see Barry Roland lay out Greg Day with a front kick to his chest.

Barry swings back around and stands over Kase. "You stop it!" Barry screams. Kase writhes on the ground, groaning. Barry crouches over him, like he might kick Kase's face off.

"Don't," I say.

Just then the big security bouncers from Jonny B's are on Barry. They wrestle him to the ground, pin him on the pavement.

"Adam! Adam! Help!" he cries.

I stand, braced against the wall. I hear cop sirens in the distance.

FORTY-SIX

BARNEY WAS A DOG

I lie on the floor of my bedroom. Professor Mike, Renata, and both girls came to pick me up from the police station in Mankato. Renata screamed at me. She has only done that one other time, when I fought the kid in Philly and she grabbed my shoulders and shouted, "I can't have a violent child."

Here we are again. She heard I attacked Kase Kinshaw. She heard that Barry had to fight to save me. She cried, "How could you do this?"

I can't explain. I am a bad person. I make people hate me. I hurt people I love. Look what I did to Barry. I should be taken back to the nuns or thrown out on the street.

There are no charges filed against me right away, because the police are still talking to witnesses. There are no charges against Kase, either. I didn't see him at the station at all.

I did see Barry, though. He was in a bad state. The police wouldn't release him to Renata. He had to wait for Tiffany, but Tiffany was not answering her phone. Barry cried when we left. We drove to the trailer in Northrup to find Tiffany, but she wasn't home. Merle said he didn't know where Tiffany had gone, maybe to the bar. We went to Patrick's. She wasn't there. We went to a place called the Logjam. She wasn't there.

"We can't look in every damn bar in Northrup," Professor Mike said. He looked tired, red-eyed.

Renata took us home. I was so tired, too, and unhappy about the world. I went to my bedroom. Renata left again, and she did look in every damn bar in Northrup until she found Tiffany. She drove Tiffany to Mankato to get Barry. She drove Tiffany and Barry back to the trailer. She waited while Tiffany screamed at Barry. She waited while Barry shouted back. She waited while Tiffany threw Barry out of his house. She drove Barry to our house, and he is now out in the living room on the couch. He has so far been unable to talk.

I don't want to talk, either.

Was I arrested? They put no handcuffs on me and they didn't read me any rights, but they put me and Barry in a cop car and we drove back to the station.

What if I was arrested? Mr. Doig will find out?

I roll onto my face. Mr. Doig will find out.

The Conduct Contract I signed with the Fury says I will be immediately terminated from the team if I am arrested. So I lie on my face on the floor of my bedroom.

What if no more Fury?

What if Renata decides I am violent and she can't have me?

My anger undoes me. I am the worst boy.

Meanwhile, Carli texts.

Why did this happen? Why were you even there?

I don't answer. She texts more.

I'm sorry. I should've told you what was going on. It's my fault.

I don't respond.

Listen, please. Sara and Darci got so mad at me because I canceled on going to the Mall of America with them. They spent all night Saturday taking nasty pictures at a party with everyone I know, sending them to me, saying I would never be their friend again.

I don't respond.

I'm sorry. I'm sorry. I'm sorry. PLEASE. What if you thought you suddenly lost every last friend you ever had in your life?

I lie on my face.

And I hurt my knee again Saturday because I was in Minneapolis with you. I freaked out. I decided you were bad luck. I know that's stupid. I feel terrible, man. Please.

I'm sorry.

No. I am bad luck.

Are you there? Are you reading these? I see the texts are being delivered.

I don't respond. There is a gap of about ten minutes where Carli writes nothing. And then this:

You know Barry Roland shot his dog a couple years ago, right?

What? I sit up.

I type into my phone:

What dog?

The Kinshaws' dog. Barney. Barney died.

Barry Roland killed Barney the dog? I cannot believe this.

I stand. I go to the living room. Barry lies on his back and stares at the ceiling. His fluffy mustache face turns to me as I enter the room.

"Hey," I say.

He shakes his head.

"Sorry," I say.

He doesn't say anything for a moment but then talks straight up to the ceiling. "Were you in bad danger today?" he asks.

"From Kase?" I ask. "I don't know."

"Did I lose self-control? Maybe I did? I don't like Kase, even if he isn't worth my time and heart. I'm mad at him for my whole life, but I can't kick someone because I'm mad at them. That would go against my spiritual beliefs?" He turns and looks at me again. He isn't wearing his big glasses. He squints to try to see me better.

"Kase was trying to hurt me. If it went on another second, I would have really tried to kill him, too. I lose my mind sometimes."

"You do?" Barry asks.

"I have twice in my past. It was bad, because I hurt other kids."

"Yeah?" Barry asks.

"Uh-huh. So you weren't just kicking him because you were mad. You saved me today, from Kase and from myself, too."

Barry exhales for a count of ten. He nods. "Okay, thanks." But I don't think he believes what I have said.

I sit down on the big chair next to the couch. I reach and grab the remote control. I put on the TV. There is a very old show on about four old ladies living in a house in Florida. It makes me laugh, because the oldest lady on the show reminds me of a Polish grandma. She is clever and has a dirty vocabulary. We watch until a commercial break. I turn off the sound.

Barry looks at me.

"Did you shoot Barney the dog?" I ask.

He sits up and pushes the big blanket off him. "I have

never shot a gun in my whole life? I told them that already, okay? A thousand times."

"Them? Kase?"

"And Greg and those girls and the police and everybody," Barry says. "They don't believe me."

"This was two years ago?" I ask.

"Like almost three."

"Why do they think you did it?" I ask.

Barry shuts his eyes. "Merle's car."

"What?"

"Merle drove me everywhere for a while, because Tiffany lost her license. A car like Merle had—stupid red Ford Taurus—was seen right by where Barney got shot, right by the Kinshaws' place out in the country, but Merle was at the bar and everyone saw him there and he walked home . . ."

"Oh . . . did you drive Merle's car?" I ask.

"No," Barry says. He breathes out, then talks quietly. "But maybe Tara did."

"Tara your sister?" I ask.

"Yes," he says.

"Were you with her?" I ask.

Barry shakes his head. "But Kase picked on me so bad? She doesn't like people picking on me."

"That's good," I say.

"No. No, it is not good. She is not good, okay?"

"Did she have a gun?" I ask.

"Tara worked at Scheels in Mankato. They have a lot of guns there? She used to go hunting with our dad when I was really little? She knows how to shoot."

"Oh," I say. "Tara?"

Barry nods slowly. "Another reason why I am in tae kwon do. I don't want to be bad like Tara," Barry says. Then he says, "I don't know if she did it, really."

Renata comes out of her room, even though it's late. She wears a University of Pennsylvania sweatshirt and big sweatpants. Her hair is messed up, like she has already been asleep. She smiles but looks sad. "You guys okay?" she asks.

"If you don't throw me out on the street, I'll be okay," I say.

Renata shakes her head. "I would never, never do that, Adam. This is your home . . . wherever I am is your home."

"Because you're the best mom there is," Barry says. "That's why."

He has put no question mark sound at the end of those sentences.

FORTY-SEVEN

THE LAST MONDAY

It is Monday. I don't want to go to school. I almost didn't sleep all night. When I did sleep, I had my bad dream. I worry this will be the day I find out about charges against me. I worry I will join Khalil, get kicked off the Fury.

Barry and I climb into his shit car. I have to go to school. Renata is right, I missed school last week and homework doesn't stop coming just because I am a criminal. "You have to stay focused on your main job," Renata tells me.

"What is that?" I ask.

"Student. Duh," she says.

She isn't calling me names, just reminding me of the truth. There is chemistry to deal with and a book called *The Red Badge of Courage* in English.

Barry is also a mess. He went home Sunday afternoon, but Tiffany told him to go away. He has caused her too much trouble. "She's done with me," Barry said during Sunday dinner.

"I think she's legally bound to care for you," Professor Mike replied. "You're sixteen? You're a minor?"

Barry looked down at the kielbasa sausage on his plate. "I'll actually be eighteen in May?" he said.

"But you're a sophomore?" Professor Mike said.

Barry nodded.

"You're not an adult yet. This isn't right," Renata said.

"Uh-oh," Professor Mike said. "You're almost an adult."

"You can stay here as long as you need to," Renata said.

Professor Mike stared at her with big eyes.

"I went to kindergarten a year late?" Barry tells me as we drive to school. "And then they wouldn't let me pass first grade because I couldn't recognize letters? I can now, though."

"That's good," I say. "That's dope."

"Yeah," he says. He is nervous like I am. I think he has tied his karate headband on extra tight. Who would want to go back to this school after what happened at Jonny B's?

When we enter the school, my biggest worry is seeing Kase Kinshaw. He is not in the entryway and he is not in the commons area, sitting at the table where he often does. He is nowhere to be seen. My second-biggest worry is seeing Carli, because I didn't return her texts after I asked Barry about Barney the dog. I can't deal with her. She is not in the commons. Sara and Darci are there, though, huddled over a table.

I walk faster. Barry keeps up. We turn a corner, to the spot where we have to split up and go to our separate parts of the building. Right then, Derrick Oppegaard, who pounds the drum in the pep band, runs up to us.

"Dudes," he says. "Holy balls. You kicked Kase Kinshaw's ass!"

I shake my head, because I know how Barry is feeling.

"Yeah, you did! My cousin was at the movie theater, and she took a picture of Barry getting tackled by these big guys. It's because you kicked Kase's ass!"

"Bouncers tackled Barry," I say.

"I didn't want to kick his ass," Barry says. He reaches up and pulls on his karate headband.

"He deserves it. He's a butt munch."

"A what?" I ask.

Barry pulls his karate headband off. "I have to go to my class?" he says. He scurries away fast, holding his headband in his hand.

All day, I see no Kase Kinshaw. He isn't at school. Greg Day isn't at school, either. Carli is. I see her between classes in the afternoon. She stops in the hall. Stares at me. Spreads out her arms in a gesture that maybe says, *What are you doing, you dumbass? Because I'm right here . . .*

The bell rings. I don't see her again.

And then at home, there is a big, big relief waiting for us on the voice mail. There will be no charges against me and Barry, because an old man who was with his granddaughter in Jonny B's said the little guy (Barry) was protecting the tall guy (me) from getting beat up by the big guy (Kase). That was all the Mankato police needed. They closed the file.

I'm not sure why there are no charges against Kase, though. Didn't the grandpa say the big guy was beating up the tall guy?

It doesn't matter. I ask Renata to look at the D-I Fury Conduct Contract. She reads it and says I am clear. I have not broken any stated rule. I didn't smoke. I didn't drink. And I wasn't arrested. Unlike Khalil, I have basketball.

To celebrate no charges, Barry and I go running on the Red Jacket Trail. It rains, but Barry runs barefoot. He doesn't talk the whole way. He sleeps on our couch. Renata washes his clothes, because he only has one pair of jeans.

Barry doesn't seem like he's in any mood to celebrate.

FORTY-EIGHT
3:17 A.M.

"I like Barry, but do you really have the resources to take care of him?"

I hear the voice, a whisper, coming through the wall. I look at the clock on the little table next to my bed. It is 3:17 a.m.

I can hear Renata talking, but her voice is too quiet to understand.

"I have two daughters, Renata, and so much emotional responsibility already."

The voice is Professor Mike. He is in Renata's room. Renata says something more. She sounds stressed out.

"I don't know. I don't know. I have to think about this," Professor Mike says.

Our house creaks. I hear him leave her room. I hear him walk softly down the hall. I hear the front door shut quietly. *There goes Professor Mike,* I think. *He is going away from us. There goes Regan and Margery.*

FORTY-NINE

THE LAST TUESDAY

On our car ride to school Tuesday, Barry tells me many kids came up to him to congratulate him the day before. This has made him even more sad. He is not wearing his karate headband now. He says he doesn't deserve the honor of wearing his karate headband, because he kicked Kase Kinshaw out of hatred.

"What about protecting me? Isn't that what you wanted to do?"

Barry says, "Yeah, okay, but honestly I really wanted to kick Kase, too, therefore I disgraced my teacher and shamed this holy place."

"We were in Mankato. That's not holy."

"The holy place is a line from an old TV show called

Kung Fu." Barry sighs. "The holy place is wherever you are."

Once again, the school contains no Greg Day and no Kase Kinshaw. In many ways, this is better. In one way, it is maybe not so good. Barry Roland wants to tell Kase Kinshaw that he's sorry. He wants to ask for his forgiveness. Of course I think this is stupid.

Carli Anderson is at school. I try to avoid her not because I am mad, but because I don't know what to say. We pay for our bad choices. Me and Carli are now broken. Life is hard, and you can't count on people. That's what I said to Renata at breakfast. She shook her head at me like I am crazy.

Carli has different thoughts than I have, too.

During chemistry, where I receive an F on the quiz I took the week before, Carli comes in. Mr. Burton stops the class, whispers to her, then motions for me to come to the front of the room. I don't leave my desk. "Come on, Adam Reed, move," Mr. Burton says. So I uncurl and go up front.

"You know Carli, I imagine," Mr. Burton says.

I nod.

"Carli and I ran into each other at the yearbook bake sale this morning and somehow ended up on the subject of you. You both play for the same college-bound basketball organization?" he asks.

Again, I nod. *College-bound?* I don't know about that.

"What is it called?" he asks.

Both Carli and I say, "The Fury."

I look at her.

She says, "D-I Fury, for Division I college prep."

"Aha," Mr. Burton says. He turns to me. "And Carli tutors Division I Fury players in math and science. Isn't that right?"

"Uh-huh?" I say.

"Yes. That is true," Carli says slowly, looking to the side and also blushing. She sounds exactly like she is lying.

"So why aren't you taking advantage of her services, Adam? She's a very good science student. She knows this material. She could really help you."

"I don't know," I say.

"Well, how about this?" Mr. Burton says. "You have no choice in the matter now. The only way you're going to pass this class is if you get help. I'm going to require you to work on chemistry with Carli for two hours a week for the rest of the semester."

"Oh," I say.

"If you do, I'll give you extra-credit points, but my guess is you won't need them. You're smart enough to do this. I think the reading slows you down."

"Uh-huh," I say.

"Go out in the hall and make a schedule." Mr. Burton points at the door. Carli's face breaks into a big smile.

But out in the hall the big smile drops from her face. She turns and pokes me in the chest hard.

"I like you," she says. "I'm sorry I messed up. Do you like me?" she asks.

I am stunned and words are stuck in my mouth.

"Do you, Farmer? Do you?" she asks.

"Yeah," I say.

"Then accept my stupid apology and get over it," she says.

I don't respond. She pokes me hard.

Barry once accepted my apology. Haven't I said I should be more like Barry?

"Okay?" I say.

"Okay," she says. "We'll meet Friday and Sunday for chemistry and whatever other shit we want to go over, because we're buddies and that's what we do. Spend quality time together. Do you understand?" she says.

"Okay. Okay. Yeah," I say.

She leans. She whispers, "I am a person, and I make stupid mistakes sometimes. I'm really, really sorry."

"It's okay."

"Now go tell Burton we have this all figured out, please."

"Okay," I say.

Then she is gone. There is no limp as she walks. Just big, powerful strides and the lingering smell of honey in the hall.

Before I go back into the room, I text Khalil:

You were right. Carli is ok.

I hope he sees it so he knows I am thinking of him.

FIFTY

11:26 P.M.

The phone buzzes in my hand. It startles me, because I am asleep on the couch. Barry has taken my bedroom for the night. He looked so tired at dinner, Renata suggested he could use some privacy. He said no, but I said yes.

I fall back asleep, but the phone buzzes again. How do people ever sleep enough after they get phones?

I look at the screen. It is Khalil. I sit up fast. I am so happy to hear from him. The phone buzzes again and again. All from Khalil!

Sorry didn't text back, bro. Mom took phone for few days cuz trouble.

You hear about trouble? It's bull but bad.

Mr. Doig won't let me play. Says I'm terminated.

I text as fast as I can, so he knows I am here.

What happened????

I can see on my phone that Khalil is typing. It takes a long time for this message to show up.

Cuz my little bro lonnie got accused of stealing cheetos and it wasn't him but he had on the same hoodie as the kid and of course he black and cop thought it was lonnie so they chased him to the house and when they banged on the door, I said lonnie you gotta talk to them and tell them what you know, but he was shaking and shit and I got scared as shit too so how can I blame the little dude for that? Lonnie wouldn't talk and I opened the door and don't know why but I told the cop lonnie was unavailable to talk but lonnie was lying on the floor crying right behind me and then another cop showed up and he was pissed and they arrested me for obstructing justice dude. Even before we got to the station they got the actual kid for steeling cheetos and they let lonnie go but not me cuz I was obstructing justice even though there was no justice situation at all!! City attorney to decide next week if they pursue the charge against me. Stupid lonnie just had to talk to that cop and it woulda been fine but lonnie what can I say? Mom told us to stay away from cops cuz they will mess with us and maybe worse. Shit, bro. Mr. Doig says I'm just a thug criminal now I guess because I broke the contract. I think I am kicked off for good.

I sit for a moment on the couch and stare at this message.

My guts turn and my eyes hurt. I remember what Tasha Tolliver said in the hot tub. *Trouble is out looking for all black kids right now . . .* but isn't trouble looking for me, too? Isn't trouble looking for Barry? I almost type back about how the cops took me and Barry in on Saturday because we got in a fight, but then two things come into my brain at one time.

First, the cops just let us go. No arrest. No nothing. There was a real justice situation, right? Kase Kinshaw grabbed and ripped my 76ers shirt and he punched my ribs. I got a bruise like my dad used to give me. Then Barry Roland kicked two guys. If Khalil gets in trouble for trying to be nice to his little brother, shouldn't me, Barry, and Kase be in much bigger trouble? It makes no sense!

The second thing that comes into my brain is this: don't tell Khalil, because you don't want Mr. Doig to find out about you and the cops.

Shit, bro, I write. *I don't wanna play without you out there.* This is only part true, because I would rather play with him, but also, I want to play no matter what. I can't lose basketball.

Khalil types his message back.

I'm scared schools pull my scholarship offers cuz I'm not like Devin nobody cares that much about a five-foot-eleven dude. I will commit to North Dakota State tomorrow if they promise not to pull my scholarship. If no basketball I don't know if there is a future, bro.

Yes. Yes. This I know.

Even though I don't believe what I am writing, I text Khalil:

You will be out on the court with us soon, bro. Don't worry. It will be dope out there and we will kill Owens boys and this will be a bad dream.

There is about a minute where it looks like Khalil is writing back, but all he replies is this:

Don't think I'll be on court so good luck. Better go sleep.

FIFTY-ONE

THE LAST WEDNESDAY

Again on Wednesday, there is no Kase Kinshaw in school. Maybe Barry has done a great favor for everyone? Maybe Kase will stay out of school for the rest of the year? Not that I am happy. How can I be happy with Khalil on my mind?

Barry is not happy, either. Renata had to talk him into going to his second-to-last tae kwon do practice before he tests for his next black belt on Sunday.

"I'm not honorable enough to be a tae kwon do master?" he said during breakfast.

Renata stood up so fast her chair tipped over backward. "That is not true, Barry," she said. "You are a wonderful kid. Wonderful, do you understand? I have never seen you be anything but honorable. And I will be so upset with you if you don't follow through on your test. You will go to your class tonight!"

Barry then stood up. He placed his right fist in his left palm and bowed to Renata. She bowed back.

I think I have many weird people in my life.

The school day feels normal, and I begin to think more about Saturday. There will be no Khalil on the floor with us. I have to get over this. There will still be Devin and Rashid and Marques and Trey. There will be Charlie, too. Together we will take on Kyle Owens and his cousins, and we will find our flow. They will chase the ocean. We will destroy them. I try to gather my focus. During study hall in the library I pull out my phone and tweet @KyOw23 that the Fury will crush him to the ground.

@KyOw23 responds: *@PolishHooper not a real baller. #keepyourdayjob*

A few minutes later I receive a text from Devin. It is the first time I have heard from him since we played the TC Tigers. He doesn't know about my drama. He doesn't know about Carli and Kase Kinshaw and Barry.

He writes:

Stop the trash talk, Farmer. The game is not what matters right now.

It matters to me, though. Kyle Owens has disrespected me as a human being. He has called me a head case and says I don't understand basketball because I am a foreigner and that all I do is run and jump. He is Kase Kinshaw, but on the basketball court where I can fight back legally. I will not keep my day job!

I don't know what that last thing means, though.

FIFTY-TWO

7:21 P.M.

Professor Mike, Regan, and Margery show up at the house with two pizzas from Pagliai's in Mankato. It is the best pizza ever. Professor Mike kisses Renata on the cheek as if he never visited her at 3:17 a.m. Regan and Margery jump on me like I am Hooper the Dragon.

Professor Mike even high-fives Barry when Barry comes back from his tae kwon do practice saying he has mastered his form and has mastered his board breaks and he will use his final practice just to settle his mind. He is ready for his second-degree black belt testing.

I am surprised by all of this. Professor Mike and Renata fought at 3:17 a.m. I heard them. Why is he here?

FIFTY-THREE

THE LAST THURSDAY

As soon as Barry and I walk in through the front doors and into the commons we are greeted by Mr. Sanders, the vice principal. He jumps a little when he sees me. "Well, hi, Adam," he says.

"Hi?" I say.

Then he looks at Barry. "Uh, Barry, I'm going to have to ask you to come with me right now, because, well, I suppose we all have to talk."

"We?" Barry asks.

"Who?" I ask.

"Me, Principal McCartney, you Barry . . . your mom, although we haven't been able to reach her."

"Tiffany isn't really my mom," Barry says.

"No?" Mr. Sanders says.

"She's not too good," I say.

"Mrs. Renata's sort of my mom?" Barry says.

"Mrs. who?"

"My mom has been watching him," I say.

"Does she need to come talk?" Barry asks.

"Yes," Mr. Sanders says. "If she's taking care of you."

Barry pauses. He blinks. He looks at me for a moment, then looks back to Mr. Sanders. "Why do we have to talk?"

"I think you know," Mr. Sanders says.

"Yeah. I think so?" Barry says. "Because I kicked Kase?"

Mr. Sanders nods. "Come with me."

I start to follow, too, but Mr. Sanders says I should go to class.

How can I go to class? What is the point? Do they think I will concentrate?

I don't. Not in English, not in social studies, not even in gym. All I can think about is Barry. I get no news, even though I text Renata, who just texts back, *Not now. In the office. I'll fill you in later.*

It isn't until before lunch when I find Carli standing at my locker that anything becomes clear. "I heard what's happening," she says. "I'm sorry, dude."

"What? With Barry? How did you hear?"

"Darci. I guess Kase doesn't feel safe with Barry here, because of his dog and Barry beating him up. Kase's dad is petitioning the school board to expel Barry."

"Expel?"

"Like, when a dude gets two technicals or a flagrant. You know, kicked out of the game."

I just drop my head into my hands.

"I'm sorry," Carli whispers.

FIFTY-FOUR

5:47 P.M.

"How could they ever believe you'd kill a dog?" Renata asks.

We all sit around the big table in Professor Mike's dining room. Barry Roland looks like he will die. His face is pale and his glasses are more bent-looking than normal and they have slid down his nose.

"I wouldn't hurt anything," Barry says so quietly.

"Except you kicked those boys," Margery says.

"Well, sounds like that was self-defense. Or at least defending your good friend here, right?" Professor Mike says.

Barry stares at the floor.

Renata smiles at Professor Mike, reaches and holds on to his arm. I am very glad to see this. Then something occurs to me.

"Why shouldn't Kase get expel?" I ask.

"Expelled," Renata says.

"Okay? Expelled. Because he called me and Barry 'fag' and 'retard' and 'refugee' and he tripped me in the halls and he ripped my shirt," I say.

"When did he trip you? Did he really call you those names?" Renata asks.

"Uh . . ." I say. The red sea floods into her face.

She stands up. "Why didn't you tell me?"

"I don't know," I say.

"Okay. Okay. Maybe I should petition the school board to expel him, huh? Would you like that, Barry?"

Barry shrugs. "Maybe I can go back to the other house and lie down?" he asks.

"This isn't a done deal, Barry. We're going to figure out something. We've got until Tuesday to figure this out," Renata says.

Barry is suspended from attending his classes until the school board hearing.

"Meanwhile, you've got to keep your head straight. You've got that big tae kwon do test on Sunday. You stay focused on that," Renata says.

Regan jumps out of her chair and shouts, "Barry the Shinja will break wood with his bare feet!"

Barry stands up. "Thank you. I'm going to go back to the house?"

"Of course," Renata says.

Two hours later, Barry and I jog through the almost total dark of the nighttime Red Jacket Trail. His bare feet slap on the cold pavement. The sliver of moon lights his fluffy face.

"If I get kicked out of school, do I work at the stables forever?" Barry asks.

I don't know how to answer this question.

"I deserve it. I kicked Kase out of hatred," Barry says.

There are no question marks by these sentences. But I say, "No, bro. You do not deserve this."

FIFTY-FIVE
THE LAST FRIDAY

I walk to school, because Barry is still asleep in my bed. Renata has early morning conferences with students, and Professor Mike has to take Margery and Regan to the elementary school. I don't want to walk.

In fact, I don't want to go to school at all.

I step down the steep hill past Trinity, where students are hustling to get to their early morning classes. I turn left and get onto Center Street, which runs between Trinity and Northrup High School. I think of Kase, because he might be at school without Barry there. I don't want to think of Kase. My phone buzzes in my pocket. I pull it out and am very happy to be getting a call, even a call from Devin Mitchell, who is not easy to talk to.

"Hello. Hi?" I say.

"Dude. Farmer. Listen, I have to . . . I want to tell you something I'm planning," Devin says.

Devin doesn't sound like himself. He is speaking fast. His voice is higher than normal. I feel nervous hearing him. "Okay?" I say.

"You know that Khalil is a damn good human being, right?"

"Yeah?" I say. It's true.

"What Mr. Doig is doing to him can't stand, man. It just can't. Doig has no idea what it means to grow up without everything getting handed to you. His family is like mine. Rich for generations before him. Plus he's white."

"Okay?"

"He doesn't know what it means for Khalil to have this on his résumé. 'Got kicked off a top AAU squad because of a scrape with the law.' That sound familiar?"

"No."

"It's the kind of line you hear all the time on ESPN when some poor black boy doesn't get drafted or loses his scholarship offer."

"Oh. Uh-huh."

"It's the curse, dude. The curse."

"Is the curse because racism?" I ask.

"So deep in their racism they don't even know it."

"Trouble is looking for black kids."

Devin doesn't talk for a moment. Then he says. "Yeah, which is shit. So, I'm going to do something."

"What?"

"And I hope you join me."

"What?" I ask.

"Me and you can't get hurt like Khalil can. So we have a responsibility."

"What do you want me to do?"

"Don't show up tomorrow."

I stop walking where I am, which is in the middle of the intersection of Third Avenue and Center Street. A car honks at me. I jump. I run to the other side of the street. "Don't show up for the bus?" I ask. "Don't show up to play our game?"

"That's right. That's what I'm doing. Won't tell my dad until the last possible minute, because he's going to bug so bad. But I'm not going to play for Mr. Doig if he treats my brother Khalil like this."

"Oh shit," I say. "Oh no." Devin Mitchell doesn't know about me. Devin doesn't know what is happening in my life. He doesn't know how my brother, Barry, is getting his ass kicked out of the building. He doesn't know how I couldn't even read English until basketball started to organize my brain, how I couldn't say full sentences in English until only two years ago. He doesn't know that I am nothing except another boy like Barry if I don't play. "I'm sorry," I whisper.

"I gotta go to school now."

I hang up on Devin Mitchell.

I run toward school.

Me and Renata watched so many biographies about her favorite jazz musicians, okay? I saw a lot of stories about bad racism in the old days. Is this the same thing? I can't believe it.

I sprint.

How can I battle all of history? I have so many troubles of my own!

There is no Kase at school. I take my test. I tell Carli I can't study chemistry, like she was planning for me in the evening. I need to go to the basement and do my dribbles and practice my footwork. Tomorrow I will face Kyle Owens and the rest of the Minne-Kota Stars. Tomorrow I play basketball.

I walk home from school alone.

FIFTY-SIX

I AM NOT ALONE, PART I

Carli follows me in her SUV. I walk on Center Street. She drives maybe five miles per hour behind me. Cars are honking. She doesn't care. They must pass her.

"Come on!" she shouts out the open window. "Get in my car! You want me to get arrested for slow driving?"

A man in a very big SUV, much bigger than Carli's, pulls up behind her and lays on the horn without stop. The honk pierces the air and continues. It vibrates in my brain.

"Okay. Fine," I say. I run out on the street. She stops. The man honks and shouts the f-word. I leap into the SUV, and then she pulls over and parks. "What are you doing?" I shout at her.

"Hi there, buddy!" she says. She smiles her Carli smile.

"No," I say, because I won't accept her Carli smile. "Why are you causing trouble in the street? I have enough trouble!"

Carli nods. "Yeah. Okay. I just wanted you to get in my car," Carli says.

"It worked. Can I go home now?"

"Well, I guess. I mean I know you have to practice your quote unquote dribbles and everything, but I'm guessing you also haven't practiced your jump shot all week, and you're going need that tomorrow, right? To beat the Owens boys? So I thought maybe you'd want to go up to the gym and shoot?"

She looks at me with her eyes wide, like she is an innocent girl, but she is pulling all my levers. She knows how to. "Okay," I say slowly. "But don't make me talk about nothing."

"Anything. I promise. I won't make you talk about anything," she says.

"When I get upset, I start to forget my English skills."

"Dude," she says quietly. "You're fine. You talk great."

Then she drives. We stop by her house, and she gets basketball clothes on. We go to mine and I change. There is no Barry or Renata or nobody . . . anybody for me to talk to, so I text Renata and let her know where I am.

She texts me back that she and Barry are with a lawyer.

This is more heavy news.

At least Carli and I are able to find court space in the Trinity athletic facility. Happy college kids play volleyball

282

and basketball and badminton on other courts. But they are not me. Here, in the gym that should be my home, I have no energy.

Carli warms up. "The swelling is gone in my knee. That was a bad couple of weeks."

"Yeah," I say.

She begins to hit three-pointers as always.

My shots are short. My legs are jellyfishes.

Five minutes in, Carli gives up on me. She picks up the ball and says, "Hey, man, I'm sorry about Barry. I'm sorry you're in the middle of all the bad blood in my crappy town. I totally caused you to be here. It's my fault."

I shake my head. "Kase messed with me before you."

"No. He started messing with you because I told him you were a baller back in October. I told all my friends I thought you were cute, which pissed him off, too. I guess he has a crush on me, but he's not my type . . . whatever. I guess I put him on you, man."

"Really?"

"And he hates Barry, of course. And you're tight with him."

This is surprising news about Kase, yes. But I don't really care. The heaviness I feel is not only about Barry. I don't know if she knows what's happening to Khalil. She doesn't know about Devin, I'm sure, how he wants me to disobey my coaches, to not show up for the game at all. "Uh," I say.

"Is something else going on?" she says more quietly. "Tell me."

"Do you know about Khalil?"

She nods. "It's not fair. My dad talked to Mr. Doig last night, but he won't budge. Dad seriously might resign from the Fury. He's been on their board for ten years, but this is too much."

"Your dad is not the only one who is mad."

She begins to dribble the ball. She pops it back and forth between her legs but never takes her eyes off me. "You're mad?" she asks.

"I don't know," I say. "So much bad happens, how can I be mad? If I get mad at everything, all I'll do is be mad."

"Yeah, but this?" she says. She dribbles in a circle around me, so I have to keep turning to see her. "You know, Khalil doesn't mess around. Like, he actively tries to not mess around, tries to steer clear of any trouble. Plus, he's a great teammate. He's nice to everybody, right?"

"He was not so nice when I first met him," I say, but I don't even know why I'm saying it. He was much nicer than Devin or Rashid.

Carli stops and dribbles the ball hard into the floor. "Dude. Come on. Now he's kicked out, and that hurts your team, it hurts him, and he's your friend. It might even hurt his chances for a scholarship, which he's been working for since he was a little kid."

284

I hate to think of Khalil as a little kid who is dreaming of basketball. So I think of Devin instead. "Devin isn't going to play tomorrow. He wants me not to play."

Carli catches the ball. Holds it. "Whoa. Mr. Doig could kick you off the Fury."

"I can't lose basketball."

"Well . . . you wouldn't be losing basketball. Just the Fury."

"I have to play against Kyle Owens."

"Yeah?" Carli says. "I want to see you play Kyle Owens, too, but he'll probably kick your ass because Khalil and Devin won't be on the court."

"No. I'll kick his ass," I say. "He's going to pay."

"Pay?" She smiles. "Farmer, I think you gotta chill and think straight." Then she dribbles in a tight circle right around me. She bumps me with her hip. "Guard me, man. Come on," she says.

FIFTY-SEVEN

I AM NOT ALONE, PART II

Again. Again. Again.

I am me. I am in a tall Warsaw apartment building with a big window and black darkness outside. The window reflects my 76ers jersey back to me, but I am small, maybe eight years old. It is daytime, but the air has filled with this ink from an octopus. The ink has spread and blotted out all light. The ink starts to leak in through cracks in the cinder block. I back away from the window. I back away into the apartment, but the ink knows where to find me. It chases me against a wall. I scream for my dad. He does not answer. The ink envelops me. I fight, but there is nothing to fight, no substance. I am drowning. I am drowning. I am drowning.

"Adam! Wake up!"

"What? Huh?" I sit. I am on the couch in the living room. It is dark except for the TV. Barry is asleep on the floor. Regan is asleep on the big chair. The TV is playing an episode of *Avatar: The Last Airbender*. The bald boy's head is glowing on the screen. Margery stands over me holding a pillow. "Did you hit me with that pillow?" I ask.

"You were yelling, and I couldn't hear the TV," Margery says. "That's rude. You're not the only person in this room, you know."

"What time is it?" I ask.

"I don't know. It's late time. Just stop yelling."

"Okay. Sorry."

"That's okay." She pats my forehead, then goes back in front of the TV.

Then I think.

I think more.

Margery is right. I am not the only one in this room. There are more people in Renata's house, too. I can hear Professor Mike's snores coming from down the hall. And guess what? On the other side of campus, Carli sleeps in her bed. Coach Anderson is there, too. I am not alone in Northrup.

I feel light as a feather.

I am not the only one here!

"I love that bald airbender kid!" I say to Margery. "He's so great!"

"Shut up!" she says.

FIFTY-EIGHT
I AM NOT ALONE, PART III

It is Saturday morning. Barry goes to work at the stable. He seems even smaller than normal, like he is a deflating balloon. The lawyer told him and Renata that there's not much they can do about him getting expelled. If there is documentable behavior that repeatedly violates school bullying policies, the school board is able to say good-bye to Barry. Just like that.

Professor Mike got very angry when he heard this. "Bullying? This guy?" He pointed at Barry, who was hunched over dinner, already losing air at the table. "He's the gentlest kid I've ever met!" Professor Mike is now a supporter of Barry. Maybe it was a dream when I heard him complaining to Renata at 3:17 a.m.

Anyway, with no Barry available to give me a ride, Renata

is to take me to Chaska so I can catch the bus to the game in Saint Cloud.

I have spent the morning listening to jazz on my phone, earbuds in. Regan and Margery have been making art projects, but they hide what they're doing whenever I come in. I find this a little annoying.

I have turned off all notifications. If @KyOw23 makes bad tweets about me, I don't want to know. I have also turned off my ringer and the vibration, because I don't want to hear from Devin pleading with me to disrupt my basketball career. He is the rich guy, not me. He is the muscleman who can dunk from the free-throw line, not me. He is the big-time recruit with touch from the three-point line, not me. I have to play this game against the Owenses. I have to honor basketball, my passport.

When the time comes to get in the car, I am very surprised that Margery and Regan are already sitting in the back seat. Both of them are wearing Philadelphia 76er T-shirts, like I like to wear.

"Where did you get those?" I ask Margery.

"We like them because Philadelphia was important in the Revolutionary War," Margery says.

"Not because of you," Regan says.

"What?" I ask.

Professor Mike also climbs in the back seat with them. "Since you're heading north, Adam, we decided to spend the day at the Mall of America," he says.

"Oh, okay," I say. I slide into the front seat and pull the chair up so Professor Mike has room. My knees are in my chest, and I am more annoyed. Whatever. I put my earbuds back on and listen to Thelonious Monk, *Monk's Dream* album.

Thelonious takes me away from the drama. He puts me in a different world. The album runs the whole time we are in the car and keeps me from worrying about Regan and Margery when they kick and punch each other near Belle Plaine. It keeps me from worrying about Barry or Khalil or even Devin. I visualize shooting shots, like soft birds flying from my hands, over the top of an outstretched Kyle Owens. I visualize leaping in the air, cramming Kyle Owens's shot back in his ugly face. The Monk album ends just as Renata pulls into the parking lot of Chaska High School.

She drives to where the small Fury bus is parked. There is also a school bus to carry the 14, 15, and 16U boys' teams to Saint Cloud. The 17U team gets to go on the nice one that has video screens hanging from the ceiling.

When I pull out my earbuds, Margery is marveling at how nice the high school is. "It looks like a spaceship," she says. This is true.

Then I stop paying attention to her, because to our left I see Devin Mitchell climb out of a Cadillac that is parked in the lot. I think this is his dad's car. Devin has come to the game. He wears headphones. He doesn't say a word to whoever drove him, but slams the door and walks to the bus. His face is not the kind of face I want to talk to. I am sure he doesn't want to talk to me, or probably anyone.

I get out of the car, say thanks, give the girls a wave.

"We'll pick you up," Renata says.

"Bye-bye, Mr. Basketballs!" Regan says.

"Bye-bye, Hooper the Dragon!" Margery says.

"Uh-huh," I say. Then I go to the bus.

Devin is sitting in the last row. He looks up when I climb on board. He motions me back. When I get there, he says, "Pops says Khalil isn't my business. He says he won't let me go to Saundra's birthday party if I don't 'get my head on straight' and play this game. My head is fine, but I'm not going to do that to my sister."

I nod.

"By the way, thanks for hanging up on me," he says. "I won't forget that."

I nod. My heart sinks into my guts. "Sorry," I whisper.

He puts his headphones on again. I walk back to the middle and slide into a chair. Coach Cliff and Mr. Doig climb on the bus. Rashid, Charlie, Trey, and Marques all sit around me. They listen to their own music. There are no players in back near Devin.

I lean and look out the window. Renata, Professor Mike, and the girls are already gone.

On the bus ride, Coach Cliff sits and stares forward. He looks unhappy to me. Mr. Doig is doing the coaching. He shows a video about the San Antonio Spurs basketball team. Mr. Doig's voice comes from his big nose. I don't like it. "Many Spurs players are foreigners, like Adam. Some are four-year college players. Some are one-and-done street players, but they all fall in line with this system that wins championships. See that?" Mr. Doig says, pointing at the screen. "Look familiar? That's the motion action we use in our sets."

I'm the foreigner. Who are the four-year college players? I wonder. Who are the street players on this bus? Maybe Devin will be a one-and-done NBA guy, but he's no street player. Also, I lived in America before I learned basketball. Maybe I'm not really a foreigner? I don't like Mr. Doig with his names.

The Spurs run very good offense, though. The ball fires around from dude to dude. Tim Duncan, who is almost seven feet tall, and is now retired from the NBA, was a very good passer. I see that. So what? I'm a dude who hangs up on his friend when he is upset. That's who I am. A selfish guy, Adam Reed.

I put in my earbuds, turn on Dave Brubeck, rest my forehead on the window, and shut my eyes. The drive to Saint Cloud is just about an hour, and I don't want to watch people who are better people than me playing basketball.

At some point, Rashid sits down in the chair next to mine. He taps my shoulder, and I open my eyes. "Mr. Doig just said you're playing Khalil's spot, okay?"

"Point," I say.

"Running the show," Rashid says. "Make sure I get it down in the post so I can posterize Kyle Owens's ass." He smiles.

"Yeah, okay. Good," I say.

You'd think I'd want to be the one to posterize Kyle Owens, but there's something wrong with me. I shut my eyes again.

Rashid stays in the seat next to me, and I fall asleep, only to awake when the bus makes a sharp turn and my head bounces off of Rashid's shoulder.

"We're here," he says.

The bus pulls into a giant parking lot next to a large coliseum with big parking lots all around. There are several buses like ours parked in big lines. There are teams of basketball players in warm-ups walking in packs. There are white vans with the logo of TV stations from Minneapolis painted on the side.

"Why is the TV here?" I ask.

"Devin and Khalil never get to play against the Owens boys, except in AAU. News covered this game last year, too. We only won by a bucket, so it's important," Rashid says.

"Except no Khalil," I say.

"We got a farmer and we got me!" Rashid says. Then he shifts his attention out the window past my head. He points. "Hey, Adam Sobieski. Those kids got a sign with your name on it."

And then I see a strange sight. I almost can't believe it is real. Two little girls with hair cut short at their chin and big brown eyes hold giant poster board signs. They jump up and down and shout! One sign has a dragon. The other has these words:

WELCOME TO SAINT CLOUD
ADAM
HOOPER
SOBIESKI!
YOUR BIGGEST FANS EVER!!

It's Margery and Regan. Professor Mike and Renata stand behind them. They are smiling and waving at me.

"They drove fast," I whisper.

"That's cool!" Rashid says. "I like their 76ers shirts. That's what you wear all the time!"

"Yeah," I say. And I think I might cry because I am so happy.

I am not alone anywhere.

FIFTY-NINE

DEVIN IS NOT ALONE

We are let off behind a fenced area, so I can't hug these girls I like so much, but I wave at Regan and Margery before we go in. I can't even believe Renata is at a basketball game. The only one she's seen was my first in Philly, when I was pretty bad. I leapt and had my legs taken out from under me and landed on my side hard. She said she couldn't handle it, not the crowd, not the noise, not the violence. That game was in an elementary school gym with kids playing and about twenty people in the stands. This will be different.

The whole game is different from the other AAU games we have played. There are other courts and other teams warming up, as there were before, but our court is on the side and has bleachers pulled out on one sideline. There are lots of people already sitting in the stands. Tasha and Carli are already here, as is her dad. Renata, the professor, and the girls come in and find chairs. There's a long, tall kid sitting in the front row, too. He's wearing a red T-shirt I recognize. It says "Fear the Cob" on it and has a picture of a big yellow corncob.

Rashid and I warm up. He sees me looking at the kid.

"You know him?" Rashid asks. "He's from down by you, right?"

"What do you mean?" I ask. "I think he's from Wauzeka. I saw him on the bench at a game. Wauzeka is in my conference."

"Yeah, man. Ben Kowalski. That farmer boy is in seventh grade. He was at the Tommies Baller camp last summer. Best pure shooter I ever saw. Heard he scored like thirty a game for their jayvee, but they wouldn't move him up because he's a little fragile."

I stare at this skinny Ben Kowalski. He has a Polish last name, I'm sure. I thought he looked like he could be my little brother last time I saw him. He smiles and waves at me. He's still a little kid. I remember how he cheered when I dunked against his team. Here he is again.

"He plays on the Heat 16U. Maybe we'll get a chance to see him later. Fun to watch," Rashid says.

Fear the Cob.

It's all coming around, like a big circle. When I played

Wauzeka back in February, I already had basketball, didn't I? I've gotten much better in a few months, but even then I could jump and jam and I was on my way.

What didn't I have the last time I saw Ben Kowalski in his "Fear the Cob" T-shirt? I had no Carli. I had no Khalil or Devin or Rashid or Tasha. I had no visits to Minneapolis to go against old guys who play basketball like jazz musicians or to sit in a big church, as part of the Mitchells' big family, to watch Saundra play the same classical song that put me on a chair next to Renata in Poland when I was a kid. There wasn't even any Professor Mike when I saw this "Fear the Cob" boy. Margery and Regan were two weird little girls who sat in trees. I have so much more now.

I bounce a pass to Rashid. I watch Devin bounce a pass to Trey.

I look up in the stands and see Carli, who told me I had to talk. I look and see Renata, who protected me so I could find basketball and Barry. Wow. Renata has made my life possible. Carli has taught me how to have friends just by being who she is. Barry is my brother. Khalil was becoming my brother. Devin was becoming my brother.

The Minne-Kota Stars arrive just then. Holy cats, they are so tall. Three are giant blond kids from South Dakota who Carli mentioned and Rashid texted me about during the week. I recognize them. Several boys look like Owenses, but I'm not sure. At first I don't see Kyle. Really, I half expect

Kase Kinshaw to jog onto the court, because he and Kyle have become one guy in my head, but I am off base with this expectation. Kyle Owens is the last guy on the court. I remember him, of course. He looks nothing like Kase. Kyle Owens has floppy brown hair, not a short buzz. He is about my height and skinny and not filled with muscles like Kase. He is also bouncy and happy looking. He sees me, smiles, jogs over, and says, "We are such dicks on Twitter, dude! I'm just joking, okay? Don't kill me on the court. I already told Joe that if he cheap-shots you like he did during our playoff game, I'm going to bench myself!"

"Ha-ha," I say. "No worries. I want to play basketball, not have a hockey match out here!"

"Good. I like my teeth!" Kyle Owen says.

I think Carli would like my joke. I look into the stands. She waves at me because she's seen me talking to Kyle. I continue to pass the ball back and forth with Rashid. Kyle is not the kid of my nightmares. But then something else. He stretches nearby.

"What's up with Khalil Williams?" Kyle asks. "Why'd he go to jail?"

I catch the ball and turn to Kyle. "No. He didn't go to jail. He's probably not in trouble, really, but . . . but . . ." I don't know what to call Mr. Doig. A coach? An owner? "This Fury board member guy is not letting him play."

"That sucks, man," Kyle says. "Khalil is cool. I was

298

surprised when I heard about his gang thing."

"Gang thing?" I say. "That's not true."

"No way, man," Rashid says, because he's heard. "He didn't go to jail. He's not in any gang. That's stupid."

Kyle nods. "Someone said it on Facebook," he says. "I guess nobody should believe that source, huh? Anyway, I played against Khalil a lot, and he's about the happiest guy on the court, right? I love that guy."

"Me too," I say.

I look at Rashid. He shakes his head. We must be thinking the same thing. How would that message get started? Khalil in a gang? Khalil, who tries to keep away from all trouble? He was in his house. His brother was scared. That's all that happened.

Just then Coach Cliff blows the whistle. We move into our shooting warm-ups. For just a moment, Devin and I meet up at the back of a line.

"Kyle Owens heard Khalil was in jail because of being in a gang," I say.

Devin freezes in place, puts his hands on either side of his head, squeezes, then looks up into the stands. His dad, mom, Saundra, and several other friends have just climbed up and taken seats. Devin is almost groaning. Only I can hear. "If Mr. Doig just . . . if he just supported Khalil instead of punishing him . . ."

It's my turn to take a layup. I go, but I can't do it. I miss.

Carli makes a face at me.

Through all of warm-ups, I don't hit a single shot. Hard life is creeping onto the court. Before, never. Before the court was what made me forget all about it.

There is a real buzzer here. It sounds. The Fury jog over to our bench. Mr. Doig hugs a clipboard and stares over his glasses at us. Coach Cliff talks quietly. "Do what we do. Farmer has point. Devin, I want you to jump, but you're in the two. Trey, Charlie, you guys keep moving, keep moving the ball. Don't think any on that side can stay with Rashid down in the post. Keep that in mind. And remember, yeah, they're the Owenses, but we're the Fury. We got this."

The buzzer blows again. Me, Rashid, Trey, and Charlie jump from our chairs and jog onto the court. Devin sits for a second, then stands, too. He walks to the court. He and Kyle Owens bump fists. Then Devin says, "No."

The ref gets into position for the jump. One of the tall blond South Dakota boys goes to the center circle. Devin should jump, but he's shaking his head. He stands ten feet away. Kyle is next to him, looking confused. The ref blows his whistle, but Devin doesn't move. He stares up at his parents in the stands.

The ref blows his whistle again. "Come on, Eight," he says to Devin, referring to the number on his jersey. "Let's get this show on the road."

Devin turns to Mr. Doig. He says, "You don't know

anything. You don't care about us. You go ahead and ruin Khalil's whole life just because being white and rich makes you think you have the keys to the damn world. But you don't know anything, man." Devin sighs hard, then jogs off the court and into the hallway where we came in.

I look at Rashid. I look at Kyle Owens. I look up at all these people in the stands, some with phones ready to capture the jump, two with TV cameras, everyone stunned silent, because the main dude they came to see just ran off the court. I look at Devin's dad. I look at Devin's mom, who is glaring at Devin's dad. I look at Renata. She is very confused. I love her. I look at Carli. She is smiling like Carli smiles. She knows. Her dad stands next to her. He nods at me.

I look at Mr. Doig and say, "I've been through a lot. I've been treated unfair. I know what it smells like. This is unfair. I support Khalil." I jog off the court toward the hall. Rashid follows me. So do Trey and Charlie and every player left on the Fury bench. And here's the part I will never forget for as long as I am able to dribble a basketball. We are only in the hall for a few seconds when Kyle Owens and his cousin Joe, who ran me over in the playoff game and made me lose my mind, arrive. Then so do another Owens kid and the three blond boys from South Dakota. Everyone from both teams. In just a moment, we are all gathered in the hall next to the gym. We stare at one another. Stunned. We are quiet.

"What do we do?" I ask Devin.

Devin's mouth hangs open. His eyes are so wide. Tears start to come up and run down his cheeks. "Thank you," he whispers. "Thank you, guys. Bring it in."

We move into a huddle. We put our hands together and hold on.

"We gotta support each other like this our whole lives," Devin says. "This time is for Khalil Williams. We will see him back on the court with us soon. Khalil on three. Farmer, you lead it."

I nod. "One, two, three, Khalil."

Khalil.

I say it again: "Khalil."

Khalil.

I say it again: "Khalil!"

Soon after, I ride home with Renata, Professor Mike, and the girls. Not a single member of the Fury 17U team takes the bus. We all find different ways. I don't know if we'll ever play together again.

Renata turns to me at the last stoplight before we leave Saint Cloud. "That is not what I was expecting. I don't even really know what happened. But I think I'm proud of you."

"Yeah," I say. I'm so tired. But I have to talk. "If you guys didn't come with the Sobieski Hooper signs, I wouldn't have had enough courage. Thank you."

"They are great artists," Professor Mike says.

"You are a good guy, too. I'm glad you don't abandon us because of Barry."

He turns and looks at me. "No. I won't."

"Renata, Barry is right. You are the best mom around. I like Sobieski back in my name, but I would like to be called Adam Sobieski Reed, because you're my mom and I'm very proud that you're my mom."

Renata turns and stares at me. She says, "You're my son, okay? Forever."

I nod, and I am so happy again.

"Remember when you all shouted 'Khalil' in the hall?" Regan says. "It echoed through the whole gym. They stopped all the other games. That was awesome."

It's true. It was awesome. It was in news reports all over Minnesota, too.

SIXTY

BARRY IS NOT ALONE

It is Sunday, about an hour before Barry Roland goes up for his second-degree black belt. Since the "game" the day before, all members of the Fury "community" received this email from Mr. Doig where he calls himself "we":

Dear members of the D-I Fury Community:
Our intent is to help these boys and girls become the best young men and women they can be. Discipline is an important aspect of that training. We have always had a zero-tolerance policy for bad behavior. Each player signs a contract committing himself or herself to being good a citizen while they are members of this community. If they break this contract their position with the team is

immediately terminated. Until now, we have never had reason to second-guess this policy.

Before our 17U boys took it upon themselves to walk off the court to protest the way we treated the Khalil Williams situation, we felt sure we handled it the right way, operating in accordance with the written rules, even though several of the team's coaches and advisors suggested this situation might be special.

Because of the 17U boys' protest, we have reviewed Khalil's situation, and we do believe the police may have overstepped common sense with regard to Khalil. Khalil should not be charged with obstruction due to a case of mistaken identity. No crime was committed involving Khalil or his family as far as the record shows. The police were simply looking for someone else and Khalil was caught in the middle.

We do want our boys and girls to know that we support them on and off the court. Not only does the Fury reinstate Khalil Williams immediately, we are also providing him with the services of a lawyer to make sure this unfortunate charge does not become a part of his permanent record. We have a long-standing relationship with Khalil, and we welcome him back with open arms.

Please know that each and every one of our players has a special place in our hearts, and we will always attempt to do right by them.

Sincerely,
Karl J. Doig
Executive Director
D-I Fury Basketball

Devin says the letter is bullshit. But I don't think it's bullshit. What Devin did made something that wasn't fair become fair. I am thankful to Mr. Doig for doing right.

Khalil is out of his mind with happiness. He is all over Twitter thanking us and the Owenses and all of the Minne-Kota boys. He is also saying again and again that he was never involved in a gang. Whoever suggested this about him and whoever repeated it should feel sad and ashamed for what they did.

But now, I am thinking so hard. Look what Devin did. He had some big strength because his family and basketball gave it to him. TV news stations came to record him play! Maybe nobody cares about me like that in the state of Minnesota, but in Northrup? Maybe I can use my passport, my little strength, to save Barry from being expelled?

How can I help my brother?

Regan and Margery are in the living room with Barry. He looks healthier and happier wearing his karate uniform and his black belt and his headband. This morning, he didn't want to get ready, but Regan and Margery were on him like flies. He could not stop them. The more they buzzed at him and said things like, "You are going to leap like a leopard, Master Barry," the more he smiled and grew bigger and got a better color in his cheeks. Regan and Margery are forces of nature. They can climb the pine tree outside to its tip-top and swing back and forth. They can find a way onto the roofs of the college buildings. And they can grow your spirit and fortitude with their bare-knuckle buzzing. They are great. Now Barry is practicing his second-degree black belt form, which has eighty-two different moves and takes almost four minutes to complete. The girls are cheering for his every turn and kick, and I am back in my bedroom.

How can I help?

There is no Northrup game for me to stop, to say, "I won't play basketball if you don't let my furry pal Barry back in school!"

That doesn't seem like a good idea anyway. I want to play, so it's not a real threat.

Could I say I will transfer to Wauzeka to play with Ben Kowalski? "Fear the Cob! If you do not let Barry in school, I will join forces with the skinny Polish boy, and the Wauzeka Cobbers will beat you stupid for the next two years!"

I wonder who I am going to say this to? The principal? The school superintendent? The school board? Who is on the school board? I don't even know, but I picture businesspeople like Kase Kinshaw's dad.

Wait. What about Kase Kinshaw's dad?

He said how much he enjoyed watching me play basketball when Renata and I were at Patrick's. If I told him I was leaving school and Northrup basketball would be bad again without me, would he drop his petition to have Barry expelled?

No. That's stupid.

He thinks Barry is a dog-shooting boy who beats up his son. Rick Kinshaw wouldn't give up the safety of his Kase in exchange for my good basketball. The real trouble is, Rick Kinshaw doesn't know the truth, the real Barry, the gentle boy.

I wish I could get Kase's dad to meet the real Barry. If he saw how good and pure-hearted Barry is . . .

Maybe I could get Rick Kinshaw to go to Barry's test today? If he saw Barry in action there, he would see the purest form of Barry there is! How could I get Kase Kinshaw's dad to do that?

I will make a threat! "I won't play basketball in Northrup ever again if you don't come see my boy Barry kick some wood in half!"

Sounds like a crazy idea.

Yes. So crazy.

But what else is there? I take big, deep breath. I will have courage. I will try it.

I call Carli to find out where Kase lives.

"You're going to go over to Kase's house?" she asks. "Seriously?"

I tell her why. She is not impressed by my logic.

"Why do you think Mr. Kinshaw gives a crap about your basketball?"

Because he said he did at Patrick's!

Kase lives outside of town, so I need a ride. Carli offers it. Problem? There is now only forty-five minutes before Barry's test.

On the way out the front door, I say to Renata and Professor Mike, "I'm going to see if Kase Kinshaw's dad will come watch Barry do his test."

"Whoa. Wait," Renata says.

"Who?" Professor Mike says.

"The father of the kid involved in the incident," Renata turns to him and says.

"Wow," Professor Mike says. "I don't know, pal."

"He doesn't know Barry. This way he might know Barry and see that it is all crazy and wrong."

Renata looks sad. "He's not going to come to Barry's test, Adam. There's no way."

"No. There's a way. He likes my basketball playing, remember?"

Carli pulls outside in her SUV. Regan shouts, "That girl is here." I run between Barry and Margery and out the front door. Barry's eyes are huge underneath his glasses.

"You assist me so many times," I say to Carli as I climb in.

Carli blinks at me. She shakes her head. "We're a good

team. We're good for each other."

"Dope," I say.

"Why do you say that all the time?" Carli shouts.

We drive into the country.

There is only a half hour to go before Barry's test when we turn down a drive into the woods. There are tall pine trees on either side of the SUV and rocks and ravines heading up to the crest of a river bluff. The woods open into a big yard with a giant stone house in the center. It has large windows and a brick roundabout driveway.

"This is a lot of money," I say.

"Kinshaw Construction builds a lot of stuff," Carli says.

Right then, Kase and his dad walk around the side of the giant house. Each is wearing a baseball cap and a flannel shirt. Each is carrying a big stack of wood in his arms. They both stop and watch as Carli's SUV approaches.

Carli pulls up next to them. "So?" she says to me.

My heart is pounding. "I better talk, huh?" I say. I open the door and climb out.

Kase blows air out of his mouth and looks to the side. His dad squints his eyes at me. "I'm surprised to see you here," he says.

"Yeah. Oh boy. I'm surprised to be here," I say. "But it's urgent, okay?"

Kase looks at me. "What could you possibly want?" he says.

"I want you . . . I mean, I want your dad to come to Barry

Roland's black belt testing today."

Mr. Kinshaw turns, walks three steps, and places the wood he was carrying onto a stack of wood next to their garage. Then he turns back to me. "And why would I do that? Barry Roland used his martial arts training to crack my son's ribs."

I look at Kase, who is holding much heavy wood. He can't be so injured, can he? I say, "If you go . . ." I want to say I will play basketball for Northrup next year, but it's too ridiculous. Instead I say, "If you go, you'll see how hard Barry is trying to be a better person. What happened last week was my fault, not his. He was only involved because he thought Kase was hurting me."

Mr. Kinshaw looks at Kase, cocks his head, shuts his eyes, then looks back at me. "Was Kase hurting you, Adam?" he asks.

I take in a breath. Kase looks at the ground. What can I say? I choose not the truth, because I have bigger goals here. "No. No. Kase was just messing around. Barry misunderstood what was happening."

Kase looks back up.

"The police reports said you and Kase were fighting, too," Mr. Kinshaw says.

"No. I think we were more joking, okay?" I say. "Witnesses didn't get it."

"Really?" Mr. Kinshaw says.

I nod. "Please, Mr. Kinshaw. Barry Roland is a very honorable guy. I want you to see him work. I want you to see how hard he tries. It will only take an hour."

"Maybe we should see what Barry is up to," Kase says. He is staring at me.

Mr. Kinshaw turns to his side. "Okay. We'll do it."

Carli leans out of the window. "Hey. We don't have a lot of time."

A moment later, I am sitting in the back seat of Carli's SUV. Kase Kinshaw sits next to me. His dad is in the front with Carli. They are making small talk, but I can barely listen. Kase and I just cooperated to get his dad to see Barry do tae kwon do? What the crap?

The parking lot in front of Bob's Champion Tae Kwon Do Studio is completely full. In fact, there is not much parking nearby on the street. Carli pulls around the block and then we all walk quickly to make it on time.

Regan and Margery both wear their 76ers shirts again. This must be our team shirt. I am wearing one, too. They have saved a seat for me next to Renata. I tell Carli and Mr. Kinshaw that I'll go sit with them. I'm really doing this not because I don't want to be by the Kinshaws, but because I don't want to draw Barry's attention toward Kase. What if Barry looks for me before he starts his pattern, sees Kase, then loses his concentration?

All the seating around the mats up front is taken. There

are people backed against the walls. Barry and the two others who are going for their belts must be warming up in another room. Bob, the owner, comes to the middle and introduces himself and then the grand master from Mankato, who is an old white tubby guy with a white beard like Santa Claus.

Bob introduces the first test person. It is a woman who must be Renata's age. She goes and does her pattern, which is like a dance. She bows. Then a couple guys in their karate suits stand and hold boards. The woman breaks these boards with different kicks and punches. One board she can't break, so they swap it out with another board, because maybe it is defective. This next one she breaks, and then she bows, and everyone applauds. The Santa Claus grand master asks her some questions. She ends every answer with sir, just like she is talking to Mr. Doig. She has gained her blue belt. Everyone applauds loudly.

Then a young kid with a pile of floppy hair that gets in his eyes, who is maybe in middle school, does his thing. It is just like what the woman before him did, except he forgets his pattern in the middle and does not recover. He starts. He stops. He starts. He stops. He turns very red and bows and apologizes. The grand master Santa Claus speaks quietly to him and then the boy bows to the audience and leaves the mat. Everyone applauds, because even if he failed this time around, he gave it a good shot.

Bob turns down some of the lights.

The whole place becomes very silent.

Bob walks to the center of the mat.

He speaks.

"All of you who take classes here know what a great inspiration Barry Roland is to me. Before he started with us, Barry had never done anything athletic in his life. He was just a troubled teen who smoked cigarettes and maybe drank too much beer, isn't that right, Barry?"

Barry stands on the side of the mat. He bows, which I guess means yes, what Bob said is all true. I never knew the Barry who smoked or drank beers and he never told me he did, so I'm surprised.

Bob continues to speak. "But before Barry came to us, he also watched hours and hours of an old TV show called *Kung Fu*. Most of my young students come here because they've watched those Ninja Turtles or maybe the Power Rangers. They want to kick butt. That old *Kung Fu* show is more about justice and learning to control one's inner demons. Barry came to us not so he could kick butt, but because he wanted to learn to be a better person. And, oh, what a good guy he's turned out to be. He has done everything we've asked. He's a fine, natural martial arts practitioner. He is so disciplined in his preparations. He never misses a class or an opportunity to get better. And, most important, Barry is a wonderful friend. He volunteers with our kids' classes. He helps me run the elder kicks program. I'm just as proud of him as can be. I know whatever hurdle gets in his way, my buddy Barry Roland is going to succeed. No matter what hurdle, now or in the future."

Barry shuts his eyes and nods.

"I know most of you are here to support him, too. Am I right?" Bob says.

There is a lot of whooping and applause.

"Well then, let's just do this thing. Wait till you see what he's got to show you. Okay, Barry . . ."

For the next four minutes, Barry treats us to many kicks and punches and spins and leaps. He shouts (HI!) and holds on to terrifying poses. He crouches. He breathes. He flows like the ocean. Toward the end, he leaps many feet off the ground and swivels in the air, kicking and punching. He looks like a movie, he is so good. Then he puts his fist over his chest.

The grand master Santa Claus smiles and nods.

Barry puts his right fist in his left palm and bows.

Everyone whoops and applauds more.

Then the board breaks are even crazier, because they involve a whole bunch of those other students holding boards in different spots on the mat. Barry breathes and concentrates for maybe thirty seconds before he punches, kicks, kicks, then leaps off the bent knee of a classmate high into the air and kicks through a board that is maybe seven feet off the ground. The kid who holds this board is standing on a chair, bracing the board at chest level! When Barry lands, everyone jumps out of their chairs and cheers and shouts. Barry is one amazing tae kwon do guy.

After the grand master speaks to him and then ties his new belt on him, all the kids in the crowd mob Barry. He high-fives everyone, including Regan and Margery. Finally, I think he will come talk to me and Renata, but he doesn't. Instead he walks quickly past to where Kase and his dad are standing.

I watch. He talks only to Kase.

Kase turns red in the face. Is he mad? I can't tell.

He and Barry shake hands. Barry and Kase's dad shake hands. Kase's dad spots me watching. He nods at me. He, Carli, and Kase leave.

Barry comes over.

"What happened?" I ask.

"I told Kase I was sorry that I kicked him last week? I told him I acted from anger? I told him I deserved to get kicked out of school because I broke my vows when I kicked him? I told him I love dogs and I would never hurt a dog? I told him that what happened with Barney scared me so much and made me so sad that I came to tae kwon do to be a better man and person and that has changed my life forever, then I said I hope he can forgive me for everything I did wrong."

"But . . . but Kase has been a bad bully, bro," I whisper.

"Yeah. He just said in front of me and his dad that he was

the real bad guy. Not me. I think Kase Kinshaw cried? It was pretty weird."

Then we all go to Patrick's to celebrate Barry. We get the biggest table in the whole place, because my family is now six and if you add Bob, his wife, their daughter, and the grand master Santa Claus—his name is Jerry—there is ten. It's almost like a Polish wedding party going on in Patrick's, because we are so loud and making so many good jokes.

While I eat pizza, I get a text from Carli. This is what she says:

You did it. Mr. Kinshaw called the school board president on the way home. Barry won't hear officially until tomorrow, but it's done. You're a superhero, dude.

Barry Roland may not be Shinja, but he is the real superhero.

But I do know I am something more than just me. I know what injustice feels like. I know I will fight injustice, and sometimes that means a protest and a battle, like what Devin did, but I think many times that means just being a good, kind person in the world.

For instance, Barry Roland can fight. He knows how.

But more, Barry Roland is gentle and kind. I believe that's why so many people came to see him break wood and spin and kick. I believe that's why he will never be abandoned when things get tough for him.

We should all learn from Barry Roland.

At home, before I go to sleep in my bed, Renata comes in and says, "I'm so proud of you, Adam. I always worried that your trouble . . . the trouble you had when you were younger . . . would define you. But look what you've become."

"I have so much advantages," I say.

"You have so *many* advantages," she says.

"Yes. So I will, I promise. I'll do good."

Renata, my mom, kisses me on the forehead.

SIXTY-ONE

WE ARE HOOPERS

But that's not the end. Don't be fooled. Just because I am Polish and a friend and a son and a boyfriend—an official fact in the minds of the school, because we went to the dumb prom together—and a brother, you might get lost about what this is. But don't get lost.

I am a hooper.

Devin, Khalil, and Rashid come with me to the Anderson Center at Saint Thomas University. We have been playing together so well. The D-I Fury 17U team competed in four Nike Elite Tournaments. We played on the coast of Virginia, in Indianapolis, Atlanta, and Los Angeles, and guess what? We motion our competition into the floorboards, and then we fly through the air and dunk the ball on their sad heads.

Four total tournament victories.

These guys and me? I think we can beat anyone in the country.

Here's some reality, though. I am a good part of this team. But I am not Devin. I am not Khalil. They have minds that are connected through the whole game. When one hedges on D, the other helps and destroys any easy lane. When one cuts to the basket, the other has already launched a pass that will land softly in the cutter's hands. Although sometimes I become part of the ocean with them and flow, often they are in a different part of the world from me.

Next year, when I am their age? I will be in that part of the basketball world, I promise.

But today we aren't playing. We have time off before the Nike Elite Championship Tournament, the Peach Jam, in South Carolina. Right now I am wearing a Minnesota Timberwolves number twenty-two jersey, not my Fury number thirty-four. Today we are fans. I follow Khalil into the stands.

We climb.

The game is about to begin. The All Iowa Attack looks like a good team while they warm up. They are quick. They speed to the rim. They leap high for rebounds. Their passes are zipped on a rope. I'm a little afraid.

But you know what? Katy Vargas and Tasha Tolliver are amazing players. Katy is a point guard with eyes in the back of her head. Tasha has all the smooth moves in the post. And, finally, they get their two-guard back. Carli Anderson received the doctor's permission, and she's going to play her first real game since the AAU season finale eleven months ago. Her hair is in two braids. Her muscles fire as she shoots warm-up threes.

Whoa. I have never seen her in her uniform. She is the most beautiful person to me. I trip on the stands while climbing and have to catch myself because I'm only looking at her, not looking where I'm going. She is perfection. Her stroke is so easy. She almost doesn't miss.

Me and Carli have practiced so much together. Last week her dad ran us through cutting drills, made her go 100 percent, and the next day she wasn't even sore. "You're ready. Might have something to do with how much time you two spend working out," Coach Anderson said.

Me and Carli also train in tae kwon do. We take a weekly class from Barry, who is now the number one employee at Bob's Championship Tae Kwon Do Studio. Maybe I will become Shinja?

Devin, Rashid, and Khalil sit down and watch over the court. I stay standing, so excited to see Carli out there.

"Dude," Devin says, "Carli should give you some more shooting lessons."

"She's so much better than you," Khalil says.

"She's the best shot ever," I say back.

"I can't hit like that," Khalil says.

The girls huddle. The buzzer sounds. Here I am, Adam Sobieski Reed. My friends stand, too. The girls walk around the center circle. Katy gets in position on one side. Carli gets in position on the other. Tasha moves to the center. She is greeted there by a giant girl with black hair tied back. They bump fists. The ref walks between them holding the ball. Katy and the Iowa girl next to her elbow each other, push against each other. Carli is crouched. The girl next to her seems to hold her breath.

The ref blows her whistle. She tosses the ball up.

Tasha leaps above, swats the ball to Katy. She catches and spins from her defender, dribbles, sprinting toward the basket. Her girl goes with her, bumping against her hip. Carli's defender sprints to protect the basket, too. Carli, so light on her feet, runs unseen to the right wing. She gets to the three-point line as defenders converge on Katy, and Katy leaps and lofts the ball out from under the basket. It lands in Carli's hands.

And I know what's coming. I've seen her practice it again and again.

Carli squares, pauses for a breath, jumps, and releases the ball a moment before she reaches the pinnacle. The ball rotates, arches, begins its fall . . . accelerates and *swoosh* . . . it slides through the net, barely making a ripple.

Khalil and Devin leap and shout. Rashid spreads his arms

in victory. I sit down and put my hands on my head. It took her all of five seconds.

Carli jogs back on defense. She points at me. She smiles so wide.

I have never seen anything so beautiful.

Yes. We are hoopers.

Now. That's it.

That's how we end.

ACKNOWLEDGMENTS

First of all, thank you to my agent, Jim McCarthy. It feels like I've grown up with you, Jim. Thanks to my editor, Ben Rosenthal. There aren't exactly truckloads of Midwestern sports fans in this business. I'm so, so lucky to be with you. Thank you to Jason Darcy for reading an early draft and for knowing way too much about basketball (someone needs to publish your eighty-page screed on the history and societal implications of moving screens in today's professional game). Thank you to Nicole Overton for reading a draft in the middle of the process, for catching what I couldn't see well. For catching what I should've clearly seen, but didn't. For just generally helping *Hooper* so much.

Thanks to my maternal grandpa, Oscar, for leaving

Eastern Europe when people were getting killed. He farmed in Minnesota. Worked in factories in Iowa. He and Grandma Elinor made a good life for their family. They made my amazing, adventurous mom. Thanks to my paternal grandma, Yvonne, for fleeing Belgium right ahead of the Nazis. She went first to Brazil. She ended up in New York, where she made a good life working as a translator for everything from cookbooks to bank contracts. She learned a lot of languages while moving across the globe. Thanks to my dad, Max, who, as a baby, sat in the arms of the SS while my grandparents were interrogated. He got to Brazil, flunked math in eighth grade, went to an American school, and ended up immigrating to the United States when he was eighteen. Thank you to everyone who welcomed my family with open arms.

For *Hooper*, I feel especially indebted to the following authors and their books. Sherman Alexie for *The Absolutely True Diary of a Part-Time Indian*. Jason Reynolds and Brendan Kiely for *All American Boys*. Tamika Catchings for *Catch a Star*. Alice Goffman for *On the Run*. J. D. Vance for *Hillbilly Elegy*. Ta-Nehisi Coates for *Between the World and Me*.

Read many books and you will see deeply into many lives. You will be a better person for it. That's a pretty good reason to read books.

Turn the page for a look at Geoff Herbach's
Cracking the Bell

CHAPTER
1

SEPTEMBER 28: CRACKING THE BELL

Football has been my medicine. It has given me a singularity of purpose. It is the tower I built, on which I stand and see everything around me.

I'm a defensive player, but that doesn't mean football is simple seek and destroy, like some people might think. I captain the defense, which takes smarts, especially the way I play the game. I'm not some firing missile. I'm a smart bomb, communicating subtly, like through fungal mycelium, to a network of other smart bombs, my killer teammates.

On the field the world goes into vignette mode on Instagram. I'm in this dark tunnel except for a brightly lit place right in the center where everything makes sense. I shout an alignment, read how the offense sets up, call out adjustments—verbally,

1

with my eyes, with hand gestures—signal plays to watch for, react to action in the backfield, take on blocks.

The world makes sense on the football field.

Even on September 28, apparently. In fact, as soon as we left the locker room, my bone-tired heaviness, my thoughts of my sister, Hannah, and poor Mom and Grandpa John . . . they went away and all there was in front of me was grass, jersey, helmet, the mechanics of Lancaster's offense lit in a bright Instagram vignette.

Screw Lancaster. I'm not a kind person on the football field. Yes, I play smart. But after I make my reads, I am free to destroy.

In the fourth quarter of a heavyweight bout that featured far more defense than offense, we led Lancaster by six points.

But as time fled, Lancaster had the ball.

They are really good. They are the monsters of the Southwest Wisconsin Conference. They drove the length of the field—their huge linemen, having finally exhausted our front seven, paved the way for Jimi Jentz and Jake Brogley, their fleet-footed running backs. With just over a minute left, they moved all the way down to our twenty-two yard line. But I didn't lose faith. I knew this business. I knew my place in it.

I'd studied so much film. I had a research paper full of evidence proving they got conservative when they hit this part of the field. Most teams who played them lost confidence, lost their will to fight. Most teams got run over easily. Why would Lancaster do anything risky? Most teams laid down and lost.

Not us.

In the huddle, I was my most pure "second life" self. I nodded, looked into everybody's eyes, pointed at each one of my teammates. "Not us. Not us. They will not run us over," I said. "We bend. We don't break."

My teammates huffed and snorted. They nodded, returned my gaze.

"Let's go. Now," I said.

And I was right about conservative. Of course. Lancaster called running alignments three plays in a row, certain we'd lay down. But each time, I lined us up like a hammer poised to hit. They couldn't move at all. One yard first play. A yard loss second. No gain third.

My heart pounded. The vignette was blinding.

Dave Dieter, our defensive coordinator, pumped his fist, gave me the thumbs-up. Very few knew, but Dieter let me call most of the game by myself. Essentially, Dieter was cheerleading, and I did his coordinator job.

On fourth down, Lancaster had to go for it, even though they had ten yards to go. There was no other choice. Images from the film I'd watched riffled through my mind. I knew that their playbook would open up in this situation. A pass was coming, and I knew which one.

Then Coach Dieter tried to grab the defensive reins. He signaled in a set, shouted for the corners to stay back off the line of scrimmage.

I shook my head, tried to shake him off.

Dieter signaled the set again.

"Ignore Dieter," I said in the huddle. "Don't play off the line. It's an option route to Clay. He's the guy, right?"

Everyone nodded.

"Press on the damn edges."

"You sure, man?" Matty Weber, the free safety, asked.

"Can't have Clay running to the damn sideline. We don't want him stopping the clock if he gets a first down. Make him cross in front of me," I said. "Funnel him right at me."

The corners nodded. They broke huddle. They lined up tight.

"Back off! Back off!" Coach Dieter screamed.

My heart slowed. I crouched.

"Back off!" Coach Dieter cried. Our corners didn't budge.

"Red. Red. Red," Lancaster's quarterback shouted. "Hut. Hut!"

Dakota Clay, Lancaster's all-state tight end, got bumped off the line by our outside linebacker, Knutson. It was happening just like I thought it would. Our corner was between the hash and the sideline and Matty Weber was shaded to that side to double Clay. Instead of running out and up the field, Clay rode the bump and dragged across the middle.

I stayed crouched, made myself small, baited Lancaster's QB into thinking the middle of the field was open. It worked perfectly. Lancaster had spent the entire game running every play away from me, keeping me from being a factor. Not this time. The QB threw the ball. It left his hand on target, right at Clay. I exploded forward, accelerated like rockets were attached to my ass. I didn't break down for the tackle at all, because I knew exactly where the ball would be. At the last moment, I uncoiled on Dakota Clay. I exploded into him at the same moment the ball reached his hands. It was brutal, crushing, like a pickup truck blowing a country intersection. Clay cried out. The ball bounced away. The crowd leaped to its feet, screaming.

Even though a few seconds remained on the clock, all we had to do to win was take a knee. Game over.

After the hit, apparently Clay lay on the field groaning.

I didn't hear that part. I'd done something I shouldn't do. Really bad technique, failed to keep my eyes up, dropped my head down when I made the hit.

Eyes down. Head down. Absolutely terrible technique.

I have a tendency to drop my head when I want a hit to be remembered. Once in my career, sophomore year, the resultant collision caused my eyes to roll back in my head, my sinuses to drain, and my ears to ring like a French cathedral on Sunday morning. No, not just bells. I heard the shriek of a witch for the first time. I'd worked hard to counter my intuitive style of play after sophomore year and had avoided that kind of collision, although I did hear the shriek of a witch one other time, junior year, when a receiver cracked back on me, hit me at full speed while I wasn't looking. Man, I worked so hard to avoid that kind of contact.

I'll tell you this, I'd never dropped my eyes on a 240-pound superathlete before. The back of my helmet had ricocheted off Clay's ribs and shot my face down into the turf. Crash. For a count of three, I think, I was totally out (looked like that on the video—Kirby Sheldon showed me later). Twiggs ran onto the field and raised his arms, signaled the coaches for help, because for that three count I looked dead. But before anyone could check on me, I was awake. I pushed myself off the turf and ran to the sideline like nothing had happened. On film my teammates slapped me on the helmet, jumped up and down, and high-fived each other around me.

I don't remember it.

This is what I remember: witch whistles screamed in my ears. What sound would steel make if it was torn apart slowly? Witch whistles. Got more intense. The whistles came from ten places at first, then combined and became a single dying girl shrieking without breathing. Constant deadly shriek. The sky above turned orange, yellow, blue, red . . .

What's happening? What's happening?

That's the last thing I remember thinking. Or seeing. Or hearing. The last thing for many hours. I don't remember the good-game line, or hugging Dad and Grandma Gin in the stands, or riding the bus back to the high school, or telling Twiggs and Riley I had to go home to see Mom, because she hadn't made it to the game, or driving home, or going to bed, or getting up and vomiting.

All that was gone from my head, my cracked bell leaking it away. The contents of my second life leaking away.

CHAPTER 2

FOUR YEARS AGO, IN JULY: HANNAH DIED

Because Grace, who was my girlfriend back when I was an eighth-grade criminal, works for Grandma Gin at Dairy Queen, Mom wouldn't let me work there anymore. To make money, I clean gutters and paint houses with Joey Derossi, a twenty-year-old dude who was my sister Hannah's weirdest friend.

He is a wild card but isn't wild. He's just weird and I like him more than just about anybody, not only because he reminds me of how funny Hannah was.

In my second life, we drove around in his old GMC pickup truck. He played whatever music he'd gotten into (usually from the 1960s or '70s, but sometimes new stuff—as long as he could get it on CD or cassette—Joey lives as analogue

1

as possible, no smartphone, electronic notebook, laptop, internet). He talked about whatever strange idea he'd been reading about at the library. Last summer, he began asking me to write stuff and read it to him. He wanted to examine my deep perceptions. Doing that writing—and I wrote all the time—felt good, but also shook me up. Yes, I like Joey Derossi more than anyone my age, except for maybe Grace.

This is how the weird writing thing started.

Last summer, after I began having a recurring Hannah dream, Joey gave me one of those green-and-white composition notebooks you can get at Walmart for a dollar. He said, "Grab a pen. Write that shit out. Write about your feelings, bro. This is the greatest gift the great eyeball in the sky gave to all us humanoid primates down here. The ability to reflect and write out all our big-brained-ape shit."

"Seriously?" I said. "I don't really want to."

"I'm your pal, man. Listen to your pal," he said.

"No thanks," I said, handing the green notebook back to him.

"Bullshit. Riggles and Twine don't care if you're struggling. But your real pal, aka me, wants you to be as mentally healthy as you are physically magnificent."

Joey Derossi. A freak of nature. I did think it was funny he called my best friends over at school, Riley and Twiggs, "Riggles and Twine." I also thought maybe he was right about this gift from the "great eyeball in the sky" (this is what he called his version of God). When my first life broke completely, back when I was fourteen, the social worker at the group home I was sent to asked me to write stuff, too.

Anyway, this is the first thing I wrote for Joey Derossi. I started writing it in first person, because why wouldn't I write about myself in first person? But Joey—who is probably a genius—made me go back and write it in third person.

"That way you get out of your own path. You gotta get out of your damn head!"

Okay . . .

Four years ago in July, Hannah Died

The phone rang just after 10 p.m. Isaiah's mom and dad were in the living room watching a Kevin Costner movie on Netflix. Something about baseball, which thirteen-year-old Isaiah thought was stupid. This was during the summer between seventh and eighth grade, when Isaiah was small and dirty and liked to eat peanut butter right out of the jar (sometimes with his finger).

Instead of watching the stupid movie with his boring parents, he played Temple Run II *on his phone. Although he was physically attracted to Scarlett Fox—the character with whom he played the game—he kind of hated* Temple Run II. *It took too long to die once you got good and when you did die you had to start over from the beginning, so it took a long time to learn how to deal with the challenge that killed you. It gave him a big headache. Sadly,* Temple Run II *was one* of the few games that still worked on his piece-of-shit Galaxy, and he needed to be doing something with his damn brain.

There was tension in the air. His sister, Hannah, who had always been the good kid in the family, had skipped her shift at Dairy Queen to go to Blackhawk Lake with her new boyfriend, Ray Gatos. The dude seemed so nerdy to Isaiah. But apparently Ray had some criminal intentions? Or a criminal mind? That's what Isaiah's parents said anyway.

"That kid is a bad influence," Mom whispered before the movie started. "We better keep our eye on him."

It really didn't seem possible to his parents that Hannah would have chosen criminal behavior, missing her DQ shift, on her own. Grandma Gin owned Dairy Queen. Hannah hadn't just skipped out on a fast-food job; she'd put her own grandma into a crap spot on a busy summer night (Isaiah had been forced to work for two hours, which made him mad, except the new girl, Grace, was at Dairy Queen, and he liked her weird sense of humor and also, if forced to admit it, how she smelled when she was sweaty), and Grandma Gin was not one to forgive and forget, so Hannah would be in trouble for a long time. . . .

Hannah wouldn't invite the wrath of Grandma Gin into her life, would she?

Scarlett Fox, who looked a little like the new girl, Grace—kind of pouty and pointy—burst through the temple ruins, jumping over massive holes, sliding under fallen trees and bursts of fire, picking up all the tiles, and avoiding the giant *creature that chased her and wanted to tear her to pieces.*

The landline rang in the kitchen. Isaiah figured it was Hannah, finally. He didn't even look up from his phone. He didn't want to hear Mom's screaming. But Isaiah did look up when Mom failed to scream. At first, Mom said yes, yes, yes? Then she gasped. Then she began to cry oh no, oh no, oh no, again and again.

"What?" Isaiah asked. "What?" he shouted from his bedroom.

"You know there's no way Ray Gatos forced Hannah to go, right?" Joey said to me after I read it aloud to him. "No way he was the one pushing her. It was other way around with those guys. Ray Gatos was like a cute little teddy bear Hannah carried around with her. Bro, she owned Ray Gatos."

"Really?" I asked.

"Yeah, man. Yeah. All you people think Hannah was some angel, but she wasn't, okay? Don't get me wrong, she was about as nice as a human being could be. She was sweet to a weird-ass high schooler like I was, right? But come on. She was fun. Hannah was, like, 'Hannah the Adventurer.' She was a little bit half-cocked and good to go, you know what I'm saying?"

"No."

"She loved to live her life. That's all. Nothing evil. She was just out there doing stuff."

"That's a new perspective," I said.

"Always good to see things from different angles, bro.

How about you imagine her at the end, in that car, loving life, not worried about breaking those rules too much?"

So I did. One Saturday afternoon two weeks before football started, while we were out in Hazel Green working for an old lady Joey had known since he was a kid, Joey cleaned gutters on a ladder above. I sat on the old lady's lawn with my green notebook and wrote this . . .

Ray Gatos drives his Toyota Corolla on the rolling county road. "I can't believe your grandma let you off work tonight," he says.

"Yeah. Ha ha. Seriously," Hannah, who sits next to him, replies. She blushes. She is not a great liar. She doesn't want Ray to worry she might get in trouble. To take her mind off things, she sticks her hand out the window and lets it ride the hot air currents of a falling summer night. Whatever trouble she'll be in, the day was worth it. The whole day had been amazing. Grandma couldn't hate her forever, right?

At that same moment, Steven Hartley (33), leaves the Boulder Junction Tap and stumbles to his new Ford F-150. The man is broken, drunk, loaded to the hilt. He climbs in, turns the ignition, and puts his head down on the steering wheel. "I can't do it," he sobs. Then he takes a big breath, lifts his big head, whispers, "Screw this." He flips the truck into drive.

Meanwhile, the sun sets red over the Driftless Area, that weird, rolling landscape in southwest Wisconsin that the earth-grading glaciers somehow missed. Everything runs red to orange and green in the fields and a perfect light shivers along the road.

Ray and Hannah have not been drinking, like some of their friends were out by the lake. They're not about that. They are quiet, and totally in love. They swam together in the lake. They hiked down into a valley and up across a high ridge that gave them a view of the entire park. They kissed up there for the first time.

And now, in the car, they listen to Sufjan Stevens, the Michigan *album*, because it's Hannah's favorite, because the sweet, rolling songs remind Hannah of home, of rolling Wisconsin country. The open windows let hot farm air pour in, wet earth, growing corn. It is perfect. Her hand rides the currents.

Ray's Corolla crests a hill near Rewey, about fifteen miles northeast of Bluffton. The song "Alanson, Crooked River" comes on. It's not even a real song, just a dozen tiny bells ringing together, like the sound fairies would make playing in the tall grasses along the road. "I love this," Hannah says.

They cross into an intersection. The pickup truck driven by Steven Hartley comes from the right, runs a stop sign. Hannah doesn't even have time to scream. In a flash of steel and light, Steven Hartley's truck blows the Corolla to hell.

Steven Hartley of Arthur, Wisconsin, dies in a blink. He's so confused as the Ford's engine cuts through him.

He has a blood alcohol level of .19, which is more than

twice the legal limit. He is in the middle of a divorce. He has a two-year-old daughter named Melanie. Everyone is confused. The dude never drank. Never.

Until he went to Boulder Junction Tap. Then he did drink.

He kills Hannah while fairy bells play.

I read my thing to Joey while he drove us home from Hazel Green.

He had to pull over.

He stared out the window for five minutes without saying a word.

Finally, he looked at me, and said, "Yeah, bro. I bet that's exactly how it happened. You nailed it. The goddamn fairy bells, right?"

CHAPTER
3

I awoke thinking about my written version of Hannah's crash. Or trying to. I kept sort of passing out. I wanted to remember it. I rolled to get out of bed. I couldn't. I reached for my green notebook, which was stuck under my bed. But the room spun and the woman, the witch, stirred, shrieked. I couldn't get my fingers around my notebook's edges. I rolled back onto my pillow, swallowed hard. I had a terrible taste in my mouth. My head pounded.

What is going on? What is going on?

I shut my eyes tight. *I am injured.*

Shrieking, like the sound of a girl losing her life?

Hannah is dead.